NUCLEAR DRAGON

KEN CARODINE is a Naval Academy graduate and Desert Storm veteran currently serving as the commanding officer of a fifty-member US Navy Reserve unit. Ken is the winner of the 1997 Rose Trilogy Award for Best New Work. Since leaving active duty in 1989, he has worked as an information systems professional. He is now a managing consultant for a software company in the Dallas, Texas, area.

AVAILABLE NOW

Termite Hill
Tom Wilson

A Reckoning for Kings
Chris Bunch and Allan Cole

Distant Valor
C.X. Moreau

The War That Never Was
Michael Palmer

NUCLEAR DRAGON

KEN CARODINE

ibooks
new york
www.ibooks.net

DISTRIBUTED BY SIMON & SCHUSTER, INC

ibooks, inc.
24 West 25th Street
New York, NY 10010

The ibooks World Wide Web Site address is:
www.ibooks.net

Original title: *All the Tea*

Copyright © 2000 Timberwolf Press, Inc.

Cover Design: Raul Carvajal

ISBN: 0-7434-9759-7
First ibooks mass market printing December 2004
10 9 8 7 6 5 4 3 2 1

For Andrew, Victoria & Jill

Thanks and Acknowledgements:
Ms. Jill Olhausen
CDR David Fisher, USNR, USNA '83
CDR Richard "Spike" Martin, USNR
CDR Peter Carrier, USNR, USNA '79
LCDR Timothy Brown, USNR
Ms. Reeta Santos-Selene
Prof. Doug Edsall, USNA, Physics Department
Prof. Marlene C. Brown, USNA, English Department
NR COMSEVENTHFLT Det. 111, Current Members & Alumni
Mrs. Mary Kay Grasmick
Ms. Ginger Scheopp
Ms. Paula Wiley
Mr. Robert Jeffrey Reid
Mr. Brad Loewen
Ms. Laura Castoro Parker
Mrs. Catherine Rogers
RMI Bernice Bonar, USNR
Ms. Brenda Russell
Ms. Carol Woods
Mr. Patrick Seaman

CHAPTER ONE
WEDNESDAY, APRIL 7TH

Government District
Tokyo, Japan
8:00 PM
23:00 PM, GMT

He stepped out of the train station as he had a million or two times before. *Cool tonight*, he thought. Yuen Xin Li pulled his dark wool overcoat tighter. *Not much difference in the weather between here and home, at least what I remember of it.* However, the similarities ended there. *Not much longer now. Not much longer now.*

A thin veil of fog whisked around as he and others near him walked through it. His clouding breaths joined it as he exhaled. Yuen knew it would soon grow thick enough to hide almost anything.

Something pulled his gaze upward and he remembered his childhood in Manchuria. He recollected trying to count all the stars in the sky but not being able to because of the number. Tonight the cloudless sky hung above him like a black velvet curtain. He couldn't recall the last time he'd seen anything but Venus at sunset.

He turned to walk the kilometer or so to his office building and joined the masses on the still–busy sidewalk. The noise and fumes of passing vehicles filled his ears and nose. The sounds of cars, trucks, and motorcycles competed with the voices of those he passed while the aroma of dinner wafting from a restaurant on the other side of the street fought with the automobile exhaust.

I've missed so much. My parents' deaths, my aunt's cooking. I hate the food here. Not much longer now. This was his sixteenth year in Japan.

Yuen studied the faces of people who passed by. The fatigue in the eyes of the dark–suited businessmen struck him with less ferocity than did the short, almost skin–tight, skirts on the women who walked next to them. *Decadent cows. Whores, all of them. They deserve this society.*

He'd grown up hearing stories about the Japanese. His relatives had spoken of them as if they were ten–foot–tall monsters. After so many years among them, he now knew, at least, that none of them grew to that height.

Soon, Grandmother. I will avenge what these bastards did to you and to our family. Soon they will know.

Fellow pedestrians bumped and shoved as they walked past him. *Stay off me, you pigs!* In some cases, he used his torso to shove back. He even elbowed a few. His heart raced and his hands sweated more and more with each step. As his anger stood ready to boil

2

over, he placed his hand on the Makorov pistol inside his overcoat pocket. *I hate you animals.*

Yuen slipped his hand around the pistol grip. The sight of the International Trade and Industry Ministry building and a policeman looming in the distance had the effect of a well–brewed tea. His grip on the pistol stock relaxed. Yuen exchanged smiles with the police officer. *You stupid ass. I could kill you right now.* He concentrated on the silencer and extra magazine in his left coat pocket.

Four guards manned the gate to the headquarters directorate of the Ministry. Two stood their watch just outside the gate while the other two watched from the inside of a bulletproof glass–enclosed guardhouse. They controlled the switch that opened and closed the gate to the high black fence encircling the large white marble building.

The two patrol guards came to attention as Yuen approached. They saluted when he was within six paces. "Good evening, Tanaka San," they greeted with respect.

Yuen smiled back and nodded at them as he pulled his wallet from the inside pocket of his overcoat. He opened it to his Government ID Card and held it up for their inspection.

Yoshi Tanaka, his handlers had given that name to him. He remembered how strange it used to be to hear others call him that. His handlers assured him that in time the discomfort would pass. After all these years, even through college and a successful career in the Government, he still smirked each time he heard it.

"Good evening, Sergeant," Yuen responded in his

second, now almost first, language. "Pleasant night, don't you think?"

"Yes, Sir. A little late work tonight?"

The guards were nice kids, even for Japanese. The one talking to him was from a farming community in Hokkaido. The other one was from Okinawa. Yuen knew the question came out of kindness rather than concern for his late arrival. After coming across the find of his espionage career, Yuen Xin Li had been sure to slowly adjust his hours to allow the maximum opportunity to take what he needed without detection.

"Yes. I'm afraid that our work only continues to grow in scope, no matter what we do."

The guard nodded. Then he waved to his counterpart in the guardhouse. Servos snapped on and the black entryway slid to his left to permit him access.

Yuen noticed the door to the station was propped open with a steel chair.

"Is that a proper thing to do?" he asked officiously.

"Sir, the steam heating system is not working properly. We can't turn it off and it's getting too hot in here."

"Well, don't let it stay like that too long. I can't let it be said that I allowed the guard detail break security rules."

"Yes, Sir," the sergeant answered for his men.

Yuen nodded. "Goodnight, men," he said to them.

"Good evening, Sir."

Yuen smiled openly to himself once he was past them. *That was the last time I'll ever have to go through that charade.* He put his face back on as he entered the building.

Yuen knew that his rise to the rank of Deputy Assistant Minister for Administration had come by no coincidence. Infiltrating the Japanese had proven easy, much more so than the Russian, British or American governments. Perhaps it was the proximity to Mother China, or even the commonalities of cultures and physical appearance. Either way, Yuen knew that his ability to stay in office and rise in rank through the political and economic turmoil of the 1980s was due to forces and powers beyond his view, but they were there just the same.

He pressed the button for the elevator and the doors slid open immediately. Yuen eyed a surveillance camera move toward him as he stepped into the lift. *Everything is as it should be.* He pressed the button for the sixth floor and the doors closed.

Yuen pulled the pistol and silencer from his pockets and put them together. Having worked in the same building for so long, he knew all of the security blind spots. He even knew how fast the elevator moved between floors. The gun went back into his coat as the floor indicator blinked his arrival.

Yuen took a step and found himself struggling for balance. He slipped on the tiling as if treading on ice. He flailed with both arms to keep from falling, but to no avail. He landed on his back with a heavy thud. As he sat up, he realized the floor beneath him was soaking wet. "Damn it!" Even through the pain coming from his backside, he heard his voice echoing down the corridor.

The sharp pain came from his coccyx bone. He rubbed at it, but the ache didn't subside. He rolled to his right to pull himself up on all fours. Water from the floor had soaked through to his knees. As he reached for a nearby chair, the sound of approaching footsteps pulled his attention down the hallway.

"Oh, Sir. I'm so sorry!"

Takei rambled down the hallway as fast as he dared with the slick floors. The old man, bald and stooped, had a bony frame that reminded Yuen of a skeleton. He made his way over to Yuen with a shuffle.

"You old fool!" Yuen, now on his feet, shouted as he slapped the old man across his face. "You damn near killed me!"

Takei bowed his head.

"Put up a fucking sign before you really do kill someone!"

Yuen hobbled down the corridor. He felt for the gun. It was okay. *I ought to just shoot that old bastard right now.*

Takei had a dubious reputation at the Ministry. As a very young man, he had been a soldier in the Great War. Most of Yuen's co-workers treated him with great disrespect while a very few gave him much deference, even for a janitor.

Yuen made his way to his outer office at a much slower pace than normal. On the way there, he leaned against the wall, file cabinets, almost anything he could find to take some of the weight off of his lower back. *Damn him.* His tailbone ached more with each step. *The bastard is probably one of the ones who raped my grandmother. I hate these animals.*

Within moments after he inserted his key, he was in. He leaned against the wall to rest a bit as he closed and locked the door. For the next two hours, he would need as much privacy and security as he could get.

Both rooms, the outer area where his secretary normally sat, and his office, were relatively dark. Only light cutting through closed blinds allowed him to see her desk and his doorway.

He limped the last few feet to the inner office and let himself in. Yuen rested for a moment against the closed door. The short distance had felt like a marathon.

Finally inside his inner sanctum, Yuen flipped a switch and overhead fluorescent lights flickered on with a crackle. He pulled the pistol from his overcoat and placed it on his desk. He slowly pulled off his overcoat and draped it over one of two adjacent guest chairs.

Yuen leaned against the top of his metal frame desk to get to his chair on the other side of it. "Umm," he moaned as he eased into a gray high–backed chair. His tailbone hurt. Yuen was sure something was broken.

He placed the pistol with the attached silencer in the top drawer. He pushed it shut as he inserted a key into the lower right drawer and opened it.

He unlocked the file drawer and pulled it open. Red folders immediately caught his eye and he smiled. An unknown cohort had done his or her job well. Nothing, no logs, no cameras, nothing connected his office with these files. Everything was going according to plan.

Almost five months earlier, Yuen was carrying out his dutiful function of reviewing personnel payroll summaries when something caught his attention. Figures simply just didn't add up. Someone was doing a very good job, although not completely undetectable, of either stealing money or conducting some sort of covert activity.

Yuen arrayed the contents of the folders across his

desk. Very soon, working papers marked with Government Security stamps covered his desk. He smiled to himself as he turned on his computer and flatbed scanner.

The scanner, far from the newest technology, took up almost as much space as the computer monitor on his desk. With the recession firmly in place, getting his supervisor to authorize the purchase of the used equipment had been nothing short of a miracle.

He eased back in his chair as the machines finished booting up. The Japanese version of the Windows operating system seemed to take forever. Yuen had heard that the Chinese incarnation of the operating system was much faster. It was low on a list of things he longed to see for himself.

The scanner whirred loudly to let him know it was warmed up and ready. *You'd better not die on me, you inferior piece of capitalist shit.* The noise was almost deafening. Yuen Xin Li leaned forward with great discomfort to grasp the mouse. Several clicks later, the scanning program was up and he was ready to begin.

He examined the stack of paper. *Should take about forty minutes.* He placed the first one on the scanner.

Large displays of buttons guided him through the process of moving a hard copy page to the electronic medium. A graphical computer program, or wizard, prompted him to carry out each step.

"Scan a new page?" it prompted.

Yuen clicked on the "Yes" button.

"Is document on scanner?" the wizard asked.

Again, he clicked "Yes."

The scanner whirred as a bright light crept out of the box's edges. When the noise stopped, the screen flickered and the prompts disappeared. The monitor now presented an image of the original document still on the scanner.

Yuen read each line, checking it for accuracy. He nodded and reached for a new page. He replaced the document on the scanner glass and closed the lid to repeat the process.

He was in the middle of his tenth or eleventh sheet when something caused him to look up. Perhaps it had been movement in the doorframe, or just a change in the light. He hadn't heard him over the scanner, yet there stood Takei, his mouth agape. Even that old fool knew that copying documents with red security classification stamps didn't look appropriate.

"So, you've come to clean my office?" Yuen asked as he reached into his desk drawer.

"Yes, Sir." Takei's eyes were still fixed on the desktop full of papers. "Also came to apologize for the wet floor."

"That's okay. I think this office is clean enough." Yuen raised the pistol and fired a single shot. The old man's brains splattered the door and wall of Yuen's office and the adjoining entryway. "Your apology is accepted."

Yuen stood and hobbled around to the edge of his desk. He smiled as he pumped four more 9mm rounds into Takei's already expired body.

"My grandmother was forced to be a Comfort Woman for you monkeys during your 'Great War'. You may not have been there, but your brothers, or your cousins, or your friends were. I may even be *your* great grandson. What I would give to wash the Japanese blood from my veins." He pumped one more round into Takei.

The smell of gunpowder and the hot lead cooking the old man's dead flesh reached Yuen's nose. He inhaled a chestful of air to take in the aroma more deeply. "I feel much better," he said as he let it out.

The sound of the scanner clicking on to stay warmed up pulled his attention back to his desk. He looked back down at Takei's bleeding corpse and then the desk again.

He shrugged before limping back to the desk. *Scanning all this shit was getting just a little tedious anyway.* Yuen grabbed the papers, not bothering to keep them in order or even aligned, and shoved the lot into a briefcase. He turned back toward the door after he closed the briefcase full of papers. Reaching for his coat, he pulled it on.

The extra ammunition was in the left pocket. Yuen reloaded the pistol. He looked at Takei once more before stepping over him to leave the room. He didn't bother to switch off the lights on his way out.

The elevator ride down passed without event. Yuen knew that eventually the other janitor would seek out his partner. When he found him, all hell would break loose.

The doors slid open and Yuen grimaced as he tried to walk normally. The guard in the security station was sure to be watching him leave the building. Yuen Xin Li's hand tightened around the pistol stock.

Yuen pushed on the main door and exited the Trade Ministry for the last time. He managed to keep up the façade as he walked down two flights of stone steps to the sidewalk. The Guard Station loomed ahead.

Yuen raised his hand to wave and the two in the station turned to smile at him. His tailbone screamed. Taking normal strides quite simply was the most excruciatingly painful experience of his life. He finally had to stop for a moment.

Yuen looked up to see one of the station guards standing to scrutinize him closer. *Got to keep moving.* He started up again and the guard eased himself back down.

"Everything okay, Sir?" the Sergeant asked. The door to the guard station was still propped open.

"I slipped on a wet floor inside. I may have hurt my back."

"Do you want us to call an ambulance, Deputy Minister?"

"No, no," Yuen forced a smile. "I think I'll just go home and soak in a bath."

The man nodded and pushed the button to open the gate.

Yuen now made no effort to hide his discomfort. He leaned against the guardhouse as the gate opened for him.

Come on, damn it. Hurry up! He mentally shouted at the gate.

When it was open enough for him to get through, he still didn't move. *Can't give them the impression that I'm in a hurry.* He remained still until the gate was all the way open.

As he stood on his own to walk through, the two men patrolling on foot came to attention. With the first step toward the gate, an alarm from the Ministry Building sounded. Yuen pulled the pistol from his coat and fired single shots at the two guards. They each fell with 9mm bullet holes in their foreheads.

The two men inside the guardhouse normally would have been protected behind the bulletproof glass window. However, Yuen, with a deftness that impressed even himself, slipped back around to fire multiple shots through the open guardhouse door. Blood from the fallen guards splattered the windows and control panel.

Yuen put the gun back into his pocket and hobbled away without looking back. The alarm claxon resonated in his ears as he crossed the street toward his train station.

CHAPTER TWO
THURSDAY, APRIL 8TH

Project Blue Flame
Reactor Control Room
6:30 PM
9:30 AM, GMT

"Somebody shut that damned thing off! I can't hear myself think!" Doctor Robert Deitrich shouted.

The claxon that had for the last five minutes alerted everyone at the facility fell silent. A dozen men and women in white lab coats sat or stood at consoles banked with lights, dials, buttons and computer monitors. The standers shifted from one leg to the other. Those lucky enough to have seats moved around in their chairs in vain attempts to find the best position. Though the trapezoid–shaped room, about thirty feet square, easily accommodated the scientists and their instrument panels, his own comfort was the last thing on Deitrich's mind.

He glanced across the open area at his colleague, Doctor Stanley Loewen. Like most of the crew,

Loewen worked at his console with an all–consuming fervor. A little 'out there', Loewen wore his bushy blond hair long, and sported an earring. The applied mathematician and physicist, besides holding several advanced degrees and citations, also looked and dressed like a 1980s–era rock star.

The claxon started up again. "Shit's hitting the fan," Deitrich muttered to himself. He looked over at the fusion reactor's Tritium Monitoring Panel to his right. Analog needles buried themselves to the right. Now in full overload, the reactor was producing too much power and, consequently, too much heat.

Red lights, constant and blinking, peppered the instrument panels. Deitrich's PC now displayed horizontal temperature bar graphs. Two of them indicated the temperature rate of change. The third showed the metallic torus' skin temperature. At this rate, it would explode in a few moments. Deitrich checked his display. *We've got maybe a minute or so before this whole place becomes a big lava pit.*

"Stanley?" Deitrich called into his headset.

"Yeah?"

"What the hell—"

"Hold on a minute. I think I've got something," the younger scientist said, cutting him off.

Somebody, Deitrich didn't look up to see, nor did he care who, shut off the alarm again. He watched Loewen, seated a few feet away in front of him at the primary control panel, check one set of readings, then another.

"The electron–neutrino injector is stuck shut."

Deitrich noted the confidence in Loewen's voice. If anyone could have figured that out, Loewen was the person. "What do we do?"

"Bleed helium exhaust. As much as we can."

He also noted Loewen's characteristically calm demeanor. Such was his way. Today's event numbered as their fiftieth or sixtieth emergency since the project's inception. The 'Loewen Cool' was legendary.

Some might attribute this to upbringing or religion or some other esoteric thing. Deitrich figured it had more to do with Loewen's involvement with the project. Doctor Stanley Loewen had designed and built the fusion reactor.

Deitrich nodded as he pointed at the circuit board behind him. Two junior members of the team turned and started typing on two small keyboards that extended outward from the instrument cabinets in front of them.

Deitrich knew that venting the super–heated helium to the atmosphere above would cool the reactor in time. They still had to find a way to open the injector. He checked his instruments again.

"We're at max exhaust, Doctor," Professor Murray Rawlins announced.

Deitrich only nodded as he took off his headset. He climbed out of his chair and went over to Loewen's station.

"Having fun yet?" Deitrich asked.

The longhaired, thirty–six–year old scientist didn't bother looking up. He did, however, take the time to pull his hair back and tuck it underneath his lab coat collar.

"Temperature's on the rise again," Rawlins reported from the back of the well–lighted room.

"No, Stan. I'm not."

"Stay cool," he replied. Loewen's tone was almost melodic.

"Tell that to the reactor," Deitrich quipped.

The claxon started again. This time, several of the technicians abandoned their stations. Deitrich watched with wide–eyed amazement as they ran toward the door.

"Let us out!" they shouted when they found it locked.

"Shut up! Get back to your stations!" Deitrich shouted as he went back to his console.

The facility, a very high–tech building, had a computer system that monitored the spaces for fire, flooding, and other unusual events. Fire doors with magnetic locking mechanisms acted to isolate key spaces in case of emergencies. Deitrich pulled up the system's interface and disengaged the lock on the Reactor Control Room door as well as the others in the lab.

"If this thing blows, there's no where on this island to run!" he shouted at the personnel still at their stations yet eyeing the door.

Two of the technicians still standing at the entryway glanced from their stations, to Deitrich, to the door, and back to their stations again. They eventually moved toward the Reactor Control Room's interior.

Deitrich got up and went back to Loewen.

The scientist's computer now displayed a schematic diagram. Deitrich spied the label on the bottom on the screen. They viewed the components adjacent to the control circuitry for the injector.

Loewen frowned, stroked his chin, and sighed.

"What?"

"I'm going to cycle the power going to that assembly," Loewen said.

"But how do you know if you can power it back up?"

"I don't. But if I can't, it won't matter."

Loewen's matter–of–fact tone didn't help the basketball–sized anxiety tumor in Deitrich's stomach. He almost preferred the singsong tone of a few seconds prior.

Deitrich caught himself nodding. Loewen was right, of course. If something didn't go right and soon, he and everything around him would soon be a big smoking hole.

Loewen turned in his chair. "Tony, Dolores," he pointed at two wide–eyed techs. "Shut down circuits A–11, H–25, and M–24!"

The man on the left, Tony Swinson, turned around and flipped two switches. Next to him, Dolores Shinozaki flipped the last one.

"Now, switch on M–24," Loewen said to Shinozaki.

She complied and took a step or two back from the panel and toward the door. She shot Deitrich a nervous glance.

"H–25, now!"

The male technician flipped the switch and the claxon started up again.

"No, don't do that," Loewen ordered as Professor Rawlins went to shut it off. "We need to know when the sensors start reading normal again.

The man eased his hand back from the reset button.

"Okay. Hit A–11."

Swinson didn't hesitate. He flipped it immediately. A few electrical sparks flew from the surrounding switches when it went to the ON position. Swinson jumped back with a start. He stood a little behind Shinozaki.

Loewen's display now showed the same temperature bar graph that Deitrich had viewed at his station. With the exception of the claxon and eight heartbeats, silence gripped the room.

"Torus internal temperature is falling!" Rawlins shouted from the rear of the room after a moment that felt like an eternity. The claxon stopped sounding almost as soon as the words left his mouth.

The remaining technicians and Deitrich cheered. Several gave each other high–fives and thumbs–ups.

Loewen only smiled to himself. "I told ya, stay cool," he said to Deitrich. He reclined in his chair and pulled his hair from underneath his coat.

Deitrich smiled back as he pointed at the sweat–soaked spots in the armpits of Loewen's lab coat.

Loewen looked down to examine the stains before grinning away his embarrassment.

CHAPTER THREE
THURSDAY, APRIL 8TH

Tokyo, Japan
Tsukuda–jima Port District
10:30 PM
1:30 PM, GMT

Yuen Xin Li sat across the street from the fishing boat docks in the relative comfort of a stolen black sedan. The tinted glass, while it made watching the agreed–upon meeting place a little difficult, also made it hard for passers–by to see the owner's body lying on the floor of the back seat.

Still in pain from the fall the night before, Yuen had used a cane to help him walk. The Japanese woman whose car he now occupied had been stupid enough to assume this meant he was no threat to her.

He, like most things he had ever done, planned the act of taking the car. From the first moment he watched the woman get on the train, his mind had started working. Two hours later, a simple knife blade inserted at the base of her skull had kept her from screaming or struggling. A darkened and empty parking lot acted as an able ally. With his injured back, getting her beefy carcass into the car had proven to be the most difficult task.

He smiled as he puffed on a Western cigarette. *One of the few good things about that society*, he decided. Yuen let the smoke linger in his lungs before blowing out a thick gray cloud.

Avoiding the authorities who searched for him had proven easy. Since no one knew his real name, he simply used it. He possessed all of the necessary credentials, even a properly stamped Chinese passport. On several occasions, he had simply walked right through the police checkpoints.

His contacts had communicated the meeting place earlier that morning. A series of telephone calls from pre–determined phone booths allowed him to get a message to the Executive Committee. They, in turn, responded in the same manner.

The rusting, dark brown exterior of the fish–processing plant across the way looked as abandoned as it should be. Large white lettering that at one time had probably borne the name of a company was no longer legible. The windows and other openings in its walls were all dark.

A high chain–link fence, covered in about the same amount of rust, served as the only barrier. It extended down the street as far as he could see in both directions. Only a single–bulb light pole guarded the entryway.

Several dozen fishing boats bobbed in the mix of dusk and streetlight. A few of them had lights to illuminate their empty decks, but most sat dark in the evening mist. Their rigging swayed with the wind and the rocking decks.

Yuen checked his watch. No one had entered either the boat yard or the building in the almost three hours that he had been watching. If his appointment was coming, he or she was already inside, waiting for him.

He glanced down at the passenger seat and the briefcase full of documents he planned to turn over. The expression of shock on Takei's face, as well as the faces of the guards, ran through Xin Li's mind again. He smiled, but only for a moment.

He checked his watch again. *It is time.*

Grabbing the handle of the briefcase, he opened the car door. The dome light gave him just enough illumination to see the heavy form of the dark–haired body lying on the floor as he got out. "Stupid cow," he mumbled as he slammed the door shut.

A gentle rain started falling as Yuen crossed the street. The cold air didn't help. He turned up the collar of his overcoat and pulled it tighter. The cane occasionally slipped on the wet surface.

The sound of a distant siren pulled his attention away from the yard for a second as he looked down the street. It wasn't coming his way, whatever it was. The sounds of distant horns, automobile engines, and other city noises soon obscured the siren.

Moisture and the smell of fish permeated the air, nearly suffocating him. The aromas of newly caught and rotting catches fought each other. He looked up to see dark and puffy clouds filling the sky. More rain was coming.

The tempo of raindrops hitting objects around Yuen picked up a bit. Metal objects gave off little pings at first until they all blended in the downpour. Soon whole droplets snaked their way down differing courses on his face, overcoat and briefcase. Moisture soaked through the collar of his overcoat and crept into his shirt and down to his shoulders and chest.

Just in time. He reached the side doorway of the warehouse. A small metal awning gave some protection from the weather. The raindrops thrummed against it as he scanned the pier and surrounding area. *All clear.*

Darkness engulfed the entryway. Yuen fumbled for the knob. He found it on the second grasp.

As he pushed the door open, it squeaked on its hinges. He peered into the murky space on the other side with wide–open eyes. *Something isn't right here.* He drew his pistol.

"Comrade," a male voice said out of the pitch–blackness. "You will not need your weapon." A flickering match drew Yuen's attention to the right side of the cavernous space.

"How can I be sure?" He pulled back the hammer.

"Now, now, Xin Li. Don't tell me that you don't remember your old schoolmaster?"

The man held the match up to his face as he lit a cigarette. Yuen squinted. The man had a few more wrinkles, but it was he, all right.

"Come in, Xin Li. We have much to discuss," Master Fong instructed. Then he flipped a switch and a desk lamp came on. Fong was seated in a chair. Another chair sat across a small wooden table from him. The old man and the furniture near him seemed to hover in the darkness.

Yuen pulled the door shut and made his way over to the chair. He used the back of his hand to wipe the last raindrops from his face.

Fong smiled as Yuen arrived at the table and chair. He eased down the hammer on the pistol and put it away.

"I can't believe they sent you. How long has it been now? Twenty years?" The old man creaked to his feet.

The two men hugged.

"Twenty–two. You were my best student. Please, let us sit." He did so.

Yuen looked around the room once more. Still dark, except for the area right around the old man, it seemed safe enough.

"Are we the only ones here?"

"Of course, Xin Li. Were you expecting others?"

Yuen edged onto the chair. "Well, I had thought for such an important find…"

"Let's see what you have there," the old man nodded toward his briefcase.

Xin Li placed it on the table and dialed the combination. Fong pressed the latches on either side of the black case and opened it himself.

Yuen Xin Li relaxed in the opposite chair. As the old man studied the papers, Yuen analyzed Fong. The intervening years had not been kind to his old master. Fong's glasses were noticeably thicker and his hair, once gray, was almost all gone.

On the second or third page, Fong gasped as one eyebrow went up. The cigarette he was smoking almost fell out of his mouth. Yuen's eyes met his when he looked across the top of his glasses at his pupil. "I now understand the reason for your urgency," Fong said as he began putting away the papers.

Yuen smiled.

"This is phenomenal."

"Yes, I thought so, too."

"So, what now?" Fong asked as he began to place the papers back into their red folders.

"I do not understand."

"What do we do with you now?"

"Master Fong, I have been a loyal patriot. I was hoping that I could…"

"Go home?" Fong asked as he finished Yuen's sentence.

"Yes."

Fong shifted his weight in his chair. "Yes, Xin Li. You have served the State well. You have proven yourself time and time again."

"Thank you, Master."

"But it does not excuse your carelessness with State assets."

"What do you mean?"

"By acting so impulsively, you have managed to damage our entire network here in Japan, possibly irrevocably."

Yuen frowned.

"I'm sorry, Xin Li. You have been of great service to Mother China for so long. It is a shame to see you end this way."

Yuen heard three thumping noises before he looked down to see his own blood covering his hands. *Oh, my.* He felt tears forming in his eyes. *How could he have done this?*

CHAPTER FOUR
FRIDAY, APRIL 9TH

Hobson Residence
Glen Burnie, Maryland
3:20 AM
7:20 AM, GMT

Marcia Hobson squinted, trying to focus on the blue numbers of the alarm clock beside her bed. She gave up and sat up to reach for the clock.

It didn't add up. The piercing electronic noise came from something other than her clock. It shouldn't go off for another hour. She peered across the still dark reaches of her bedroom to see a small red light blinking in time with the shrill beeping that had pulled her out of a good dream.

"Shit." She put the clock back down.

She used both hands to rub her face, and then to wipe the rest of the sleep from her eyes. Meanwhile, the pager on her desk continued screaming at her. "Yeah, yeah. I'm coming."

She switched on the lamp and threw off the covers.

Three or four staggering steps later, she was fingering the buttons to stop the noise. The digital display read, "Call Op Center Immediately."

She frowned. "Op Center. I don't know the number for the Operations Center." She sighed as if the weight of several tons had suddenly descended upon her.

Marcia sat at her desk and switched on the lamp. She reached for the National Energy Agency phone book. It was under several notebooks, pads, and fishing guides. As she pulled it from the bottom of the stack, several of the things near her cascaded to the floor. "Damn it." She made a face at the mess.

As her eyes scoured the pages looking for the number, her vision improved in the light. She found it a few seconds later and reached for the phone.

"Operations Center, Desk Watch. May I help you?" a wide–awake male voice asked.

"Hi, this is Marcia Hobson, I—"

"Yes, Doctor Hobson. We've been waiting on your call. Stand by, please," he interrupted.

Marcia's right eyebrow went up. *Wow. I never get this much respect. What the hell is going on?*

"Marcia?"

She instantly recognized her boss' voice.

"Doug Miller, here."

I know who this is, you big idiot. I work with you every flippin' day. "Yes, Doug?" She tried to keep the "Why the hell are you paging me at three in the morning? tone out of her voice.

"I need you to get in here ASAP. We've got an emergency."

"Can I ask the nature of the emergency? I've got a Parent–Teacher conference this morning and—"

"Marcia, your *big* project, whatever it is, has just suffered a major setback."

His words went through her like bullets. The sweat glands in her hands and armpits instantly started working. She caught herself on the verge of hyperventilating. "What? How?"

"You know I can't get into that over the phone. How soon can you get in here?"

She glanced over her left shoulder at the clock. "Give me a couple of hours."

"See you then." The line went dead.

She put down the phone, already second–guessing what she might have left undone. "Oh, God. Please don't let this be my screw–up."

CHAPTER FIVE
FRIDAY, APRIL 9TH

Department of Energy
Office of the Secretary
Washington, District of Columbia
5:45 AM
9:45 AM, GMT

"Sir, she's twenty minutes late. This is ridiculous. I can get someone else, someone more dependable to take over the project."

Energy Secretary Jack Langdon reclined in his chair as Doug Miller made his case to replace Doctor Marcia Hobson.

Miller, a thin dark–haired man, looked like an accountant. In his mid–thirties, he had started out his post–graduate days as a law student. Somehow he got swept up in the political process and because of some family friends, found himself with an appointment in Langdon's department.

"You know, Doug, you remind me of me when I was a young staffer about a million years ago."

"Sir, I—"

"And that's the main reason I don't can you, because you're being a real pain in the ass." Langdon's candor surprised even himself.

Miller's mouth dropped open.

"Doctor Hobson is not only a brilliant scientist and administrator, she's also a single mom, black, the widow of a Desert Storm war hero, and a local. You've got to learn, son, that in politics, you don't get presents like Marcia handed to you every day. She stays on the project and I don't want to hear any more noise about replacing her."

The real reason that Langdon didn't get rid of Miller was that, like himself, he was there through political appointment. Worse yet, Miller knew it, too. However, Langdon wasn't going to give him the satisfaction. *I hate this little twerp.*

"And on top of that, I like her," Langdon added.

Miller folded his arms and blew out a sigh.

The combination telephone and intercom on his desk buzzed.

"Yes, Tina?"

"Doctor Hobson is here, Sir."

"Send her in, please." Langdon pressed the button to end the connection and pushed his chair back from the desk.

I love pissin' him off. A knock at the door kept him from smiling to himself. "Come in."

"Sorry, I'm late," Marcia began as soon as she opened the door.

"Think nothing of it, Doctor." Langdon came to his feet and walked over to meet her. He watched as she and Miller exchanged glances and then spoke.

"How's that son of yours?"

They shook hands. Langdon made a point of using both of his to grasp and enclose Hobson's.

The attractive and medium–height woman always dressed well. Her blue suit and white blouse gave her just the right 'Washington–corporate' image. She wore glasses today rather than her regular contact lenses.

Langdon thought most people probably only saw the well–shaped female figure now gliding across his office. Anyone with the idea that she'd made it in D.C. on looks had only to see her credentials: two Ph.D.'s, one in Nuclear Physics from M.I.T., and too many citations to even mention in one seating.

"Fine, Sir. He's doing very well."

"Good. Good. Have a seat. Doug here will give us a rundown on what's going on."

Langdon returned to his side of the expansive and shiny wooden desk. His chair squeaked a bit as he sat down and again reclined. Miller and Hobson sat in guest chairs on the other side. Langdon could almost see the wall between them.

"At approximately eight o'clock Tokyo time Wednesday evening, this man stole a still–undetermined number of documents pertaining to Project Blue Flame." Miller handed Hobson a picture of the spy. Langdon had seen it earlier.

He watched her as she raised an eyebrow.

"In the process, he killed five people." Doug could have been commenting on the weather.

Marcia touched the base of her throat as she whispered, "Five?" She shook her head slightly. "Do we know anything about him?" she asked, her tone matching Miller's as she handed the photograph back.

"Yes, he's dead and the files he stole are missing."

"Dead? How?"

"Shot in the heart at nearly point blank range. Several times. Bastard got a little of what he'd handed out earlier."

Marcia Hobson shrugged her lack of understanding at his meaning.

"One of the people he killed was an eighty–year–old janitor."

"Oh? Where did they find the shooter?" she asked.

"In an alley near the bay. Japanese Intelligence has the body for investigation. Hopefully, they'll figure out who he is."

"But we've already got a pretty good idea," Langdon interjected.

"Yakuza?" she offered.

"Chinese."

"Chinese? I don't understand."

"We've known for a long time that Chinese intelligence agents had infiltrated Japanese government at several levels. Just like the Soviets did to us during the Cold War," Langdon replied.

"And just like the Chinese have done to us," she added.

Langdon didn't like the reminder. She was right, however.

"Besides," Miller added. "What would the mob, Japanese or American, want with information concerning nuclear fusion?"

Langdon sat up in his chair. "There's a second Cold War coming. Whoever can cut domestic costs and build the most weapons will win."

"Just like the last time," she added.

"Just like the last time."

"So what do we do next?" Hobson asked.

"The President, National Security Advisor, and the

CIA Director have to be briefed. We'll be watching the Chinese for any actions," Miller said.

His pride–laced voice only further agitated Langdon.

"What's the status of the project?" Langdon asked Hobson.

Miller moved to the edge of his chair. He'd been trying for months to get his nose into this thing, and now it looked like events had worked in his favor. Blue Flame had enjoyed the highest levels of security. Like its predecessor, the Manhattan Project, everyone involved was certain it, too, would change the world.

"We've been running the facility on fusion–based power for almost a month."

Miller's eyes widened at the news.

"We are roughly a year ahead of schedule," she added.

"You did it? You actually did it?" Miller asked. Disbelief and surprise washed across his face.

"Do you have enough information to recreate the reaction somewhere else?" Langdon asked, shooting Miller an evil glance and trying to return some decorum to the meeting.

She shifted in her seat. "Yeah, I think so."

Langdon sat back in his chair again.

"Does the President know about this?" Miller asked Hobson.

"Yes, Doug. He knows everything."

Langdon almost laughed aloud at Hobson's patronizing tone. Controlling his voice, he said, "Marcia, I want you on an airplane. Get over there and shut it down. Wrap up all the data and get back here as soon as possible. I'll get some help from DOD if we need it."

"Sir, I've got a problem. Next week is Spring Break and my kid and I were going skiing. Canceling the trip isn't a problem, I just don't have anyone for him to stay with while I'm gone."

"Tristan ever been out of the country?" he asked.

"No, Sir."

"Miller, make a call to State. Get her son a passport. Marcia, take him with you."

She frowned as she spoke. "Sir, if we think a spy has shot five people...Well, I'm just wondering if it's safe?"

"Marcia, we've run a security check on everybody on that island. We're gonna run another one today. The whole place is locked down; nobody can get on or off the island without us knowing about it. Everything will be fine." Langdon smiled warmly as he spoke.

She smiled. "Yes, Sir."

"Besides, I want you focused."

"Yes, Sir."

"And Marcia, keep a lid on this spy thing."

"Sir?"

"I don't want anyone over there knowing too much. If they get wind that the Chinese placed somebody in the Japanese government..."

"I understand, Mister Secretary. But I was just over there. They, well, one of them in particular, will be curious."

"Tell them I chewed you out for not getting enough information, tell them you left your purse, hell, I don't care."

"Yes, Sir. I understand."

"This thing is still our best–kept secret. I want to keep it that way." Langdon slapped his hands on his desk.

CHAPTER SIX
FRIDAY, APRIL 9TH

The McGuire Residence
Plano, Texas
6:05 AM
11:05 AM, GMT

Ben's eyes shot open. "What was that?" He blinked in the darkness, trying to convince himself that he hadn't heard a gunshot. "Must have been a car backfiring."

Ben's neighbor had a teenager, complete with a Mustang convertible. *Of course, it was a backfire.* The sound of gunfire fit Plano like listening to Frank Sinatra belt out a rap tune.

He liked his upscale neighborhood, even if it was a little sterile. Located in the northern part of the Dallas–Fort Worth metroplex, Plano held the distinction of being one of the most affluent communities in Texas.

Claire stirred at the sound of his voice, but only for

a second. She soon fell back into her characteristically deep slumber.

Her arm draped across his chest as she came to rest her head on his shoulder. Her short blonde hair tickled his nose before he pushed it away from his face.

He stared at the contrast of their skin color for a long while. Even in the early morning darkness of their bedroom, their racial difference was clear and defined. He always reveled at how alike and how different they were, all at the same time. *A true paradox.*

Ben reflected on how their chance meeting three years before had blossomed into a marriage. He was just divorced then, from his college sweetheart. His two children were the priority: How to be apart from them and yet not let them feel he was leaving them, too. And, of course, there was work. He let the latter fill what was left of the room in his life, that is until Claire came along.

The clock's electronic shrill suddenly shattered the early morning quiet. Squeezing his eyes shut, Ben swatted at the alarm clock four times before he finally nailed the snooze button. *So much for reflection time.*

"God, I'm so tired," Claire moaned.

"Yeah. Me, too."

"Snuggle," she said just above a whisper. As her leg came to rest on his, Ben pulled his wife of just four months closer. He kissed her forehead.

"I love you," she whispered.

"Oh, bullshit. You're just after the McGuire family fortune."

"Damn, you've got me figured out. I guess I'll have to have sex with you to keep you under my control."

He smiled at the prospect. "Well, only if you think it's *absolutely* necessary."

As Claire rolled on top of him, he opened his eyes to see her lovely oval–shaped face in the morning light. Her brown eyes seemed even darker in the dimly lit room. However, her smile, oh that smile, was as clear as day. He had fallen in love with it on their first meeting and every day since. "Somebody's feeling frisky this morning," he murmured.

"Uh huh. Well, after you denied me last night, what's a gal to do?"

"What do you mean, denied you?"

"When I came in last night, you were asleep." She used her index finger to poke him in the forehead, right between the eyes.

"You could have woke me up."

She fell silent for a moment. She kissed his mouth then his cheek. "I could tell you were tired."

"Babe, I'm never too tired for you." He grinned what he hoped was his most seductive smile.

"Really? Is that right?"

"And remember, I'm a Naval Academy grad. We're always ready for action, of any kind."

"Please don't start singing 'Anchors Aweigh' again," she replied as she kissed him.

Ben used his feet to pull the covers away. Then he wrapped his legs around hers as their kisses swelled with passion and vigor. His hands intertwined with hers.

"Daddy, are you up?" A soft knock at their bedroom door followed the question.

Their embrace, among other things, faded with disappointment. The knock came again from his five–year–old daughter.

"Aren't you going to answer?" Claire asked as she struggled to pull the covers back over herself.

"Maybe if I don't, she'll go away," he replied.

Claire hit him on the shoulder. "Yes, sweetie. He's up. Just a minute, okay?" She grinned an evil grin.

"Okay. Morning, Claire," Vanessa said from the other side of the door.

"I *was* up," Ben whispered to his wife as he climbed out of bed.

"Don't think this gets you off the hook." Claire climbed out, too. By the time Ben was finished putting on his pajama bottoms, she was already dressed in hers.

"Oh, no?"

"Tonight, mister. Your ass is mine," she whispered.

She fell into his arms. They kissed again as another gentle knock came from the other side of the door.

The White House
Washington, D.C.
7:20 AM
11:20 AM, GMT

Secretary of Energy Jack Langdon wrung moist hands as he sat in the Oval Office reception area. Just a few feet away, some of the President's staff compared notes on their involvement in the day's activities. Eavesdropping on them helped take his mind off the reason for his being there: telling the President his pet project was in trouble.

From what he could tell, someone had screwed up and double–booked the Chief Executive's post–lunch workout. One of them had him bicycling with the House Minority Whip, a very outspoken Democrat.

Someone else, however, had him playing tennis with Chairman of the Senate Armed Forces Committee, a feisty Texas Republican.

Langdon caught himself leaning forward in the high–backed chair to catch every word. The Social Secretary ranted while two junior staffers cowered in her shadow.

Geez, what a shitty job.

"Jack, the President will see you now," Chief of Staff George Nelson announced.

Langdon jumped. The President's chief advisor had surprised him. Nelson, a large husky man with a deep voice, wore a stern expression. He was pissed. Langdon's impromptu visit had likely screwed up an otherwise well–planned schedule.

Langdon forced a smile at Nelson as he grabbed his briefcase and stood. The Chief of Staff did not return his attempt to lighten the mood. Rather, he spun around and marched into the Oval Office leaving Langdon to follow in his wake. The Cabinet member swallowed hard and took big steps.

Once inside, two Secret Service Agents closed the door behind him. Langdon stopped in the middle of the room while George Reynolds took a seat on a nearby sofa, picking up his coffee cup almost immediately.

"Mornin' Jack," President Albert Turner said from behind his desk.

"Good morning, Sir." Langdon caught himself standing at attention just like he had once done some thirty years ago as an Army recruit.

The President wore his reading glasses low on his nose. He looked up at Langdon across the top of the rim. At that moment, he reminded Langdon of the days when Turner had been a college Political Science teacher. With his hair more or less gray, Turner looked almost kindly. "Coffee, Jack?" He pointed toward a silver pot on a table near Nelson.

"No, thank you, Mister President."

President Turner looked across the room at Nelson for a moment. Then he flashed his gaze toward Langdon. "Now what the hell is so damned important as to get me out of bed this early!" Turner's grin belied his tone of voice. He removed his glasses and the image of the college professor evaporated.

"Sir, we have an issue with the project."

Turner put down the papers he'd been holding in his right hand. His gaze shifted from Langdon to Nelson.

Nelson looked first at Langdon with a frown, then at the President. The President looked back at Langdon. "Is it serious?"

"Yes, Sir. I believe it is."

Nelson was sitting up now. He put down his coffee cup and squinted at Langdon.

The President nodded. Langdon felt his stomach quivering. His armpits now competed with his hands in moisture content.

Turner's eyes went wide. He mouthed the word 'shit' as he adjusted his glasses. "I guess the time has come to let the Chief of Staff in on the project."

"Project. What project?" Nelson asked. He frowned as he spoke, more at Langdon than the President.

Langdon didn't speak. If the Chief of Staff didn't know already, he wasn't supposed to know.

Turner glanced at Nelson and then back at Langdon. "George, we've got some good news and, since Langdon's here at seven in the morning, probably some bad news." For a second or two, Nelson wore the 'ohmygod' expression common to many of the President's staffers.

"Yes, Sir," Langdon added.

"Take a seat and give me the bad news, Jack."

Langdon quickly filled the President in on the happenings in Japan. As he spoke, Langdon noticed George Nelson moving closer and closer to the edge of his seat on the couch.

"So let me get this straight," Nelson began even before Langdon finished his last words. "We've somehow managed to build a nuclear reactor in secret, and in a foreign country? How is this possible, Sir? Why would we do that?"

"It's not just a nuclear reactor, George. It's a nuclear fusion reactor."

Nelson wore an 'and?' expression.

"George, I realize you're just a lawyer, but see if you can follow me on this."

Langdon choked back a grin as the President started laying out his case for not only starting the project but also for breaking the law.

"We're in the Twenty–First Century and we're more dependent on fossil fuels than we have *ever* been. Even if all the oil in the world could last forever, most of it belongs to countries that don't like us very much."

"But nuclear power is way too unpopular. Look at all the problems we've had so far: Three Mile Island, Chernobyl—" Nelson countered.

"Those are fission systems," Langdon cut him off.

Nelson shot Langdon an evil glance. If looks could kill, Jack Langdon knew his head would have a place on Nelson's lodge wall.

"Quite right, Jack," the President continued.

"I don't understand."

"Nuclear fusion will provide the same kind of limitless power as a fission system but without the radioactive waste and danger."

Nelson's eyebrows shot up.

"That's right. We're talking all kinds of political capital…"

"And your legacy would be secure," Nelson finished the sentence.

Nelson nodded. "So how did you do it?"

"Are you sure you want to know?"

"Mister President, with all due respect, you only get in trouble when I can't cover your ass."

Turner smiled. "Okay, we hid the funds in economic assistance for Japan."

"Is that where the lab is?"

"Yes."

"But if it's so secret, how did you hide it there? I gotta believe this thing gives off a bunch of heat," Nelson asked. "I mean a nuke is a nuke. Right?"

Turner smiled and nodded at Langdon. "Our Energy Secretary figured that one out. Tell him, Jack."

"The Japanese, after their World War II experience, have always been a little gun–shy of nuclear power. When the first reactors were constructed over there, the government created a Nuclear Safety Research Facility to keep the masses calm."

Nelson nodded. Then he smiled at the irony.

"Oh, it gets even better," the President added.

"The Prime Minister that authorized building of the facility further reasoned that no one wanted the words 'nuclear' and 'research' on a building anywhere in their neighborhood. So, they built it on a relatively remote island in the East China Sea."

"Which one?" Nelson asked.

"Senkaku," Turner replied.

"Never heard of it," Nelson quipped.

"That's why we thought it was perfect."

Nelson finally reclined in his seat. "So how long has this been going on?"

"About five years. Before you came on board as my Chief of Staff."

"And now the whole thing's in trouble," Langdon added. "We're not ready to go public with this yet. We've still got a lot of work to do."

"Yes," the President added. "And we've got to come up with a plan, and fast."

McGuire Residence
Plano, Texas
7:00 AM
12:00 PM, GMT

"Good morning. This is Christina Appleton with CNN Headline News. Our top story this morning continues to be the execution–style slayings in Tokyo, Japan, where a gunman killed five people at the Ministry of International Trade and Industry Wednesday night."

Claire could hear the television as she stood in the kitchen. Ben loved watching the news first thing every morning. She hated that he didn't filter what the children could hear.

Seconds before, her attention had been focused on getting the bow on Vanessa's ponytail just right. "There, honey. You look great."

"What's Daddy watching?"

She rolled her eyes. *Ben, I swear.* "The news, honey. Let's go and see if we can get him to watch something else."

"Sometime Wednesday night, the man killed a janitor and three guards. Officials are said to be investigating but have no explanation of why the act was committed or who the perpetrator might be," the broadcast continued.

Claire walked into the den and shut off the TV.

"Hey, I was watching that."

"And she was listening," she replied, gesturing at Vanessa.

Ben put his hands to his temples and rubbed them slowly.

Claire was still feeling her way, trying to figure out how to be a good stepmother. The two of them had already "discussed" what was appropriate television viewing for the children several times. Ben had his ideas, however, and she hers.

"Don't you think you're being a little extreme here? It's the news, Hon."

Ben stood up. His tall, lean frame towered over his daughter's. They both had the same big eyes and wonderful smile. Ben's complexion, much darker than Vanessa's, reminded her of a big chocolate bar. As much as she loved him, he still could push just the right buttons. Like now.

"Ben, she's got the rest of her life to find out what M–U–R–D–E–R is," Claire spelled.

"Mur–der," Vanessa interjected.

Ben's eyes went wide open as he stared at his daughter.

"See what I mean?" Claire added.

He shot her an evil glance.

"Vanessa?"

"Yes?"

"Who taught you how to spell that?"

"Adam. He teaches me all of my new words," she replied.

"Hey, Dad. Where are my shoes?" Adam McGuire's question announced his arrival.

Ben rubbed his temples again, then his eyes.

"Besides," Claire started again. "With you going over there next week, I'm already nervous enough."

"I'm going to Korea, not Japan," he replied.

"Dad! Where are my shoes?"

"Adam, they're your shoes. You're eight years old. Find 'em." Ben threw up his hands in frustration.

Adam, tall and lean like his father, huffed a sigh, wheeled around, and marched out of the kitchen back toward his bedroom.

"Korea, Japan. Japan, Korea. It's all the same to me," she said on her way out of the room. "Adam, I'll help you."

"Good thing you're not working for the State Department," she heard him say under his breath as he sipped his coffee.

A loud *whack* heralded a well–aimed magazine hitting him in the back of the head. "My geography might be bad, but my aim is still good!" she shouted.

Vanessa laughed.

"You're not out of trouble, young lady. Eat your oatmeal," Ben said to his daughter.

Claire kept her smile to herself as she moved on to help her stepson.

CHAPTER SEVEN
FRIDAY, APRIL 9TH

Offices of Information View Consulting
Plano, Texas
8:00 AM
1:00 PM, GMT

His boss didn't like a lot of detail. He trusted his senior staff to get the job done without a lot of micro–management. Ben's status meetings with him usually only ran about fifteen minutes. Today, however, things were running long.

John Castlebury, a wiry man in his late forties, had started the company on a lark. Now, almost ten years later, he had successful branch offices in ten major metropolitan cities across the country.

Ben checked his watch. They'd been at it for almost half an hour now. He was leaving the next day for almost three weeks. He knew the 'old man' would be full of questions. "Can your team handle this?" he asked.

"Of course, John. We only hire the best, you know that."

Castlebury shot Ben an uncomfortable glance. "This is a big damn deal, Ben. We can't afford to screw this up."

"John, have we ever let you down?"

"No, and you've never been away for almost three weeks during a deal like this, either."

Ben shrugged. "Sorry, Boss."

"How can I get in touch with you?"

"You can't. I'll be at sea."

"Well, you called me from the Gulf of Mexico on your cell phone last year. How come you can't do that?" Castlebury stood and walked over to his pitcher of ice water.

"I don't think Sprint covers the Sea of Japan, John," Ben chuckled.

"Are you sure?"

Ben got nervous all of a sudden. He didn't like guessing and he sure as hell didn't like not knowing the answer to one of John Castlebury's questions. He took a deep breath. "No. No, I'm not."

"Find out which companies have got digital or satellite service over in the Sea of Japan. There's gotta be one or two, for sure. When you get a name, have Donna establish service for you for one month. That ought to cover it."

"John. That's a lot of money," Ben protested.

"Is it more than five million?"

He had a point. "No, it's not that much."

"Well, like my daddy always said, you gotta spend money to make money," the Texan drawled.

To tell the truth, I was looking forward to getting out of here for a few weeks, completely out of here. The idea of answering cell–phone calls while on Reserve duty didn't appeal to him. *But, they are keeping my pay and benefits going while I'm gone.* "I'll make it happen."

"Anything else?"

"Nope. That's it."

"All right, then. You be careful out there and have a good trip." He extended his hand.

Ben grasped and shook it. "See you in about three weeks."

"Don't worry, I'll talk to you before then."

Residence of Katelyn McGuire
Plano, Texas
8:18 AM
1:18 PM, GMT

"You're late," Katelyn grunted at Claire as she and Vanessa arrived at the front door.

Claire didn't respond to Ben's ex–wife. Instead, she knelt in front of the girl. "Have a nice day at school, honey. I'll see you tomorrow at your party."

"Okay. Bye, Claire." With that, she threw her arms around Claire's neck and squeezed. Claire hugged her back with affection.

Vanessa disappeared into the house as Claire stood up.

"I said—"

"I heard you," Claire whispered. "It's only twenty after eight. She's dressed and fed. What's the big deal? You don't have to be at work until nine."

"That's not the point."

"Please keep your voice down." Claire wanted to shout, but refused herself the luxury.

47

"Listen, you can rule your house, but not this one."

Claire gritted her teeth. She stared back at the short, brunette woman glowering at her, light brown eyes flashing like lasers. Katelyn's face was hard and dark.

"And another thing—"

With that, Claire turned and walked away from the front door and Ben's first wife's rage. "Have a nice day," was all she was able to get out before the sound of a slamming door caught up to her.

"Bitch."

CHAPTER EIGHT
FRIDAY, APRIL 9TH

Prestonwood Educational Services Center
Plano School Independent District
Plano, Texas
2:45 PM
7:45 PM, GMT

Katelyn McGuire dumped the contents of her food tray into the trashcan in the staff lunchroom. Even though most of the food went with the initial heave, she struck the plastic tray against the sides of the trashcan so hard that the banging noise reverberated through the air like two gunshots.

"I think you got it," Marie Rabb said, as she was about to strike it again.

Kate whipped around to see her friend and co-worker gazing back with a raised eyebrow. Rather than hit it again, she practically shoved it into the window and the hands of the hair-netted female foodservice attendant on the other side. A little moisture flew onto the smock of the worker.

"Sorry," Kate apologized. "I didn't mean to do that."

The hair–netted lady in the dirty–dish window only nodded back.

Kate lowered her head and turned away. As she marched off toward the lunchroom door, she heard Marie almost running to catch up.

"What's eatin' you?"

Marie, a native Texan, was a college classmate that had, oddly enough, ended up in the same town. Now almost seventeen years after graduation they were working together. She used her hand to push back her long dark hair. She loved Western–style clothing. Today, a denim skirt, red scarf and boots adorned a heavy frame.

"Nothing."

"Yeah, bullshit. The only person that gets you going like this is Ben. What did he do this time?"

Kate didn't respond. The silence between them was filled with the sound of their footsteps as they walked down the hall.

The Service Center, thank goodness, didn't usually have a lot of children in it, serving as an annex to the main administration building on the other side of Plano.

Kate finally stopped in front of her office. As the school district's Special Education Diagnostician, she rated her own office. "Come on in." She pushed open the door and walked around the desk.

Kate took a seat in her chair while Marie took one on her desk. She sighed. "It wasn't Ben. It was his *new* wife."

"What did she do?"

"She, she." Kate crossed her arms and then uncrossed them. "She didn't do anything."

Marie frowned. "I don't understand."

"I guess I'm just pissed off…"

"That Ben's married again?"

She sighed again. Her eyes watered, but she batted away tears. "Yeah."

"Kate. I…"

She reclined in her chair.

"I don't know what you're feelin'. God help me, I hope I never get divorced." Kate watched her friend stare at her own wedding band. "I just know that it's been two years since the divorce. It's been almost four since you guys separated. You've gotta let go of this."

Kate only nodded her head that she understood.

"Don't get me wrong. I still think he's a shit, but he's got a right to a life."

"And I don't?"

"Sure you do, Kate. The difference is, he's living his. You haven't started yet."

Dulles International Airport
Outskirts of Washington, D.C.
6:30 PM
10:30 PM, GMT

"Okay. Here's your gate," Doug Miller announced as the sedan pulled up to the curb.

Marcia's and her son's luggage almost filled Miller's BMW. She and one of her bags occupied the front seat while Tristan and several other pieces crammed the back.

"You really didn't have to bring us out here, Doug. I really appreciate it, though." Marcia was sure the Secretary had ordered him to do it.

"Least I could do. Besides, the boss told me to make sure you and the boy here get off on time." Miller cracked a wide smile, one of only a few she had seen from him.

I knew it. "Well, thanks—"

"Who you callin' boy?" Tristan Hobson lashed out from the backseat as he leaned forward. His head was almost in Miller's face.

Miller raised his eyebrow at the adolescent.

Marcia's mouth dropped open at her child's rudeness.

Shorter than his mother, and very muscular, Tristan had a dark complexion and skin–short hair. A diamond stud in his left ear caught the light from the airport buildings and other cars.

"Excuse me?" Miller replied.

"You heard—," her son began.

"Tristan, shut your mouth!" his mother ordered.

Silence returned to the car. She noticed the temperature in the car had surged upward, along with her heartbeat.

Since she'd cancelled the skiing trip, her fifteen–year–old son had been almost totally out of control. Trying to sell him on an adventure on the Japanese frontier had not gone over well. She hadn't thought it would, especially since his girlfriend would be on the other side of the world. *Teenagers, everything's so traumatic to them.*

Miller pulled his eyes away from the boy back to her. "Have a good trip," he said after a long while.

"Thanks, Doug." She feigned a smile before turning to her brooding child. "Come on, Tristan. Get out of the car." *God, I wish I could still spank him.*

Miller climbed out, too. He started getting the bags out of the car. A skycap arrived a few seconds later to load their belongings for check–in.

"Doctor Hobson?" he started. "Marcia," he started again with a less formal tone.

"Yeah?" she fumbled with her bags.

"Be careful over there."

"Is there something you're not telling me?"

"No. I just want you to keep your eyes open. I don't trust the Japs, I never have."

"Now, Doug. That's not very politically correct," she chided.

"Maybe, but my old man was at Pearl Harbor."

She nodded. "I'll be careful. But they're not the ones we're worried about."

He nodded. "Just keep Tiger here with you. You'll do just fine." Miller reached to pat Tristan on the back, but the youth jerked away.

Miller raised his eyebrow again. He sighed by blowing out his breath through an 'O' shaped mouth. The expression on his face decayed almost in a flash. He and her son exchanged glares before Miller turned and walked away. "Have a good flight," he said before he climbed back into his car.

Marcia waited to speak until her son finally turned away from her boss and back toward her.

"Tristan Hobson, you were raised better than that."

"But Mom—"

"But, nothing! Mister Miller is an adult! You don't talk to adults that way, especially not to one of my colleagues!"

"He was dissin' me!"

"No, he wasn't! You've been looking for a fight ever since I told you we were going to Japan instead of skiing. Be angry if you want, I don't care. But if you're going to act like a jerk, do me the courtesy of pretending you're not with me!" Marcia turned and walked away toward the airport building. After a few steps, she stopped and turned to see him pick up his bags and trail along after her.

CHAPTER NINE
FRIDAY, APRIL 9TH

Mediterraneo Restaurant
Dallas, Texas
6:30 PM
11:30 PM, GMT

"Here's one," Dave Ferguson continued. He loved telling jokes.

"Come on, Dave," Charlotte protested. "This is the third one. I'm sure Claire's getting tired of this."

"Oh, no. Let him go. He's enjoying himself."

"He goes on these sales trips and comes back with a whole new bunch. I swear, sometimes it's worse than living with a professional comedian. At least they get paid to be funny," she laughed.

"Do you mind? I'm trying to keep our friend's mind off of her tardy husband."

"Go ahead, Dave. Let's hear it."

"Okay, okay. New credit card commercial:

"Lockheed F–16 Fighting Falcon—$25 million; Lockheed F–117 Nighthawk Stealth Fighter—$45 million; Boeing B–52 Stratofortress—$74 million; Brand new B–2 Stealth Bomber—2.1 billion; a decent map of downtown Belgrade—Priceless."

Claire caught herself only grinning. However, an older man at a nearby table and Dave belly–laughed for the next few minutes. Dave Ferguson bowed to him when he waved.

Concentrating on the conversation proved difficult as her attention and gaze kept wandering back to the restaurant's entrance. Their table, located in almost the exact center of the posh downtown dining room, gave her a clear view of the doorway.

"How's work, Claire?" Charlotte Ferguson asked from the opposite side of the table as the laughter subsided.

Her friend's question had the effect of bringing her back to the table, if only for a moment. "Oh, pretty good. Things have slowed down a lot since we finished our ERP work."

Charlotte Ferguson's bright blue eyes flashed, complimenting her wide–mouthed smile. With her dark hair, light blue eyes and thin frame, she reminded Claire of a leprechaun. Like her husband, her Irish ancestry was outwardly and readily apparent.

"Can't imagine that was any fun," Dave added. "Our resource planning project took almost three years."

Dave, a few inches taller than his wife's five–foot, two inches, had a stocky build. A once–thick head of red hair was now thinned on top. Like his wife, Dave Ferguson's crystal–clear blue eyes accented a wide, toothy smile. The two of them were walking commercials for St. Patrick's Day and vacations to the Old Country.

"I'm all packed. Is Ben?" he asked.

Dave and Ben traced their friendship back to their Naval Academy days. After graduation, both had served as officers in the Fleet, Dave as a submariner and Ben as a surface warfare officer.

In the middle of sipping ice water with a lemon twist, Claire shook her head. "No. He hasn't even started yet. I know Saturday evening is going to be a wild trip to one store after another for this and that."

"That figures," Dave replied.

"Why?" Charlotte asked.

"Ben hates Korea," Claire replied.

"Really? Why?"

Claire shrugged first, and then looked to Dave for an answer.

"I don't know. He's not fond of that part of the world," he replied.

"Well, to tell the truth, neither am I," she admitted.

"Why? I think it's exotic," Charlotte added.

Claire only shrugged again. "He even hates Asian food. I've been trying to get him out to that new place on the Tollway. He finds some way to wiggle out of it every time."

"Did he ever tell you about his stint at the Republic of Korea Third Fleet Headquarters?" Dave asked, barely controlling his laughter.

Before she could answer that she had already heard the story, several times, Dave was already rolling with it. "Ben somehow got conned into doing a tour as the U.S. Navy's liaison to the Korean admiral's staff. Long story short, he was the only American Naval Officer in the City of Pusan for almost three weeks. Bear in mind, all of the really Western restaurants, McDonald's included, are down in Seoul."

"Did he volunteer for that?" Charlotte asked.

"I'm not sure. Anyway, one day the Korean admiral invites all of the officers on the exercise to dine in his mess. So there Ben is, all decked out in his dress uniform, sitting next to the admiral's Chief of Staff and his interpreter."

Claire reclined back in her chair as Dave rambled on. She tried not to show a, "I've heard this before," look.

"So they bring out this stuff in a bowl and put it in front of him."

"Ben?" Charlotte asked.

"Yeah. So, Ben asks the interpreter, 'What's this?' The interpreter tells him, 'It is kimchi'."

"Hmm," Claire added for effect. *Now, I know I've heard this story.*

"So, Ben takes a big ol' spoonful which immediately sets his mouth on fire 'cause this is the hottest shit anybody could ever eat—"

"Spicy?" Claire asked.

"Mega spicy. So, he practically spits it back into the bowl and shouts 'Holy Cow!' at the top of his lungs." Dave is barely able to speak from laughing so hard at Ben's misadventure.

Claire smiled more at Dave's rendition than the facts of the story.

"Anyway, the only reason we found out about it is because Ben was afraid that he'd caused an international incident. He wrote up the events of the meal in his daily Situation Report to the U.S. Navy admiral running the exercise."

"So what happened? Did he get in trouble?" Charlotte asked.

"No, the ROK admiral just laughed it off. But for

the rest of the exercise, about two weeks, he referred to Ben as Lieutenant Commander Holy Cow!"

The three of them laughed until they noticed the other patrons glaring at them.

As Claire listened to Dave tell his wife the rest of the story, she remarked to herself how fond she was of him. Prior to her arrival in Ben's life, Dave had been his best friend. Dave had stood with Ben through his separation, divorce, job and financial trials. And when he really didn't have to, he graciously gave up that role to her when the appropriate time came. In fact, Dave and Charlotte Ferguson had been their greatest supporters during their courtship and eventual marriage.

Claire found herself looking toward the door again. This time glances at her wristwatch separated those toward the doorway.

"What are you planning on doing to make the next three weeks go by?" Charlotte asked. She ran her fingers through the close–cropped hair on the back of Dave's head. Charlotte was going back East while her husband floated around the Sea of Japan.

Claire, however, was about to go through her first Naval Reserve separation. Through their courtship and engagement, Ben had command of his own unit. As Commanding Officer, he had his choice of duty assignments, and none of them had been far away from her. Both of his two–week training periods had been spent in Corpus Christi, which allowed her to visit.

"I don't know, this and that. I've got a couple of art workshops I've wanted to attend. Plus, the kids will want to come over one or two nights."

"Hmm. Well, don't go stir crazy. I usually forget

how much I miss this butt–head until he's gone." She winked at Dave as she sipped her wine.

"I'll stay busy, no worries about that. But…" Claire hesitated. She didn't quite know how to ask the question that had been cooking in the back of her mind.

"What?" Dave asked.

"I don't mean to sound like I don't think what you do is important, but three weeks? What could be so important? And why Korea? That war's been over a long time."

"Well, technically speaking the war isn't over yet," Dave began as he sat upright in his chair. "It's pretty simple actually: The North Koreans and the South Koreans don't like each other, at all. As a matter of fact, the whole place is a powder keg waiting for just the right match."

"Really?"

"Yeah. This exercise is the biggest one we have and it's designed for one purpose, to show the boys in Pyongyang what's in store for them if they get too froggy. Although over the last few years, it's been the South Koreans who have been the aggressors. Last year they had a big missile boat fight. The South kicked some serious ass that day. The North has been pretty quiet since."

Claire frowned. "So why should we care if they go at it?"

"Pick up your purse and take out your calculator."

Claire peered back at her friend with distrusting eyes as she complied with his request. "Okay. Now what?"

"Look at the back of it. Where was it made?"

"Korea," she said slowly.

"They're our second or third largest trading partner. If they go to war, we're affected. If they go to war and lose, we're really affected."

"Sorry I'm late," she heard Ben announce his arrival from behind her.

Claire raised her face to accept Ben's kiss on her cheek. "I was getting worried."

"Just a little traffic," he replied as he sat. He hugged Charlotte and shook hands with Dave before sitting. "What'd I miss?"

"Not much," Claire replied. "We were just talking about Korea and you."

Ben forced a grin and shook his head.

Dave smiled as he raised a menu. "Holy cow, everybody. They've got kimchi here."

Everyone laughed, except Ben.

"Yeah, yeah. Bite me."

CHAPTER TEN
SATURDAY, APRIL 10TH

Capital International Airport
Beijing, China
9:30 AM
1:30 AM, GMT

Fong shivered as he made his way down the open aircraft stairwell. Taking advantage of his status, Fong had waited until his black sedan stopped at the bottom of the steps to the corporate jet. He held the railing with a white–knuckled grip as he took each step.

"Welcome home, Minister," Fong's aide said, bowing.

Once on the tarmac, Fong brushed past his young aide as he took the last step from the corporate–style jet toward the car without speaking. Isolated clumps of snow and ice gave evidence that spring had yet to truly arrive.

Fong's long black coat blew up when a singularly powerful gust whisked in from the north. He moved quickly as the breeze carried away any warmth lingering from the plane. His cheeks and nose tingled. The door to his waiting black sedan was wide open.

Fong grunted as he stepped into the back seat of his sedan. He yawned and shivered, all at the same time. He aimed the door vents so that they would direct the warm air at him.

Once inside, Fong tossed Yuen's briefcase on the opposite seat as Yi closed the door behind him. He fell into the black leather folds of his own seat with a huff. *This feels good, but not as good as my bed.*

The trip to Japan had been easy. Getting into the country undetected, finding and even meeting Yuen, as well as disposing of his body had all proven uneventful. Getting out of the country without disclosing his identity, however, had taxed him more than he planned. Several last–minute tip–offs necessitated changing departure plans. *Spying is truly a young person's game.* He took off his favorite black mink hat and placed it on his lap.

"I have dire news, Minister," Yi Liu said as he climbed in the opposite door. Yi removed his hat and gloves. He sat as much at attention as the confined space in the car would allow.

"What now?"

The sedan started moving.

"Japanese Intelligence Services have picked up three more of our people. They now have a total of fifteen—"

"Damn it, Yi! I know the count!" Fong realized he was shouting when the driver turned around in his seat. He deduced the man could hear him, although a thick plate of glass separated them.

They were pulling out of the international airport

area now. The auto turned onto the thoroughfare leading back to Beijing, and his home.

Fong took a deep breath. He reminded himself that he, above all others, must show control, especially at times like these. He pulled off his gloves and stuffed them into his hat.

Fong brought his gaze back to Yi. The man, not much older than a boy, had lowered his eyes. Tall and thin, Yi's coat seemed to hang off him even as he sat. His thick mop of black hair needed a trim. With no facial hair and large dark eyes, Yi Liu looked even younger than his twenty–two years. Fong studied him for a long moment before he cleared his throat.

The young man lifted his eyes to Fong's face almost immediately. After three years of working for him, the lad truly had learned something after all. Fong nodded for him to continue.

"We estimate six cells have been compromised."

The Chinese intelligence network in Japan consisted of ten groups, or cells, of three to four people. Individual cells did not have access to location or complement information on the others. The only central point of contact was the Executive Committee. The Executive Committee, headed by a senior intelligence resource, changed its location frequently.

A few freelancers, or moles, like Yuen were only contacted in case of extreme importance or emergency. Moles typically did not make contact with the cells. But Yuen had.

Initiating communication jeopardized their ability to maintain their covers. They passed their information back to China by separate channels. The theory of operation was simple: two separate networks providing information. One could usually verify the findings of another without fear of detection. The two–tier system had worked well for almost twenty years, until now.

Fong sighed as the car continued smoothly down the road. "Which ones?"

"Kanto One and Two, Hokuriku, Kansai, and Okinawa. All at the lowest levels."

Fong rubbed his eyes as he contemplated the Japanese and their methods. "Someone is talking," he finally said.

Yi nodded.

"What do you think, Yi? Should we let this one incident destroy our entire network?"

"No, Master, I do not."

Fong nodded. "Call the Executive. Tell him that if he and his team cannot extricate themselves from Japan within an hour's notice of receiving my instructions, they are to suicide themselves."

Yi's eyes widened. "But, Master. He, he is your grandson."

Fong turned his gaze from Yi toward the monument of Mao now visible from his auto's window. "They are all sons and daughters of China, Yi. Do it, do it now."

"Yes, Master."

Fong closed his eyes and listened to Yi pick the car's phone. *Damn you, Yuen.*

Project Blue Flame Laboratory
Senkaku Island, Japan
11:05 AM
2:05 AM, GMT

"Now as we know, the reactor is based on a heavily

modified Tokomak concept, with the torus receiving most of those modifications," Deitrich rambled.

Even with a good night's rest behind them, most of the team still sported blood–shot eyes and pale expressions. The stress of the previous evening's activities even now played fresh in Loewen's mind. He guessed the rest of them felt it, too.

Team debriefs occurred whenever they experienced a "major event." The meetings included a history lesson, the events leading up to the event as well as its resolution. One of the technical writers scribed the proceedings to both make it part of the team's permanent project record, and to ensure that any new ideas would make it into existing procedures.

The meetings always started out the same: Deitrich spent five minutes or so talking about the general design of the world's first fully–functional nuclear fusion generator. This caught new team members up on basic design and features, and served as a good way for the handsome and affable Deitrich to take center stage, a place for which he seemed perfectly suited.

Loewen held Bob Deitrich in great regard. After two years of working with him, however, Loewen knew both his attributes and faults. Besides, he reasoned, his friend and colleague did not realize that he was a megalomaniac.

Loewen's solution for dealing with Deitrich's ego came through boosting his own. Loewen liked hearing words that he knew would someday be read during the award ceremony where he received the Nobel Prize for Mathematics and Physics.

"The re–designed cavity," Deitrich explained as he gestured toward his colleague," is described by formulas originally constructed by Fifteenth Century mathematician Johannes Kepler. In 1611, Kepler proposed formulas that yielded the densest possible packing of spheres. This is known as the Kepler conjecture. Doctor Loewen, Assistant Director of Operations here, used those early formulas to design our reactor."

Yeah, I dig that part, especially. Loewen smiled to himself. He hid the grin by sipping lukewarm coffee. *Doctor Stanley Howard Loewen, Nobel Laureate: I like that, a lot.*

"Our reactor, by using a small fission reactor to initiate the process and to upgrade the tritium fuel, now produces two types of exhaust: helium and hybrid neutrons or electron–neutrinos. We re–introduce electron neutrinos into the torus to assist in regulating the reaction. Loss of the magnetic field and over/under electron–neutrino injection is the greatest failure point for the fusion reaction."

Loewen reminisced about his early days back at Maryland. He was a big deal there, administrator of his own fusion research effort. Now he was a glorified research assistant, an important assistant, but an assistant just the same. Deitrich, and another man, Doctor Yashita, actually managed the project. Last evening, however, he had earned his keep. Everyone in the room, including Deitrich, knew that.

"Last night, the neutrino injector jammed in the closed position. It was like shooting hot gasoline into an engine already running at full–speed. Anybody care to theorize how the injector got stuck?"

"Yeah, we bought some shitty foreign parts," Professor Tony Swinson blurted out.

Half the room laughed, the American half. The other half did not. Loewen shot him a disapproving glance, but Swinson didn't see it. He was too busy yucking it up with his closest pals.

"Now, now, Tony," Deitrich admonished. "Let's not even joke about things like that. However, your point about an equipment failure is well–made."

Deitrich wrote it on the board behind him.

Swinson, a short man with a short man's complex, could usually be counted on for a less–than–politically correct remark. Loewen guessed him to be almost as unpopular among the Japanese as he was with most of the better–mannered Americans.

Swinson, however, was a good all–around scientist. As well as having a place on the Reactor Team, he also handled logistics for the project. Each week, Swinson flew back to the Japanese mainland to arrange for supplies for everyone. He occasionally filled "special" orders for his favorites. Loewen suspected it was that aspect of his personality alone that kept him from being hated by everyone.

"Could it have been a software or firmware problem?" Dolores Shinozaki asked. Rubenesque, the half–Latino and half–Japanese woman with exotic and striking features had been one of the doctoral students who stayed at her station long enough to assist in opening the injector the night before.

Dolores already had several advanced degrees in mathematics and physics. She had yet to complete her thesis when she arrived at Senkaku Island. Stanley knew her from his days at the University of Maryland. When he heard she needed help, he made a few phone calls.

"Good question," Deitrich replied. He wrote the distilled version of the question on the white board, too. "Anyone else?"

Ministry of National Defense
Intelligence Directorate
Beijing, China
11:30 AM
3:30 AM, GMT

Deputy Minister Fong Du So's office window faced Bei Hai Lake, a large body of water surrounded by trees, walkways, and shrubs in almost the exact center of China's capital city. Not too far from Tiananmen Square, Fong's office, palatial even by Western standards, faced the East. On most mornings, the rising sun gave the room plenty of light, and sometimes, to the old man's chagrin, too much heat.

In the almost thirty years he had held his post, many changes had occurred. The riot in the nearby square was, for him, the most disturbing of these. Like most Party leaders, Fong knew it had almost ended their way of life.

"You did very well," Fong said to Yuen's ghost. "Very well, indeed." The spymaster's eyes, through thick and dust covered spectacles, read each word of the stolen documents. Though written in Japanese and English, Fong moved through them with as much ease as if they were in Mandarin. "But the price of your actions was much too high." He glanced at the paper on the edge of his desk, the Executive Cell's final report. His late grandson's final act, on Fong's orders, was to kill himself after disposing of the other members of his team.

A knock at the door preceded his aide's entry.

"Master. General Zhao is here to see you."

He didn't bother to answer or look up.

"Can I get you some coffee?" he heard the child ask him, though he knew Yi was no child in most things. However, in this business he held the status of one just a hair above a newborn.

"Coffee. Black," he answered without looking up.

The next few pages went very quickly. He was proud of his ability to take in large amounts of information quickly. In the microseconds that followed the words on the next page meeting his brain, Fong's eyes almost leapt from his head.

"Yes, Master. Can I get—"

Fong continued reading. The words on the page almost knocked him from his chair. Fong read them again and again to be sure. *Good fortune is with me today*.

"Yes, get out and send in the General," Fong ordered.

Yi rushed out of the room. He closed the door behind him as if he were trying not to wake a sleeping child. Fong turned to the other papers on his desk.

A knock at the door pulled Fong's attention from the report detailing the death of his grandson and his team. "Come in."

General Zhao, a short, burly man, instantly reminded Fong of a walking muscle. His forest green, tailor–made uniform, complete with red epaulets, fit him like a glove. The clean–shaven officer, with his hat tucked under his left arm, marched across the room to Fong's desk. He carried a briefcase in his left hand, just below the hat. Zhao stopped a half–meter short of the desk, came to attention and saluted. "Deputy Minister, General Zhao Chin Lee reporting as ordered, Sir."

Fong came to his feet slowly and walked around

the desk to the still–saluting general. Fong returned his salute and the two men bowed and hugged.

"Have a seat, Comrade General," Fong offered as he pointed to a large burgundy–colored couch a meter away.

"Thank you, Sir."

The two men seated themselves. Fong turned to Zhao and studied him for a long moment. Major General Zhao Chin Lee held the enviable distinction as the youngest general officer in the People's Army. Zhao started his career as an infantry officer. Before distinguishing himself by leading the put–down of the revolt in Tiananmen Square, Zhao had worked with Vietnam in their war against the Americans. Since that time, the Army officer had attended several Western universities, under an assumed identity, to become one of China's leading experts in the field of computers. The General now commanded the 1st Information Warfare Brigade.

"How may I be of service to you, Deputy Minister?"

Fong held up his hand to silence the officer.

A half–second later, Yi returned with a coffee carafe and two cups. The aide placed the beverage tray on the small table in front of the men. He pivoted around and marched out with almost the same level of precision as the General. As before, just as he had been trained, Yi closed the door gently behind him.

"To your question, Comrade General. I understand that you have tools at your disposal that may be useful to me."

"My organization stands ready to assist the Deputy Minister in any way we can. What is my mission?"

"We have come into information which leads us to believe the Americans and Japanese have built a special type of nuclear reactor which could be of great benefit to Mother China."

Zhao sat up even more erect than before. His bushy eyebrows went up, too. "Fusion."

"General. I'm impressed. How do you know of such things?"

"Deputy Minister, not all of my time in the West was spent learning about computers," Zhao grinned. The smile evaporated. "But..."

"Yes?"

"It was only theory three years ago."

"Well, General. You know our friends, the Americans. They are an ambitious lot."

"Possibly too ambitious for their own good."

Fong smiled. "Yes, perhaps so."

CHAPTER ELEVEN
SATURDAY, APRIL 10TH

Ministry of National Defense
Intelligence Directorate
Beijing, China
1:30 PM
5:30 AM, GMT

Su Mai Lin, in her fifteen years as Fong's protégé, had earned her place as his most–trusted aide and deputy. Thin and wispy and in her late forties, one could usually find her chain–smoking the strongest tobacco available.

Mai knocked and, unlike his orderly, waited for his permission to enter.

"Come!"

"Yes, Minister?"

Fong looked up to see Mai's characteristically puffy eyes staring back at him through round eyeglasses. She wore the same stern expression that she had greeted him with all those years ago as a schoolgirl looking for a career. Today, like most days, she wore her long black hair in a single braid down her back.

"I have found something that may be of great use to us."

"Yes, Minister?"

"This is a list of American and Japanese personnel assigned to the fusion research facility." He handed her the paper. "Do any of the names look familiar?"

He watched as she studied the list. Fong loved testing his pupils, even his most talented. At eighty–five, he figured if his memory was still sharp, theirs should be even sharper. Those who couldn't measure up did not work for him for long. Although he knew this was far from a real test.

Her eyebrows went up. "This one," she pointed. She coughed, sending a brief puff of cigarette–odor across the desk. For a split second, Fong thought she even smiled. Was the cough designed to cover it up? Fong let the odor linger in his nostrils for a moment. He missed tobacco. He'd left it behind as the years passed, per his physician's orders. The time to discuss the asset and her reaction to the name would come later.

"Very good, my young friend. Contact him. Activate him. Make sure that he knows he is to be ready when we are."

"I'll see to it."

"And Mai." His words acted to cut her short as she turned to walk away. "Unlike Japan, this resource is not part of an intelligence network. This has the highest precedence. He is replaceable."

"I understand, Master Fong." With that, she marched out of the office.

Fong lowered his gaze to the papers. After a

moment or so, he looked up and followed her with his eyes. A smile ran across Fong's chapped lips. Touching her was something else he had given up due to his age.

Mai, as smart as she was ruthless, would someday be his successor.

Commander, Seventh Fleet Reserve Unit
Naval and Marine Corps Reserve Center
Carswell Joint Reserve Base
Fort Worth, Texas
0800 Hours
1300 Hours, GMT

This was Ben's third Exercise Ronin Blitz experience. The fleet exercise simulated the defense of Korea against an all–out land attack and a limited sea–based assault.

"One more time, folks. This is the biggest exercise in the Pacific Theater. The active duty side is counting on us. If you've got any thoughts that the next two and a half weeks are going to be anything but hard work, think again. Any questions?" Captain Tom Anders asked as he scanned the room.

"Why am I doing this again?" Dave whispered to his friend.

"Because you love your country and you're just a Homeric, heroic son–of–a–gun," Ben replied.

"Oh–h–h–h."

Anders, their commanding officer, was an airline pilot in civilian life. Now in his mid–forties with a medium build, the silver–haired former F–14 pilot led the Reserve unit of more than two hundred men and women.

Ben liked his CO. He appreciated Anders' direct nature.

Ben watched as the Ronin Blitz briefing continued. "I shouldn't have stayed up so late," he said in a whisper through a yawn to Dave Ferguson, who sat in front of him.

Nearly the entire unit crowded into one of the center's larger instruction rooms. The lucky ones, and that was a relative term, sat on non–cushioned, school–style seats while others took up space against all four walls.

"For those of you going on this tour for the first time, I want to introduce a few key players," Anders started again. "First, the Battle Watch Captains. These four people will be running the Flag Command Center during the exercise. You folks stand up when I call your names," he ordered.

"Commander David Ferguson," announced Captain Anders.

With that, Dave stood for a moment, and sat down.

"Captain Penny Worthington," he called next.

The petite brunette pilot stood. Also a commercial airline pilot on most days, Captain Worthington was a Naval Aviator when in military uniform. She waved to the throng as she reseated herself.

"Commander Ben McGuire." When he heard his name, Ben came to his feet and gave the same type of wave that Worthington inspired.

"Captain Steve Marx." Marx was the last of the Battle Watch officers, and Anders' voice took on a tone of finality with Steve's introduction. Marx's call sign, or nickname, in the unit was Groucho. Suitably, the dark haired, muscular Navy Seal sported a bushy, dark moustache and an unusually quick wit.

"Captain, are you sure you want me on this one? I might inadvertently start a war and end this bullshit once and forever."

Anders only smiled as he shook his head. "Take a seat, Groucho! I'll let you know later."

Marx shot back a wink at his commanding officer before taking his seat.

"Okay, people. Let's get the day started. Shots, orders, nit–noys. Let's get all the bullshit taken care of and get out of here to spend some quality time with the family before we check out tomorrow," Anders said.

Ben laughed to himselcf at Anders' characterization of details as 'nit–noys'.

With that, their Commanding Officer nodded at his Executive Officer, who called, "Attention on Deck!"

The silence of the room gave way to a hundred or so men and women getting to their feet to stand at attention while Captain Anders departed the room.

Johnny Jack's Kids' Place
Plano, Texas
7:20 PM
12:20 AM, GMT

"Girls and boys, ladies and gentlemen," Claire hammed it up show–biz style. "It is my great pleasure to introduce to you one of the world's greatest magicians."

Vanessa, twenty of her closest friends, and her brother all sat cross–legged on the floor. Most of them wore brilliantly–colored birthday hats and smiles to match the festive mood. Claire noticed that even Kate wore a happy expression.

"He has journeyed far—"

"How far?" piped up Adam.

"At least as far as Fort Worth," Claire shot back at her stepson.

The crowd giggled.

She started again, "He has journeyed far to join us. Here he is, the Great Benjamin!"

Parents and children alike, even those not in Vanessa's gathering, applauded as Ben made his entrance. Dressed in traditional hat, coat and tails, Ben bowed and smiled as he cruised across the room.

"For my first trick, I will make a rabbit come out of my hat," Ben announced.

"Ooooo," went the audience.

Ben grinned and removed his top hat. He flicked his arm and a magic wand appeared in his right hand.

The throng applauded. Little Vanessa beamed at her father's performance.

He held the hat in front of him. "You see. It's just a simple magician's hat." He put his hand inside for effect. Then he placed it on the table with the opening down. He tapped it once, twice, three times and lifted the hat. When nothing appeared, the kids exploded in laughter. Claire laughed, too.

"Let's try it again, shall we?"

Ben repeated the action. This time when he lifted the hat, a tiny stuffed bunny appeared.

Everyone applauded and Ben took a bow. He shot a quick glance at his wife and Claire only shook her head.

"He's pretty good," one of the other moms whispered.

"He's a clown," Claire replied with a laugh.

"For my next trick, I will make this deck of cards disappear," he announced.

I can't believe he's going to try it. He hasn't gotten it right in two months.

She watched, almost holding her breath, as he set up for the trick.

Ben held the deck of cards up in his left hand. Then he passed his open right hand in front of them from top to bottom and then back up again. When he pulled his right hand back down again, he did so in a quick motion and the deck disappeared.

The crowed exploded in applause. "I can't believe it," she said aloud.

As Ben accepted the crowd's approval, the deck fell from somewhere on his person to the table in front of him.

Again, the room exploded, but this time in laughter.

She saw the frustration on his face. He had practiced most of the night to get even that close. *Poor Ben.*

He took a deep breath and shrugged. He forced himself to laugh, too.

Claire focused on Vanessa and Adam. They hadn't started laughing until their father had.

"For my final illusion, I will require a volunteer," he announced. Quiet returned to the room. He looked around for a short time, finally turning toward his daughter in the front row. "You. What's your name?"

"Daddy, you know my name," Vanessa replied.

Again, the crowd howled in laughter.

"Work with me, kid. This is show business."

Vanessa laughed.

"Come on up, young lady."

She stood and walked up to her father.

"Tell everyone your name."

"I'm Vanessa," her little voice said, just above a whisper.

"Is today your birthday?"

"Yes."

"Are you ready for a neat surprise?"

"Yes."

"Okay. I have here an authentic magician's blindfold. Can I put it on you?" Ben asked.

She nodded and her father placed the covering over her eyes.

Ben turned her around three times as Claire brought out a brand new pink and baby blue two–wheeler. She stopped the bike right in front of Vanessa.

"Abracadabra!" Ben shouted as he pulled off the blindfold.

Vanessa's eyes and mouth opened wide together. Then she started jumping and clapping her hands. "It's just like the one I wanted. Thanks, Dad!! Thanks, Mom! Thanks, Claire!"

"You're welcome, honey," Ben replied. "Happy birthday."

CHAPTER TWELVE
SUNDAY, APRIL 11TH

Narita International Airport
Tokyo, Japan
8:22 AM
11:22 PM, GMT

"**W**e are very unhappy that you did not tell us that you were assigned to such an important project," the voice on the other end of the phone said.

He checked the surrounding area before speaking. The airport held its normal bustling crowd. Men and women walked briskly in both directions. Nearly all of the travelers carried luggage of one form or another, some more than others. A familiar airport scene.

However, the bank of phones nearest to him was relatively unoccupied. The nearest people were one and two phone booths away, respectively. He'd have to watch the volume of his voice, but not as closely. "It's not my job to keep in touch with you unless I'm working on something for you," he fired back.

"Besides, you people always seem to find me, anyway."

"That's right, Doctor. We do. And don't forget that," she warned.

Her voice had changed over the years. It was raspier now, older. She still had a thick accent, though. At one time, her Japanese sounded almost natural. Now, even though every verb and syllable was perfect, he could hear the native Mandarin clearly.

I wonder if she's still beautiful. Of course, I was a lot younger then and she was older than me, by more than just a few years. What the hell? I'll ask. "So, Tu Lin, if that's even your real name. Do you still like it on top?"

The question must have caught her off guard. She was silent for almost a full thirty seconds.

"What's the matter? Nothing to say? Tell me, do you still do that thing with your tongue?"

"Silence. Shut up, you pig!" she shouted. Anger filled her voice.

"Uh, ooh. Did I say something you don't want recorded?"

Silence again.

"Isn't your libido what got you into this mess?" she asked finally. The coolness had returned.

"I was young. You were a good lay. I'll bet you still are."

"You will stay in contact with this office for the next few weeks," she said in a measured tone.

I must have really gotten to her. She's trying to calm herself and change the subject. This is fun.

"Do you remember those nights in my dormitory room? You were—" he paused.

"We will require daily reports."

"Phenomenal. That's it. You were phenomenal."

"If you don't cease this talk of sex, I will contact the authorities and tell them you have been a traitor for more than twelve years."

Bitch.

"What's the matter? Haven't you anything to say?" Sarcasm leaked from her voice like juice flowing from an overripe tomato.

"No. As a matter of fact, I was just thinking."

"Oh, yes? About what?"

"About the fact that I haven't heard from you in almost three years. And that you've got to want something very important after being away for so long. You won't call the authorities." He paused, both to get his nerve and for effect. "You need me."

Silence.

"And before I do one more thing, I want a little more of what got me into this mess all those years ago. I want you in my bed."

"That is an impossibility," she snapped back.

"Then call the police."

He could hear her shouting back at him as he hung up the phone. The polite and well–rehearsed Japanese language gave way to ranting in Chinese.

He checked his watch. *Time to go.*

9:00 AM
12:00 PM, GMT

The fourteen–hour flight had gone well: no turbulence, lots of food and quiet, and above all, lots of sleep. Since the beginning of the Blue Flame Project more than two years earlier, Marcia Hobson had made the Washington–to–Tokyo jaunt sixteen times.

Still not used to it. She yawned her way down the corridor leading away from Customs.

"So, Ma. What's next?" her son asked. He trailed a step or two behind her.

She glanced up to see two familiar–looking men in business suits. Marcia took a deep breath. *Time to deliver some bad news.*

"We meet some people from my office over here and we fly out to the laboratory."

"Another airplane? Aw–w–w, man," he whined.

"Helicopter," she replied.

"Really?" His voice perked. "Cool."

"Marcia," Doctor Robert Deitrich greeted her.

"Hello, Bob." They shook hands.

Hobson liked Deitrich. A true academic, he lived to educate himself. The list of degrees and credentials featured schools like Rhodes, MIT, and Stanford. Uncle Sam had recruited him during his senior year in high school. Scholarships, internships and choice assignments culminated in his assignment to Blue Flame.

Not only did Deitrich possess one of the best brains in the world, his thin but muscular frame made him nice to look at, too. Dark hair and eyes, a full beard, and a killer smile all worked together.

He kissed her hand after shaking it.

Marcia felt the same tingle in her nether regions that she always got around him.

As he brought her hand down from his lips, she reaffirmed the only reason that she had not done something about her attraction to him. A gold wedding band glistened in the light. The jewelry blinked at her like a lone country–road stoplight on a dark night.

I wonder if he knows—

"Welcome back to Japan," Doctor Yashita said.

The greeting sounded forced. It matched the expression on his face: forced. At any rate, it brought her back to the present, and the task at hand.

Marcia reached for Yashita's hand to shake it.

Jitsuyo Yashita had never made his dislike of the partnership between Japan and America a secret. Openly critical, even defiant, he and Marcia regularly ended up on the opposite sides of issues.

"Thanks, Doctor Yashita. Gentlemen, this is my son, Tristan.

Yashita, even though he regularly pissed her off, was brilliant. Like Deitrich, he had been educated in the world's best schools. As well as English, he was also fluent in Spanish, German, Chinese and Italian. In fact, aside from an occasional phrase, his English was free of any traces of an accent.

"Welcome to Japan, Tristan—" Deitrich began.

"What brings you back so soon?" Yashita asked Marcia, cutting off his colleague.

She pushed out a smile to cover her growing anger. "I think we'd best have that conversation later." *What I really want to say is, "Quit being a shithead in front of my kid!"*

"I don't understand why you're back so soon. You were just here—"

"Doctor. Shut up. This is my son. We're in the middle of a public place. Our project is classified. Shut the hell up!"

All of the men, including Tristan, lowered their eyes and heads, almost at the same time.

"Now, let's get going." Marcia stooped to pick up her bag.

CHAPTER THIRTEEN
SUNDAY, APRIL 11TH

National Security Agency Headquarters
Government Network Monitoring Center
Fort Meade, Maryland
1:45 AM
5:45 AM, GMT

"This is making me nuts," Harvey Walters said more to himself as he scratched the top of his head with his fingernails. "That haircut is gonna feel so good tomorrow." He was sure that his thick mop of blonde hair looked more like a bird's nest, especially after two hours of playing with it.

He checked the clock, only another hour to go until his watch ended. All around him, other Technology Watch Officers monitored their consoles or talked on telephones. Tonight, like every night, the NSA's Information Security Organization kept vigil on the U. S. Government's growing web of networks.

Tonight, however, like most nights, the watch had been dull and uneventful. In this regard, Harvey knew his job bore a striking resemblance to that of his brother's. While he was in his third year at NSA, his brother was an airline pilot with ten years of flying behind him. Standing watch at NSA, so far, was years of boredom punctuated by moments of sheer terror.

Harvey thought his Operations Center looked like half a dozen others he had seen in the Washington Area. The room featured several large–screen monitors on a main wall, low lighting, and several dozen workstations on tiered rows. Each workstation included a late–model desktop computer, a telephone with several lines, an ergonomic desk and chair, and a desk lamp. A cubby for research documents, CD–ROMS, and procedural manuals bracketed a seventeen–inch flat–screen color monitor.

Harvey found himself focusing on one of the flags hanging from the ceiling. One for each of the fifty plus one for each of the territories decorated the upper reaches of the high walls all the around the room. The white stars forming the Big Dipper on the flag of Alaska had always intrigued him. *Why pick that constellation instead of the North Star or Orion? Could I see it all the time if I lived there?*

The electronic chirp of his telephone only managed to pull part of his attention away from his musings on life in the fiftieth state. He picked up the receiver without taking his eyes off the flag. "Walters."

"I can see you're really busy," Holly McNamara joked.

He turned in his seat to see the cherubic face of his girlfriend. She sat three rows behind him. "Is it that obvious?"

"Yeah. You look a thousand miles away."

"Two thousand, actually. What's up?"

"I've got something up here. Can you come up and take a look?"

"Hmm. Now there's an invitation a fella can accept."

"Just come up here, will ya?" The line went dead.

Harvey frowned. *That was weird.* She normally joked around, even at work. Not giving some kind of response wasn't like her. He logged out of his workstation.

In the moments it took for him to walk up to her row, Holly had already garnered a few visitors. Fellow watch–standers and even the Watch Supervisor stood nearby, a frown on his face and his arms folded. Harvey felt himself slow his pace as he approached.

"Walters. Glad you're here," Mike Davies greeted without looking away from Holly's screen.

"What's up?"

Holly's slender shoulders and long dark hair were opposite him now. He focused more on her backside than her computer display. *Too bad the back of her chair is so wide*, he thought.

"Looks like we've got an intrusion."

Holly's screen displayed two windows. The frame on the left displayed a series of letters, dashes, numbers, and more letters. The series ended with the letters NEA. The other simply showed an IP, or Internet Protocol address. The NEA window showed the server's responses to that of the user's commands.

"NEA?" Harvey asked.

"National Endowment for the Arts or the National Energy Agency," Holly joked.

Nobody laughed.

"What are they doing?"

"Right now they're just looking around," Davies replied.

"What are we doing about it?"

"As soon as we can figure out where that IP address is, we'll either cut 'em off or move 'em."

Harvey nodded. Cutting them off was simple enough. They would remotely configure the firewall to not let in data requests from that IP mask. Moving them was just a bit more complicated.

Holly's phone rang. "Holly McNamara."

Harvey caught his gaze drifting back toward the Alaskan flag. *Probably just a bunch of college kids hacking for fun. The FBI would be beating down their door by morning.*

"You're shittin' me!" Holly shouted into the phone. "Are you sure?" she asked a few seconds later.

His attention and his gaze were back now.

"What?" Davies asked.

She put up her hand to silence him. "Yeah, yeah. He's right here. I'll tell him."

Holly put down the phone. "The server belongs to the National Energy Agency. It's somewhere in the Pacific Theater. The user is out in the Pacific, too."

The three computer scientists exchanged glances; the techies conjectured among themselves.

"Holly, give Walters here your seat."

"Yes, Sir."

The two lovers exchanged places and Harvey went to work. Moving the user, or in this case the intruder, meant they would have to intercept and respond to his commands without his knowledge. If successful, Harvey would move him to a fake server so they could gather information on the user such as his location, type of information sought, as well as what kind of software protocols he was using to figure out their passwords and firewall protection.

"How's it coming?" Davies asked after a few moments.

"Okay. I've got the name of the meaconing server set. I'm about to switch him over."

Walters glanced over his shoulder to notice that nearly the entire seventy–member watch section angled for a view of his activities. "This is not a porn site," he said to them.

Only a few chuckles came back as he continued working the keyboard.

"Chinese?" Holly asked Davies.

"That's where I'd put my money," he replied.

"Shit!" Harvey exclaimed as his fingers moved even faster against the keyboard.

"What?" Davies asked.

"They've started a download," Holly answered for him.

She was right.

"Damn," Mike Davies sighed.

Somebody was going to have to make the call to keep them on or not. Keeping the intruder on to gather his data meant they would lose information, perhaps classified information. Cutting him off now would save the information, but also let the intruder know they were on to him. Everyone there knew Davies was that someone.

"Have you managed to get any monitoring done," Davies asked.

"Maybe a minute or two," Harvey replied without looking up.

"Cut him off," Davies ordered.

"But—"

"I know, Harvey. We can't take the chance."

Harvey did as Davies asked. A few keystrokes later, the window on the right with the mysterious IP address went black.

"I've reconfigured the firewall," Harvey announced after a few more moments.

"Harvey, you and Holly write up the report," Davies replied as he waded through the throng.

Harvey nodded as he stood up from the workstation. He looked at the crowd around the booth. "Aren't you people gonna at least throw money?"

They walked away, shaking their heads.

"Come on, that was the most excitement this place has seen in weeks. That's gotta be worth something," Harvey pleaded with laughter in his voice.

Holly patted him on his butt. "Don't worry, I'll give you something for your efforts."

Harvey Walters and Holly McNamara spent the remaining forty minutes of their watch and the first two hours of the next completing their report. The gang in the Analysis Group would take their information and observations and make it part of a much more detailed report. Pulling together the few moments of captured data into a cogent document would take weeks. Harvey ran a spell check on the nearly fifty–page document before hitting the envelope icon to send it to Analysis.

"Ready to go home?" she asked.

"Oh, yeah." Walters stood and walked over to her. "You know that vacation we want to take?"

"Yes?" She put her arm around his waist.

"What do you think about going to Alaska?"

"Alaska? It's too cold. I was thinking more like Hawaii. Why?"

"Just thinking."

Project Blue Flame Energy Laboratory
Reactor Control Room
Senkaku Island, Japan
3:06 PM
06:06 AM, GMT

The second and third cup of coffee didn't help her jet lag. Marcia Hobson couldn't shake the feeling that she was in a dream. As she moved around the room waiting for the project administrators to join her, her eyes kept crossing.

Deep in the lab complex, fluorescent lights cast the room in harsh light. White floors and surfaces gave the room a bland, almost sterile feel. *And that humming sound...God, it's almost deafening.*

Technicians occasionally walking by or speaking with each other helped keep her awake, but only barely. She eventually took a seat at the secondary control console.

Doctor Yashita pushed open the door.

Both happy and sad to see him, she sat up in her chair. *At least having him in here to talk to for a while will get my mind off how tired I am.*

"Please have a seat, Doctor."

"Thank you."

He moved with purpose, with no spare motion. He went directly from the door and sat down. He sat at the front edge of the chair, making sure not to use the backrest. Predictably, out came the pen.

It was a Mont Blanc, one of the more expensive ones. Hobson had heard that the Emperor or Prime

Minister had given it to him many years before when he was still an honor student.

Yashita made a point of playing with it whenever he was in her presence. Over the knuckles or through his fingers, he even used it to play with the hair in his eyebrows. Yashita loved that pen.

"So, things are well?" she asked.

"Yes."

Silence.

"And your lovely wife and children. Are they well, too?"

"Yes."

What the hell was I thinking? This guy hates my guts! Talking with him is like getting a root canal, something that should be done quickly and with a lot of anesthesia.

They sat in silence for a long, long time. Seconds seemed to turn into eons. Only the voices of the technicians conducting their work gave Hobson any indication that time was indeed moving along.

"Sorry I'm late," Deitrich announced his arrival. The pneumatic door closed behind him as he reached the console.

Thank God.

"Sorry, I was on a call. I've got to head back to Tokyo tonight. It seems my wife is sick."

"Is it serious?" Hobson stood to shake his hand.

"I don't think so. She's been fighting a fever for the last few days. I think it's turned into the flu. You know, chills, vomiting, etc. I just want to see for myself that she's okay."

"I understand. When do you think you'll be back?"

"Well, if I can get out of here in the next few hours, I plan to be back in a couple of days. If that's okay?"

"Yeah. That should be fine."

She gestured for Deitrich to have a seat at the console as well.

She reseated herself and opened her notebook.

"So, Boss. What brings you back out here?" Deitrich asked, grinning through his beard.

She got tingly again. However, she pushed it away. There was business to do. "Are we still on track for this phase of the project?"

Both men turned toward each other at almost the same time. Then they turned back to her.

"Yes," Yashita replied.

"Yes, we are," agreed Deitrich.

She nodded her head. "What about that problem the other day?"

"Well," Deitrich began. "After we figured out we had a stuck injector, the rest of it was pretty cookbook. If it happens again, we'll know what to do."

"Good." She sat up in her chair and rested her elbows on the console. "We'll have to shut down the lab and move it to another location." She made every effort to keep emotion out of her voice as well as keep eye contact with both men.

"And why are we doing this?" Yashita shot back.

"All that I can say is there have been some events that have made our mutual nations nervous."

"Can you be more specific?" Deitrich asked. "It must have been something big." Deitrich pulled at his beard down near the right side of his chin.

Marcia knew his mind was racing.

"Do we know when we'll restart the project?" Deitrich probed further.

"Not at this time."

"Hmm."

"How long will it take to shut down the reactor?"

"At least five days."

She frowned. "Can't it happen any faster?"

"I don't think so, Marcia. We've conducted a number of simulations just for this eventuality. Five days is the best we've been able to do."

She nodded.

"I think this is precipitous," Yashita interjected. "Where will we move the work?"

"Most probably to Sandia Laboratory."

"Ha, I knew it. You Americans have been scheming to get the fruits of this project for yourselves since the beginning!"

"Doctor. I'm not going to fight with you on this. This facility is shutting down." Keeping emotion out of her voice suddenly became very difficult.

She noticed the other scientists and technicians in the room straining to hear the conversation. After she made eye contact with one of them, he looked away. The others quickly followed his example.

"I will go to Tokyo. I will lodge a formal complaint with my government. I—"

"You can do whatever you want. As a matter of fact, why don't you fly in with Doctor Deitrich, here."

"I will do just that." He stood. "Is there anything else?"

Hobson reclined in her chair. "Yes. Don't take too long getting back here. There might not be anything to come back to."

Doctor Yashita whipped around and marched toward the door. It slammed against the doorstop as he yanked it open. Hobson didn't know it was possible to do that with a pneumatic door. He didn't bother closing it.

Marcia didn't move. She exchanged glances with Deitrich.

Eventually, the door's mechanism closed itself almost without a sound.

"I'll bet that's one personality you won't miss when this is over."

She shook her head. "I can't believe he's easy to work with. I only have to deal with him every other month or so. But you—my God."

Deitrich reclined in his chair. He eventually brought his gaze up and Hobson almost fainted when his eyes met hers. The moment passed like a sunrise.

She tried to speak. However, no words came to mind.

The buzz of someone calling on the intercom finally broke her gaze from his. "Yes."

"Is Doctor Deitrich there?" the caller asked.

"Yes. Yes, he is."

"This is the pilot. Please tell him we can leave in about half an hour."

"Thank you. I will."

She hung up the phone.

"Your pilot says he'll be ready in about thirty minutes."

He nodded as he stood. "I'll have Stanley Loewen take a look at the simulations. He wrote the program. If anyone can find a faster way, it's Stan."

"I agree."

"Marcia, I feel bad about taking off right now. But I'll check in. When will we start flying the staff out?"

"As soon as possible. The Secretary wants us out of here in days, Bob."

His eyes widened. "I'll get back to help as soon as I can."

"Thank you for your support on this." She extended her hand to shake his.

"Think nothing of it." He took her hand and held it for a long while. He used his thumb to rub the back of her hand.

That feeling came back again. Noise and movement of the others in the room flooded her mind. She pulled her hand, gently, back to her side.

"I'll see you in a couple of days," he said.

"Have a good trip."

Dallas–Fort Worth International Airport
DFW, Texas
11:55 AM
4:55 PM, GMT

"American Flight 61 non–stop for Tokyo Narita, now boarding," the announcer said as Ben and Claire cleared security checkpoint.

"That your plane?"

"Yeah." They walked at a rapid pace. They still had three more gates to go.

This was all happening too fast. The idea that he was going to be away from her for two and a half weeks hit home. After only a few months of marriage, Ben understood a lot about his relationship with Claire. He liked being with her. He liked waking up next to her. Furthermore, he knew he didn't like being away from her. *This is gonna suck.*

Ben reached out his hand and she grabbed it. They waded through the other travelers on the people mover.

Traffic had been bad that morning on Highway 121. A tractor–trailer accident snarled traffic all the way to Frisco. It took almost an hour and a half, twice the normal amount of time, to get to the airport from their home in Plano.

A few minutes later they arrived at Ben's gate. A stream of fellow passengers already jammed the jet–bridge. Ben sighed at the prospect of falling in behind them.

He pulled her close and kissed her hard. *Gotta keep it together here.* He saw her eyes growing moist. *If I don't, she won't either.*

"You be careful out there," she ordered.

"Count on it."

"I'll be waiting on you when you get home. Maybe I'll wear that new coat when I meet you. What do you think?"

"The new coat. What new coat?"

"Never mind. You just take care of yourself."

"I love you." He kissed her again before tearing himself away for the plane.

"I love you, too. Bring back some kimchi."

He turned and shook his head. Her laughter echoed in his mind as he started down the ramp. The huge lump in his throat made its way to his eyes as the plane door came into sight.

CHAPTER FOURTEEN
MONDAY, APRIL 12TH

The White House Briefing Room
Washington, D.C.
8:00 AM
1:00 PM, GMT

Jack Langdon fidgeted in his chair as he looked around the room. Moments before, he had loosened his tie for the second or third time. No matter what he did, Langdon knew his quest for comfort would be pointless for the next hour or so.

He looked over his shoulder at Doug Miller. He was as happy as a pig in shit. He smiled openly and greeted the other Cabinet aides as they waited for their boss' arrival.

"What's the matter, Jack? You look like somebody peed in your Cream of Wheat," Defense Secretary Pete Wilson said loud enough for the press on the other side of the big gate outside to hear.

Langdon only shot him a kiss-my-ass grin. Wilson's words at least took Langdon's mind off his aide.

His guest attendance at the weekly meeting of the National Security Council had him feeling out of sorts. The Secretary of Energy wasn't supposed to attend. He knew it, and most definitely, so did everyone else in the room. The fact that he had a seat along the wall instead of a place at the table spoke volumes.

He looked around the room. All the regular members sat behind engraved nameplates. The President chaired the National Security Council; statutory members included the Vice President and the Secretaries of State and Defense. The Chairman of the Joint Chiefs of Staff served as the military advisor to the Council, and the Director of Central Intelligence was the intelligence advisor. The Secretary of the Treasury, the U.S. Representative to the United Nations, the Assistant to the President for National Security Affairs, the Assistant to the President for Economic policy, and the Chief of Staff to the President all attended meetings of the Council. The Attorney General and the Director of the Office of National Drug Control Policy attended the meetings pertaining to their jurisdiction; other officials, like Langdon, were invited as appropriate.

This was the way of life in Washington. One moved up in life by following the rules. Protocol was everything.

Such had been the path he'd followed, until now. Langdon looked down at his hands. He could actually see the moisture seeping from the sweat glands.

"Ladies and gentlemen, the President," White House Chief of Staff Nelson announced.

Everyone came to their feet and two seconds later President Albert Turner entered the room. He smiled widely as he rounded the big oak table, shaking hands warmly. A photographer clicked pictures at every greeting. The electronic winder on the camera filled Langdon's ears with sound as the flash made him blink. He tried to stay focused on his surroundings.

"Good morning, Jack. Glad you could join us," the President said. He got the smile and a warm handshake, too.

"Thank you, Sir. It's an honor to be here."

The President moved on to greet several more "guests," including Miller, and regular attendees before arriving at his chair. Everyone remained standing until he took his seat.

Turner nodded at his Chief of Staff who then nodded at the photographer. The man, with the three or four cameras draped around his neck, headed for the door. Two Secret Service Agents parted to let him out, then resumed their attentive stance.

"Let's get to it, shall we?"

"Yes, Mister President. Everyone is reminded that this briefing is classified at the Top Secret level. Europe, go," the Chief of Staff ordered.

Langdon watched as several briefers stood and gave a short synopsis of the problems and occurrences in their respective territories. The lights in the room dimmed on cue and a projection system came on, displaying a split screen. The left side showed the geographic region of interest while the right featured the list of topics the analyst discussed.

As the presentations progressed, the President occasionally asked a few questions, but usually nodded or took notes. The briefing moved around the world in a mostly Eastern direction. Northern Africa, Angola, and Uganda followed by the Balkans. The Russias came next, and finally China and Japan.

"We, uh, we. The United States that is, has a developing situation in China," a skinny, dark–haired, nameless young female analyst declared. She cleared her throat several times trying to keep her tone steady. Langdon guessed she had probably rehearsed her briefing several times throughout the last few days for this moment. Standing there, she shook like a leaf in a windstorm. "Several warships recently departed an exercise in the East China Sea and headed for homeport early."

"Any idea why?" the President asked.

"No, Sir. We thought it might be a mechanical problem but satellites show the ships moving at top speed."

"What kind of ships? How many?"

"Three destroyers, a frigate and an amphibious troop carrier."

"Any troops on board?" he asked.

"No, Sir. The exercise was their regular annual gunnery and tactics trials. It was only supposed to train the crews."

He nodded.

The young woman started to sit down then changed her mind. "Any more questions, Sir?"

"No. Thank you. Let's keep an eye on those ships. Good report."

"Yes, Sir. Sir, that completes my report," her voice regained that "practiced" tone. She finally took her seat.

"Let's talk about Senkaku," the President said.

"We have a scientific installation on the Japanese Island of Senkaku." Langdon made a point of sitting at attention as the Chief of Staff began to speak. Another staffer switched the display to the Ryukyu island chain. A red circle indicated the largest, Senkaku.

"Last week, a Japanese national went on a shooting spree at the Ministry of Trade and Industry. When classified documents came up missing and the national's body showed up with bullet holes, the CIA did a little digging," Nelson added.

"His name was Yuen Xin Li," the Director of the Central Intelligence Agency began. "As far as we can tell, he's been in the Japanese Government as a spy for almost twenty years."

"Cutting to the chase," General Marksee interjected. "This guy stole information about the facility. What kind of facility is it?"

"It's a joint Japanese–American research facility," the Chief of Staff replied.

"What kind of research?" the Secretary of State asked.

"Alternative sources of energy."

Smart. If you want something to stay a secret in Washington, don't tell anyone; not even your National Security Counsel. God knows that "unofficial" sources always seemed to talk just when they shouldn't. Langdon mentally shrugged his shoulders.

All eyes came to rest on him, as he knew they would. This was not good. All the Administration needed was another story in the press about Chinese infiltration of U.S. Energy Department Laboratories.

"So, what did he steal?" the Army General asked.

"We think he's got logistics information, that's about it," the Director of the CIA said. "However, we are still looking into it," he added.

"So why is Energy with us today?" Defense Secretary Wilson asked.

"I'm considering making him an *ad hoc* member of the Council," the President replied. "With all of the interest our laboratories are generating in the media, it makes sense to me."

A hush fell over the room. Langdon himself tried to keep his mouth from dropping open. He took a deep breath and forced his face to remain neutral.

"General. I want the Navy to keep an eye on the Chinese ships we heard about today. I also want Seventh Fleet to plan a contingency evacuation of the island."

"Sir, is this a priority?" the General asked.

"No, no. I don't want to escalate any panic here. We've got that exercise coming up soon, right?"

"It starts today, Sir."

"Just make it part of the exercise. Hell, it'll give Fred Kiatkowski something real to do," the President joked.

The room chuckled with him.

Well, one thing's for sure: nobody's walking out of here knowing what we were doing at Senkaku. This is a campaign–winner, he's gonna hold it in reserve.

"I'll take care of it, Mister President."

"Okay. Next," the President moved on.

National Security Agency Director Paul Brewer cleared his throat before he spoke. "Sir, we detected a GovNet break–in last evening."

The President put his reading glasses on and began examining a small stack of briefing summaries in front of him.

"Another bunch of kids?" the Chief of Staff asked.

"No, I don't believe so. We're still investigating, but it looks like the intrusion originated from some-where in the Pacific Theater."

Langdon, though focused on the NSA Director, noticed the President's head come up.

"Any idea of what they were after?" President Turner asked.

"No, Sir. But they got into the Top Secret part of the network before we caught 'em. They were trying to gain access to one of the Energy Department's computers."

"Did they get anything?" Langdon asked.

"We don't think so. We were able to spoof them into logging onto a dummy server. They bumped around in there until they figured out we were on to 'em."

"And just when were you going to tell us about it?" Langdon snapped back.

"Anything else?" Turner asked.

His words acted to diffuse the moment. Both men turned to look at the Chief Executive at the same time.

"No, Sir. My guys are still looking into it. But it could take as much as another month to figure out where it came from or who."

Turner nodded. "Stay on top of it. But in the meantime, what can you do to protect us?"

"Not much, Sir. We can go to a higher EMCON State."

"EMCON State?" the Secretary of State asked.

"Emission Control, Ma'am. We can restrict what type of traffic is allowed to flow over GovNet. The higher the state, the more restricted the network," Brewer replied.

"Take GovNet to EMCON Level 2 until you guys get some answers," the President ordered.

"Yes, Sir."

Langdon shot Brewer a hateful glance.

CHAPTER FIFTEEN
MONDAY, APRIL 12TH

Ministry of National Defense
Intelligence Directorate
Beijing, China
5:00 AM
1:00 PM, GMT

"**M**inister, I am afraid our first attempt to infiltrate the American's network failed." The General's head hung but otherwise he stood at attention in front of the desk.

"That is most disappointing, General." Fong sat forward in his chair. "What will you do now?"

"We will try again, Minister."

"Do you think you will succeed this time?"

"Minister, we often make hundreds of attempts before we obtain any success. This work has very deliberate processes."

"So this could take months?"

"Yes, Minister. In the case of the Fulan Gong work,

we took almost two years to infiltrate their sites in the United States before we made arrests here."

"General, you must understand that we are on a very tight timetable. I don't have months or years. You must think of this operation in terms of days, even hours."

"Minister, my personnel will continue the attempts. However, I do not think I—"

"General, you have a reputation for excellence. I have every confidence that you will be successful," Fong said, cutting off his excuses. He reclined in his chair. "You have work to do."

Zhao pivoted and marched out of the room. This time he did not wait until he was out before donning his hat.

USS *Blue Ridge* (LCC–19)
Yokosuka, Japan
04:45 Hours
13:35 Hours, GMT

"Okay, let's get those overhead lights off," Ben ordered. He had the first watch of the exercise.

Although the Seventh Fleet Commander's flagship still sat in port, the task of managing the exercise's ships, aircraft, submarines, sailors, and Marines had already begun.

Ben remarked to himself how good it felt to be back aboard *Blue Ridge*. It was a strange, bittersweet homecoming. This was his fourth or fifth time aboard the flagship. The blue–tiled decks, white walls, and ornate, for a ship, furnishings seemed to only get better with age.

The Tactical Flag Command Center served as the

admiral's nerve center. The space boasted four four–foot–by–four–foot large screen display units, as well as a dozen or so computer monitors showing various types of tactical information, a number of communications circuits, and nearly twenty men and women to operate them.

As the Battle Watch Captain, Ben owned the watch section. Over the next two weeks, his primary job would be to keep the admiral, through his Chief of Staff, informed.

"Sir. What areas do you want displayed on the screens?" a yet–unidentified enlisted man asked.

"Put the entire area of responsibility on the left screen, the Korean Peninsula on the middle, and exercise area on the right," he replied. "We'll put CNN on the last one."

The lights came down and the four displays washed the room in computer–generated light. Black–painted vertical surfaces helped subdue the space even more. As the space started to settle down from a quintessential vision of Camp Run–Amok, Ben felt himself calming as well. Nothing, absolutely nothing, had been ready. He and his watch team, in just under an hour, had configured the displays, established communications, and generally brought order to the world that would be his for the next two weeks.

The six–hundred–twenty–foot antenna–covered ship served as a floating mobile command post for several admirals and generals and their staffs. From the decks of the USS *Blue Ridge*, ships, submarines, airplanes, and even foot soldiers could be directed and deployed. Without the embarked staffs, the crew was only ninety officers and nine hundred enlisted.

Those numbers usually doubled during Fleet exercises like this one.

"Hey!" he bellowed. "Where the hell is Senior Chief Ericksen?"

No one on the team of enlisted persons and officers answered. Hell, they hardly even looked up.

"Has anyone seen the Senior Chief?" he tried again. This time the tone of his voice carried the remainder of the frustration still in his bones. He even rose out of his chair at the watch console to make sure everyone could hear him.

"Sir, the last time I saw him he was headed for the Chief Petty Officer's Mess," one of the Second Class Petty Officers finally piped up.

"Great. Everything's all hosed up and my Watch Team Leader's MIA," Ben grumbled more to himself than anyone else.

He sat down hard in the chair. "Petty Officer Grayson?" he called finally.

"Sir?"

"See if you can find the Senior Chief. And when you do—"

"I'm here, Sir!" a loud gruff voice with a Texas twang cut Ben's command short.

Radioman Senior Chief Petty Officer Darren Ericksen was indeed a native Texan of the Amarillo extraction. Of medium height and muscular build, he wore the Navy Seal recruiting poster image well. As well as being one smart cookie, the light blond, blue–eyed sailor also had the most sarcastic wit Ben had ever heard.

"Glad you could make it, Senior Chief," Ben said as he coolly glanced down at his wristwatch. "I was afraid we'd have to go to war without you."

"Well, Sir. I woulda been here a lot sooner. 'Cept I got behind a train of you high–ranking zero types talking about their fuckin' stocks and bonds and investments and such. Shit, they were movin' slower than a fat girl moves through a salad bar."

Ben fought back the urge to laugh. The Senior Chief was late and the proper tone for the next few weeks had to be set. "That's all well and good, Senior. Next time, though, let's get an earlier start?"

"Aye, Sir. I hear ya." He nodded and winked.

Ben returned the gesture with a smirk.

Also a Reservist, Senior Chief Ericksen had left active duty when his wife was diagnosed with terminal cancer. In the last two years of her life, he did what he could to make her comfortable. Since her death, just a few months earlier, he had taken a more participative role in the Unit. He volunteered for almost every exercise, or training course, or anything and everything.

Ericksen explained his affinity for the Navy as getting in touch with 'an old girlfriend.' Ben, and other members of the Seventh Fleet Unit, suspected there was more to it. However, one didn't press a senior chief petty officer in general, and a Navy Seal out of good sense.

"Why don't you see if you can get this watch section properly spooled up, Senior?"

"Yes, Sir. I'll see to it." Ericksen immediately started barking instructions at the junior enlisted personnel as Ben relaxed in his chair.

"Chief of Staff is in TFCC!" someone shouted.

Ben almost jumped out of his skin as he glanced to his left to find a six foot, two inch female Navy Captain entering the space.

"Who's got the watch here?" Captain Nation barked. Her tone was sharp, anger–filled, scary, intimidating.

"I–I do, Ma'am," Ben finally got the sentence out. His heart pounded so hard he thought it would come out of his chest.

Captain Beth "Bly" Nation was the active duty admiral's right hand, or more accurately, steel fist. Nation's reputation preceded her all over the fleet: first woman to command a destroyer, first woman to command a frigate, top of her class at Command School, Department Head School, and the Tactical Action Officer Course. She had also been on the Olympic Ski Team prior to commissioning. More importantly though, everybody on the Seventh Fleet Commander's reserve staff was afraid of her, including Ben. She wore the traditional blue and gold rope around her left shoulder to signify her status.

"And your name is?"

"McGuire, Ma'am." *Why is she asking? My name's on my jacket.*

"Commander McGuire, do you always run such a noisy watch?"

"No Ma'am. I—"

"No excuses, Mister. Report."

Report? Report what? He swallowed hard. "Ma'am, the watch is set. *Blue Ridge* Engineering has assured us that all of our systems are fully operational."

While he spoke, Ben stood at attention. His gaze never left hers. He felt like a plebe again.

"This Watch Team has properly configured the space for the exercise and is ready in all regards to get underway. We have no North Korean contacts to report. All Allied Fleet exercise resources have reported in that they are ready to commence the exercise."

After he finished, Nation broke her gaze and looked around the rest of the space. Ben finally found the nerve to examine the officer. She wore her dark hair wound into a bun. Nation was broad and muscular. She had that 'well–toned, I work out everyday' look.

"Good report, Commander. How long did it take you to get everything ready?"

"About forty minutes, Ma'am."

"About? Which was it? Forty, forty–one, thirty–nine, what?"

He took a deep breath. "Thirty–nine, Ma'am."

She nodded. "Not bad. I expected it would take you more."

Ben raised his eyebrow. "Then, this was a test?"

She whipped head back toward him. Her eyes met his again. Nation frowned as she stared at him.

Not knowing what to do, Ben stayed at attention. His eyes met hers when they could, but she seemed to examine every square inch of his face.

What in the hell are you looking at? He was starting to feel less like an officer in the Navy and more like a germ in a petri dish.

He felt himself tighten his fist. *Damn it. This is bullshit.* "Something wrong, Ma'am?" he finally asked.

"Out here, we get tested every day," she replied. "Welcome to *real* Navy, Mister McGuire. Carry on."

"Yes, Ma'am."

She turned and faded into the darkness. Ben stayed at attention until he heard the door shut behind her.

"Chief of Staff is out of TFCC," the same announcer cried out.

A test? Shit, the next two weeks are not gonna be fun. God, what a sadistic bitch.

He deflated himself into his chair again. "Shit, guys. We're off to a great start."

"You did okay, Sir," one of the active duty enlisted personnel replied. "You're still on watch. She likes you. If not, you'd be down in the wardroom reading the Watch Officer's Guide."

"So this happens all of the time?"

"Yes, Sir," four of them replied together.

CHAPTER SIXTEEN
MONDAY, APRIL 12TH

Ministry of National Defense
Intelligence Directorate
Beijing, China
5:59 AM
1:59 PM, GMT

"**M**ai Lin, tell me about your time with our asset," Fong said. He reclined in his chair as he examined the woman.

Her body tensed almost as he began the conversation. She nervously pulled her cigarette from her mouth. Her hand shook so much a large clump of ashes fell to the floor.

She's going to lie to me.

Fong sat at his desk while she occupied one of the guest chairs on the other side. The ashtray that she had missed just a few seconds before was on the edge of Fong's desk.

"He was my first field assignment. While he was in his final days as a graduate student in America, I met and seduced him. Over the course of a few months as he started his Government career, I got him to tell more and more about his work. Finally, one day, he told me about classified issues, and I used the threat of disclosing his lack of good judgment to get him to work for us. Eventually, he was in too deep to get out."

Fong noted the matter of fact nature of her tone.

"And how long were you lovers?"

She lowered her head.

"How long?"

"It took almost three years to get enough leverage."

"Hmm. Three years. How often were you together?"

Silence.

"Almost every day," she finally replied.

Fong's eyebrows went up.

"So you were close?"

"He was my assignment. We were not—"

"This man shared his life with you and you shared your bed with him. You were young. You must have developed some emotional attachment."

Her voice trembled.

"Before I send you back, I need to know your weaknesses," Fong explained as he stood.

"I'm sorry, Master. This is difficult."

Fong walked around his desk to stand next to her. He stroked her hair with his hand as he had last done many years before. "Go to Japan, Mai. Use this asset. Do what you must to keep him under control. Do this and I promise you that I will allow you to kill him when this is done."

She looked up at him through tearful eyes.

"What's the matter? Does that not please you?"

She took a deep breath before smiling. "Yes, Master. It pleases me very much."

Finally, the lie. She still loves him.

Tactical Flag Command Center
USS *Blue Ridge* (LCC–19)
2330 Hours
1430 Hours, GMT

"I miss you," Ben typed. "Not sleeping very well without you," he added before hitting the SEND button.

The computer screen refreshed a few seconds later and Claire's response appeared. "You're just horny. I know, because so am I. Smile. I miss you, too. This is so neat! I can't believe you're in the middle of the ocean on the other side of the world!"

"Ain't technology grand?" He smiled as he typed the words.

Ben and Claire had arranged a meeting place on the Internet via a chat room. While others on web chatted in adjacent rooms about everything from sex to politics, Claire had found a little known and out–of–the–way place just for them. Occasionally, someone would enter and try to participate in their on–line conversation, but ignoring them seemed an effective strategy.

"How are things going?" he asked.

"Good. Heard from the kids last night. They told me to tell you that e–mails are coming."

"Okay. I'll look for them."

"What about you?"

"First day started with a bang, but it's okay, I guess."

"Anything you can talk about?"

"Not until I get home. It would be too difficult to explain here. I'll write a detailed e-mail if I get a chance."

"Okay."

"What about you?" he asked.

"I'm fine. Very lonely, only one week, six days, and twenty hours to go."

Ben smiled. "I understand."

"I can't believe you didn't get what I was saying about the coat."

"When?" Ben typed.

"At the airport."

He remembered the conversation. "Oh, yeah. But I still don't get the coat thing."

"Never mind. Well, I've got to do some work. Be careful and I'll talk to you tomorrow," she said from the other side of the world. "I love you."

"I love you, too."

"Good night."

Ben leaned back in his chair. He touched the screen with his fingers the same way he caressed her face.

"How's the wife?" Dave asked, pulling him from his musings.

TFCC was busy. The exercise was in full swing and Dave had the watch.

"Good, except she keeps mentioning something about a new coat. How's the fleet doing?"

"Okay. Kind of boring. Coat?"

"Yeah, she mentioned something about wearing a coat at the airport when I got home."

Dave turned away from his computer monitor to glance at his friend. "You know, you scare me sometimes."

"Why? Do you know what she's talking about?"

Dave shook his head. "Go to bed, Ben."

"Okay. You stay on your toes, bud. Captain Bly is liable to come in here and emasculate you," Ben joked.

Dave laughed back. "Yeah, well I gotta believe she's planning something big for me."

"She's made little visits to everyone else so far."

"Bring it on," Dave said, as he pointed at his Submarine Warfare badge. "Fuck with the best, die with the rest, baby."

"Yeah, right," Ben shot back. "I'm going to bed. See you in the morning."

Dave nodded. He picked up a phone to make a call as Ben left his side. Moments later, Ben overheard Dave harassing someone else with his sense of humor.

Ben waved at and shook hands with a few more of the watch–standers as he exited the space. He squinted in the relatively brighter–lit spaces of the passageway for a second.

When his eyes cleared, he recognized a now–familiar figure moving toward him. *Oh, shit.* "Good evening, Ma'am," he greeted.

"Good evening, Commander McGuire. How are things in TFCC tonight?"

"Busy, Ma'am."

"Well, let's see if the battle watch captain knows as much about what's going on as I do."

"I'm sure he's looking forward to it, Ma'am."

She shot him an icy glance before reaching for the door handle.

"Oh well, Dave. You've just got to be careful of what you ask for," he said more to himself than anyone else. *At least we'll have something interesting to talk about at breakfast.*

CHAPTER SEVENTEEN
MONDAY, APRIL 12TH

Aboard *Blue Flame Logistics Helicopter*
Near Atsugi Air Base
11:30 PM
2:30 PM, GMT

Doctor Robert Deitrich sat with Doctor Yashita and Professor Tony Swinson in the helicopter's passenger section. The modified CH–46 regularly ferried people and equipment between the island laboratory and the Japanese Air Self–Defense Force Base.

The twin–bladed helicopter, white in color, had ten seats in the forward part of the fuselage. The seats, made of orange–colored cargo webbing, didn't offer much comfort. They, however, were lightweight, and allowed the aircraft to carry more cargo and personnel longer distances.

Yashita, predictably, had not spoken to either of them during the entire hour and a half flight. Swinson, who was no fan of the Japanese, had not made an effort to communicate with Yashita, either.

Swinson and Deitrich spoke above the helicopter's engine noise for a while about Doctor Hobson's news and how it might affect them, long–term. Swinson wasn't as concerned about where and when the project would start again. He lobbied Deitrich for a higher profile role. He was sure a great many of the Japanese scientists would resist assignments in the United States.

After a short while, Deitrich found himself wishing he'd taken a later flight. Swinson, when it came to something he wanted, was like a dog with a bone. Deitrich, however, recognized the man's importance. Swinson had the task of receiving that week's supplies for transport back to Senkaku. This was his regular flight to the mainland.

"So you'll head back in the morning?" Deitrich asked Swinson.

"Yep. Probably in the late afternoon or evening. I've got to run into Tokyo for a while."

"One of your 'special' errands?"

Swinson's positive demeanor evaporated. "No, nothing like that."

"Hold on back there," the pilot called over his shoulder. "The tower reports there's low–level turbulence near the airfield. We'll be touching down in about two minutes."

The pilot's words acted to break the conversation. "Sorry I asked," Bob added.

Swinson only nodded.

Deitrich glanced over at Yashita as he checked his seatbelt. The Asian played with his pen as he looked out of the round window next to him. *I wonder what's on his mind.*

A few seconds later, the aircraft bounced around a

bit. Deitrich grabbed hold of the seat next to him for support. He looked out the window to see Japanese and U.S. Air Force aircraft in precise lines.

The pilot brought the aircraft down to a soft landing in front of another helicopter on the north side of the terminal. As the engine wound down, relative silence allowed the sound of unbuckling seatbelts to reach his ears. Deitrich checked his watch. *I should be there in an hour or so.*

CHAPTER EIGHTEEN
TUESDAY, APRIL 13TH

Commander, Seventh Fleet's Cabin
USS *Blue Ridge* (LCC–19)
Sea of Japan
0935 Hours
12:35 Hours, GMT

"**B**eth, take a look at this," Vice Admiral Fred Kiatkowski said as he handed her a piece of paper. He sat on his couch going through messages. Nation had just finished her morning tour of TFCC, leaving one of the reserve battle captains reeling in her wake.

The three–star admiral's roomy office and living spaces featured a large desk, two sofas, and a couple of guest chairs. A coffee table sat between the two couches.

She sat in a chair across from him as her eyes focused on the paper. "The Naval Message," a specially formatted written document, was from the Chief of Naval Operations.

"*Conduct a Non–Combatant Evacuation Operation*

(NEO) as part of Exercise Ronin Blitz. Assets from Seventh Fleet will extract up to 15 American and Japanese civilians from the Japanese Island of Senkaku. While this operation is part of the Exercise, it is to be considered a real–world event." Nation re–read the brief message and glanced up. As if we don't have enough to do," she sighed.

"Uh, huh."

The message went on to instruct Seventh Fleet to conduct the NEO within the next three days. Doing so meant ordering the carrier, and her escorts, south.

"How are we going to explain this to the Koreans?" she asked.

Kiatkowski, a tall man with silver hair and a matching moustache, shrugged. "I imagine the boys and girls at State will figure that one out. All I have to do is tell Admiral Hyun I've got orders to head down toward Okinawa."

An aviator, the admiral had a very casual style. In her first year as his chief administrator, Beth found she liked working for him. He typically let her do things her way. Nation stood. "I'll get started on this. It'll probably take Ops a few hours to put a plan together."

"Give it to the Reservists," he interjected.

"Sir, I—" His words hit her so hard she had to reseat herself.

"Beth, like you said, we don't have time for this. Besides, it'll give them something unusual to do for a few days."

Nation frowned at her boss. "If you're sure, Sir." *Why is he doing this? If they screw it up, I'll just have more to do.*

"I'm sure. They can handle it, Beth. I've worked with these guys before."

She nodded slowly. "Aye. Aye, Sir." *Great.*

Tokyo Hilton Hotel, Room 1231
Tokyo, Japan
10:00 AM
1:00 AM, GMT

"This is ridiculous," he said aloud as he checked his watch for the millionth time. *She said be here at 8:30, so I was here at 8:30. If she makes a fool out of me, I'll—*

His thoughts were interrupted by the sound of the door's electronic lock clicking open. He came to his feet as she entered the room and recognized his old lover in an instant.

Mai Lin wore black. A scarf and sunglasses accented the matching blouse and pants. A travel bag, also black, hung from her shoulder. She closed the door and pulled the dark glasses down from her face, all in the same graceful motion. His gaze met hers. He moved toward her as if she were a timid bunny. She took a large draw from a cigarette and mashed it out in an ashtray.

When he reached her, he stopped. For a long while he looked into her eyes, at her face. The creases in her face from smiles and frowns were deeper and more pronounced now. He smiled, but she did not return it.

"Am I too old for you now?" she asked in Japanese.

"Never. You are as beautiful as the sun on a spring day." He leaned forward and pressed his lips against hers. He'd responded to her in Mandarin.

For a long while she only stood there. Just when he started thinking that she would not respond, she opened her mouth and touched his tongue with hers. He felt her let the bag down gently and put her arms around him. With that, he pulled her closer and kissed her more deeply.

Mai Lin fell into his arms. He picked her up and headed toward the bedroom. All thoughts of anything or anyone else evaporated from his mind. For now, she was all he wanted.

Project Blue Flame Laboratory
Computer Room
11:00 AM
2:00 AM, GMT

"Damn."

The claxon speaker sounded again. The instrument panel window in the bottom right of the display showed four bar graphs, all in red. A "DANGER: REACTOR OVER PRESSURIZED!" message blinked in rhythm with the sound from the computer's speaker.

"Dead end?" Dolores Shinozaki asked.

"Yeah," Stanley Loewen replied. He used the mouse to push the pointer to the "SIMULATION RESET" menu on his screen.

He and Dolores sat at a desk in the back of the server room, which housed several large UNIX machines, a number of NT servers, and fifteen workstations. Loewen wore his only sweater beneath a lab coat to counter the relatively cooler air.

Loewen sighed as if the weight of the whole project rested upon him. "This is impossible." The fourth hour of running simulations was going as well as the first through the third.

"Want some more coffee?" Shinozaki asked as she stood and stretched.

"No. It'll just make me an edgy failure, rather than just a failure."

As Loewen sat back in his chair and studied the screen, he felt Dolores's hands start to knead the muscles in his upper back and neck. He smiled. "That feels good, but it's not helping."

"Oh, no?"

He next felt her mouth nibbling on his ear. "Okay, that's not helping either."

"Tell me to stop and I will," she whispered.

Loewen slowly pushed his chair back from the console and pulled her around in front of him. "You're supposed to be helping me work."

"I am." She pulled his head to her bosom.

Likewise, Loewen hugged her waist tightly. When Loewen found out about his assignment to the fusion project, he thought it a dream come true. Dolores Shinozaki, with her medium height and Rubenesque figure, was the best part of all. The beautiful, half–Latino, half–Japanese scientist pressed her body against his.

"What are you doing?" she asked as Loewen's hand moved up her back.

Loewen smiled as he looked up at her round face. He felt for and found the snap of her bra. "Taking a little work break."

"Stan," she protested. His other hand caressed her left breast through the fabric of the lab coat and blouse.

"Yes?"

"Not here," she pulled away, although not that strenuously.

Loewen pinched at the two sides of the snap attempting to open the brassiere. He pulled at it three times, his frown growing in intensity at each failure. "Man. I'm losing my touch."

This time Shinozaki squirmed like she meant it.

"I can't get it."

"That's because it's not meant to work that way," she replied.

Her words lingered in his mind for a long second. Loewen glanced at the computer and then at Dolores. He pulled away and wheeled his chair back toward the computer monitor and keyboard.

"What?"

"That's it," he said.

"What's it?"

Loewen pulled up the C++ development package and opened the uncompiled version of his program. "I can't believe I was that stupid," he mumbled.

"Stanley Loewen—"

"Dolores, listen to this. When I wrote this program, I optimized it to find anyway possible to get a reaction started and to keep it going." Loewen typed commands into the system as he spoke.

"I don't understand."

"The simulation is biased. I never adjusted it after we figured out how to create and sustain the reaction." He continued making modifications to the program.

Dolores adjusted her clothing before seating herself next to Loewen. "Glad I could help." She folded her arms and frowned at him.

CHAPTER NINETEEN
TUESDAY, APRIL 13TH

USS *Blue Ridge* (LCC–19)
Chief of Staff's Stateroom
1100 Hours
0200 Hours, GMT

"Tom, I like the plan your guys put together. Don't deviate from it too much. Keep this simple. Get out there, get the geeks and get back." Captain Nation looked across her desk at Captain Tom Anders.

"We can handle it." The Reservists' commanding officer sat in a relaxed posture, his legs crossed.

She didn't like it, but they were the same rank. "Who do you think you'll send?"

"Rumor has it that you've already met him. Ben McGuire."

"Ah yes. Mister McGuire. He's got spunk."

"You can say that again," Anders laughed.

She pushed her chair back from the desk and folded her arms. "Where's he from?"

"Alabama, I think. Why?"

"No, no. Which fleet? East or West Coast? He looks really familiar."

"East Coast. And yes, he ought to. Do you remember the Devon incident?"

"Oh, my God. That's him." A cannon went off in her head when the memory of one of the biggest events in modern naval history came to mind. She grabbed her forehead. "So that's what happened to him."

"He came to Seventh Fleet for the first time about three years ago. He's a good officer—"

"Did he tell you why he got out?" she interrupted.

"Nope. And I never asked."

Nation caught herself frowning. "I want to talk to him."

"Something I should know about?"

"This is a big deal, Tom. The CNO, maybe even the President, is watching this one. I want to make sure we're sending the right guy."

"Beth, you don't want to go down that road with him."

She didn't respond. The Navy captain only stared at him.

Anders took in a deep breath and sighed. "I'll see to it."

She nodded as her Reserve counterpart stood and left the room.

USS *Blue Ridge* (LCC–19)
Wardroom
1200 Hours
0300 Hours, GMT

The food was good, Ben decided. It was at least as good, if not better than his last three trips. He looked forward to the meal hours, and not just for the food. They gave him a chance to wind down. He liked talking with both the active duty and the reserve officers.

Meals were served cafeteria style. Once through the line, personnel went through a doorway on the starboard side of the ship and entered the dining room. Large enough to seat more than a hundred at a time, officers sat eight to a table. Enlisted mess attendants in black trousers and white golf shirts poured coffee, kept the tables supplied with clean silverware, and cleared used settings for incoming diners. The shirts featured a *Blue Ridge* Wardroom Mess logo with crossed anchors behind a golden anchor.

"Okay, here's one," Dave started.

Ben reclined in his chair as his friend started the fourth or fifth in a long line of jokes. He took the last bite of food and two seconds later one of the mess attendants came to clear his dishes away. Ben thanked her with a smile.

"This guy walks into a bar in Arkansas and orders a glass of white wine," Dave went on.

The other officers seated at the table all leaned forward as they listened. Dave had been at it almost since dinner started.

"The bartender looks up and says, 'You ain't from 'round here. Are ya? Where ya from, boy?'"

One of the other commanders snickered.

"The guy says, 'I'm from Iowa'," Dave continued. "The bartender goes, 'Iowa. What in the hell do you do in Iowa?'"

As he listened, Ben looked around the room. Blue tablecloths with gold piping covered all thirteen tables. Well–lighted, clean, and airy, it reminded Ben of the dining facility at the University where he had gotten his Master's degree.

He reflected on the changes in wardrooms since his days as a junior officer. The officer's mess now had a microwave oven, a soft drink machine and even a cappuccino maker. The Navy had gone all out over the last few years to improve the quality of life aboard its ships and submarines. The most noticeable change was the disappearance of the ice cream–maker, or Auto–dog machine. It got that name because when one pressed the lever, it poured out the dessert into a bowl or other container looking like dog–poop. Now, they had real ice cream. While it tasted better, Ben longed for the old days.

He shifted in his chair at about the same time an ensign approached the table. The young male officer came to attention when he arrived.

Ben eyed him. *God, he looks like a child. I wonder if his father knows he's stolen his uniform. Was I ever that young?*

Meanwhile, Dave continued his joke. "The guy said, 'I'm a taxidermist.' The bartender goes, "A taxidermist? What the heck is that?"

"Sirs," the young officer announced himself after standing at the table for a long silent moment.

"Hold on, Mister," Groucho ordered. "Can't you see Commander Ferguson is on a roll here?"

The kid resumed his rigid stance.

"The guy from Iowa looks around the bar and eyes the crowd. They were right out of a scene from *Deliverance*, and they were all looking at him. He swallowed hard and said, 'I mount animals.' The bartender grins and shouts to the whole bar, 'It's okay boys. He's one of us!'"

Ben and the others burst into laughter. The ensign even sneaked a grin.

"Sirs," the kid started again as the laughter subsided. "Which of you is Commander McGuire?"

"I am."

"Sir, your presence is requested in the Chief of Staff's cabin."

Ben exchanged a weighty glance with Dave. "What do you think this is about?"

"Not a clue." Ben got to his feet and pulled on his jacket.

"Enjoy," Groucho said, as Ben left the table with the baby–faced ensign.

Ben exited through the Wardroom Lounge. He smiled to himself as he passed through a gaggle of junior officers transfixed on a closed circuit television broadcast of the quintessential guy–flick, *Porky's*.

Oh, to be young again.

Out the door and up the ladder to the 0–1 Level, Ben bounded his way. With each step, he tried to come up with a reason for the COS' summons. He walked down the blue–tiled passageway until he got to the quick–acting watertight door and the wide athwart–ship passageway beyond. The no–name ensign led the way.

"Here you are, Sir." He stopped a few feet further on, near the centerline of the ship and three stars that marked the door to the Flag Passageway and Admiral's Country beyond.

"Shit." Ben squared his shoulders.

"Straight ahead, just follow the signs, Sir," the ensign said.

Ben slowly pushed up the door handle. In all of his trips out to the Seventh Fleet Flagship, he'd never been beyond the big white door.

Damn, it's quiet. He closed the door and started down the corridor.

He didn't know where the Chief of Staff's cabin was. However, every space, doorway, hatch, even most fixtures, carried a label. He proceeded down the passageway until he found her office. By the time he reached it, he'd concluded that worrying about it was probably a waste of time. "This lady's whacked," he said aloud.

The sign on the gray door read, "Knock, Then Enter." So, he did. "Commander McGuire, reporting as ordered, Ma'am."

She sat behind her desk. Even seated, she looked tall. "Come in, Commander."

Ben closed the door behind him. He marched across the expansive office and stopped a few feet short of the desk. Her two guest chairs were on either side of him. He took a quick scan around the room to note that she had enough room for two couches, a meeting table, and an entertainment stand complete with a television and stereo system. Like the rest of the Flag spaces, it also featured ivory white walls or bulkheads, and blue–carpeted decks.

"Yes, Ma'am?"

"Yes, Commander. We have a mission that's come up and we're thinking about sending you."

"Is it the NEO that I helped Captain Anders plan?"

"Yes. But before we get to that, I've a few questions for you."

"Yes, Ma'am?"

"I didn't recognize you the other day. You're something of a celebrity." Biting sarcasm filled her voice.

"I don't think I understand, Ma'am," he lied. *Not this shit again.*

"I want to know what made you turn your back on your career, and to a lesser extent, on your country."

Ben choked back his initial thoughts. *Cool. Stay cool. Play this the right way.* "No comment, Ma'am," he finally replied.

She slammed her fist against the desk and leaned forward in her chair. "I asked you a question, Mister."

"Request permission to speak candidly, Ma'am?"

She sighed. Nation relaxed her fist and slowly reclined in her chair. "Permission granted."

"Captain, ten years was a long time ago. I made some decisions that affected my personal life and my professional life for some very personal reasons. They might have been stupid, they might have been selfish, or they might have been noble as hell. But whatever they were, they were all mine. And I don't have to justify them to you, or anybody else. If you want me to go do this NEO thing, then send me. If you don't, then my watch is coming up. Either way, I'm not gonna let you treat me like a Naval Academy plebe. And that's all I'm gonna say, Ma'am."

Ben, still at attention, tried to take deep breaths to calm himself. All the time, he and Captain Nation never broke eye contact.

Nation crossed her arms. She eventually lowered her gaze. "Sit down, Commander."

"If it's all the same—"

"I said sit down, damn it."

Ben took a deep breath, picked out a chair, and followed her order.

"You always been such a disrespectful cuss?"

"Since Youngster Year, Ma'am."

She smiled, but just for a second.

"You know what we want done?"

"Yes, Ma'am."

"You'll be carrying orders from the admiral. I don't think you'll have any problems. If you do, it'll most likely be over on the bird farm," she said referring to the aircraft carrier, USS *Theodore Roosevelt*.

"I understand."

"Good. If you need anything, give TFCC a call."

"Yes, Ma'am. Is that all?"

"Yes, Commander. You're dismissed."

Ben stood to take his leave. He turned and walked toward the door.

"Commander?" she called as he reached for the knob.

"Yes, Ma'am?"

"The boys in D.C. are watching this one. Don't fuck it up. Good luck."

"Thank you, Ma'am." *Who's she kidding? This is a milk run. If it was anything more than that, they sure as shit wouldn't be giving it to Reservists.*

CHAPTER TWENTY
TUESDAY, APRIL 13TH

Headquarters, 1st Information Warfare Brigade
Beijing, China
1400 Hours
6:00 AM, GMT

"Gentlemen, this is a crucial time for our organization," General Zhao Chin Lee lectured.

His five most senior officers, two colonels and three majors, sat at the conference table. The room, darkened except for the light directly over the table's center, matched Zhao's mood since his last encounter with Deputy Minister Fong Du So.

The old man's words and attitude haunted him, even in his attempts at sleep. His past accomplishments, his family connections, his own colleagues in the Chinese Communist Party all meant nothing now. The "Old Man" wanted results and more importantly, he wanted them from him.

"I want a plan!"

A long silence swept across the room.

"The Americans have placed their mainland network in emission control—," Major Hong began.

"I already know what *is*, damn you!"

The young officer who dared utter the 'what is' fell silent and lowered his head.

"Sir, what if we try to infiltrate their network in the Hawaiian Islands?" another of them asked.

"Why would you think that network is not under the same EMCON condition?" Zhao asked. *What an idiot.*

"Sir, because the Americans must exercise operational control of their fleet," Colonel Pan replied.

Zhao sat up in his chair. His fist went up to his lips as he considered the colonel's words. "Your point has merit," he said, leaning back. "Continue."

"The Americans use a network of computers that 'trust' each other. Our best chance is to find one of those servers and use it to get to the others."

"But the American's have superb detection capabilities," one of the majors interjected. "Our best time in their systems has averaged only a few minutes."

"That was their secure systems," Pan replied. "If we confine our work to the unclassified and administrative systems, I suspect we'll have more time to look around."

"But what will that get us?" General Zhao asked. "The material we seek is classified at the highest levels."

"Yes, General. But it is also a joint effort between the Americans and the Japanese. Perhaps we can find something that will guide us to a vulnerability in the Japanese networks and systems."

Zhao sat up in his chair again. Pan was right. This

was the best idea he'd heard in days. "Start today," he ordered. "Start now."

Senior Officer Country
USS *Blue Ridge* (LCC–19)
1515 Hours
0615 Hours, GMT

"I figured she was gonna quiz you about it," Anders said. Ben's commanding officer sat in his Government Issue gray steel chair with his feet on the edge of the lower bunk. File folders and charts lay all around him.

"Well, I think we reached an understanding."

"Sounds like you did. How much time do you need to get ready?"

"Just enough to get changed into some cammies," he replied, referring to his camouflage uniform, "and drop a quick note to Claire."

"A note?" Anders' eyebrow went up.

"I know, I know. This little flail–ex is classified. I'll be vague and caring, all at the same time." Keeping the sarcasm out of his voice proved a useless endeavor.

"Listen up, Junior. If we can't get them to trust us with the small stuff, we'll never get the big assignments."

Anders' expression was firm. Ben immediately felt the weight. "Aye, aye. Sir."

"Can I take Ferguson with me?"

"No, with you gone we're gonna be short–handed on the Battle Watch."

Ben frowned at the response. Having another brain around to bounce things off was always a good idea.

"What about the Senior Chief?" Anders asked.

That was a good idea. "Okay, Sir. I'll ask him."

The growler, or ship's intercom system, squawked. Anders picked up the receiver and answered. "Yes. He's with me now."

Ben could barely make out the voice on the other end. However, he could tell from Anders' respectful demeanor that it was Captain Nation. His CO was practically sitting at attention.

"I'll let him know." Anders turned to Ben. "Captain Nation says to let you know the ship will be setting flight quarters in thirty minutes."

"Yes, Sir."

Anders climbed to his feet. "Don't let us down."

Ben nodded as he shook hands with his skipper. "Wouldn't dream of it, Sir. See you in a few days."

Tactical Flag Command Center
USS *Blue Ridge* (LCC–19)
1530 Hours
0630 Hours, GMT

"Yeah, one more thing, look at this." Dave Ferguson said, after hearing the *Reader's Digest* version of the last two hours. He had the Battle Watch. Ben had swung by to get some last minute intelligence as well as shoot an e–mail home to Claire.

The space was in its typical busy state. Officers in khakis and enlisted personnel in blue coveralls moved back and forth as well as communicated with Fleet ships and aircraft. He pulled his attention away from managing the Seventh Fleet to assist Ben.

Ferguson punched up a synoptic weather chart on one of his console displays. The image displayed a developing circular cloud pattern to their southwest.

"It's not a tropical storm, yet. But if it becomes one, it'll be big."

"What can I expect until then?"

"What am I, the National Weather Service?"

"Give me a break, Dave."

"Okay, sorry. Weather–guessers say low clouds, high winds and building seas. If you're going somewhere, you'd better get there and be prepared to stay."

"Shit. This is all I need."

"Well, look at it this way, at least you'll be off this pig for a few days," Dave replied.

"Somehow, that's not making me feel any better."

"It's not like you're gonna be dealing with the Koreans again. Lighten up, this could be fun."

Ben remembered that it had been Ferguson who'd talked him into the now infamous duty that resulted in his opportunity to sample authentic Korean kimchi. "Dave, that's what you said about that two weeks I spent at ROK Fleet Headquarters. News flash, it wasn't fun."

"This is all your fault, Ben," Dave admonished.

"How the hell do you figure that?"

"N–A–V–Y, baby. Never Again Volunteer Yourself. You never listen to me!"

"You know, I can probably get the CO to send you instead."

"Do it and you'd better sleep with one eye open for the rest of this float," Dave laughed.

"That's what I thought." As Ben checked his watch, he heard Senior Chief Ericksen gabbing with one of his pals a few feet away.

"Flight Quarters, Flight Quarters. All hands man your Flight Quarters Stations," the 1MC ship's announcing system blared. Speakers all over the ship, on every deck and nearly every space kept the crew informed as well as keeping them on a daily schedule.

"That's my ride. I've gotta get going. Still gotta get changed into my tree suit."

"Take it easy, Ben. I'll see you in a few days. And try to enjoy this." Dave cracked a wide travel–agent's smile.

"Yeah, yeah. Eat shit, Ferguson."

Ben got up from the watch console and pushed in his chair. "Hey, Senior Chief, how'd you like to get off of this pig for a few days?" He shot Dave a sarcasm–filled glance.

"Where we going?" Ericksen asked as he picked up his jacket.

"I take it that the answer is yes?"

"Try to quit acting like an officer, just for a second, Sir," Ericksen quipped back.

"Okay, okay. There's some scientists on a little island out in the East China Sea who need some rescuing." Ben never slowed his pace.

"Rescuing? Rescuing from what?"

"More bureaucratic bullshit," Ben replied halfway out of the door. "I'll meet you back on the flight deck in ten minutes. Get changed into cammies."

"Do I need anything else?" he heard the senior enlisted man shout to him from the top of the passageway.

"Yeah. Make sure you pack your sense of humor. You're gonna need it."

"Now, Sir, you know it's always packed and ready."

McGuire Residence
Plano, Texas
1:30 PM
6:30 AM, GMT

Claire McGuire was in the process of finishing an e–mail to Ben when his message arrived with the sound of a computer–generated telephone ring. She used her mouse and double–clicked the new message icon.

Claire,

Gonna be out of touch for a few days. Exercise stuff. I warned you there might be a few blackout periods. Try not to worry.

I love you, Ben.

P.S. I still don't get the comment about the coat. Please explain.

"I wasn't going to worry until you said, 'Try not to worry.' God, this really sucks."

Claire finished her e–mail although she had no idea when he would see it.

CHAPTER TWENTY–ONE
TUESDAY, APRIL 13TH

Tokyo Hilton Hotel, Room 1231
Tokyo, Japan
3:30 PM
6:30 AM, GMT

"So, you understand what you must do?" Mai Lin asked. She spoke English this time. Her speech was nearly free of any accent.

She was on her tenth or eleventh cigarette since arriving. He couldn't remember which. *I'm never going to get this smell out of my clothes. But I don't care. It's so good to be with her again.*

They'd been awake for a few hours now. Although he knew the reason for her even being there was business, and her business at that, he was happy that she had transitioned from the bedroom to the board-room with grace. Besides, they had been in bed most of the day.

Drawn curtains cast the room in relative darkness. They used the room's lamps to illuminate the space.

"Yes. I'm to disrupt communications and secure as much of the reactor specifications into one medium as possible." Now he spoke in English. He smiled to himself. It was almost like old times. During their time together, she had taught him several languages. She loved to switch in the middle of conversations just to see if he could keep up.

"This bag contains all that you will need." Still nude, she walked over to one of the bags she had brought with her. She picked it up and placed it on a nearby table.

She pulled out several articles and placed them on the table, too. "This is a radio transceiver. Do not be misled by its size. It has a range of just over a hundred miles. One of our satellites will be able to relay your signal to us and ours to you."

He climbed out from under the covers and walked over to where she stood. The transceiver was small, roughly the size of a calculator. Furthermore, it was disguised to look like a popular brand of personal information manager.

"You recognize this?"

"Yes. It's a high capacity storage drive and disk."

She nodded. "Are there many of them in the laboratory?"

"A few. Is this what you want me to use to put the reactor schematics on?"

"Yes. Try to capture as much as you can in textual and database formats."

He laughed. "It'll probably take a hundred of these to get everything. Haven't you people got anything more advanced than this? I mean this isn't cutting–edge technology. Or haven't you been able to steal anything else yet?"

She frowned. "The People of China have the most advanced science in the world. If the West has made gains it has been because of technology stolen from us."

I'll bet she really believes that, too. These people are

amazing. They've been at the forefront of technology since the beginning of time and here they are, reduced to stealing in order to get a leg up on feeding themselves.

"Mai Lin, I don't wish to engage in a political discussion. I'm on your side. Remember? Is there anything else?" he asked.

Calm returned to her voice. "If you can delay their probable departure until we can land a tactical force, that will be sufficient."

He nodded. A long silence filled the space between them. It was so thick that he could hear the cars on the street twenty floors below. He held out his hand to her.

After a long moment, she moved toward him. She grasped his hand and brought it to her mouth as she reached him.

He led her back to the bed. He climbed in first and raised the covers for her. Mai Lin smiled, laughed aloud, then climbed in next to him.

"What will become of us?" he asked in Japanese.

She stopped nibbling a long lingering second later. "Who can say? You have your wife and your life in the West. I have my career."

"Wouldn't you like to get out of this mess?"

"We cannot speak of these things. Let us enjoy the now. There is an old proverb which loosely translates to 'Don't lose the bird you have trapped trying to get a bigger one'."

He smiled. "Yes, I've heard that one, too. Well, something like it, anyway," he replied in English.

Mai Lin smiled and kissed his mouth. She rolled on top of him and then reached over and switched off the lights.

CHAPTER TWENTY–TWO
TUESDAY, APRIL 13TH

Aboard *Blackbeard Zero One*
2,000 Feet Above Sea Level
Sea of Japan
15:45 Hours
0645 Hours, GMT

When Ben visited TFCC just prior to his departure, the nuclear–powered aircraft carrier USS *Theodore Roosevelt* was twenty miles northeast of USS *Blue Ridge*, conducting flight operations. Before lifting off, Ben stood above decks with Senior Chief Ericksen. They peered into the distance for their destination but to no avail.

The ocean had a light chop. Little whitecaps disappeared seconds after appearing. The sea had lost its blue color out this far. It, like the ship he stood on, was light gray. Puffy clouds, also gray, moved by with haste. Haze–filled sea air and the roof of thick clouds made it hard to see very far. In fact, their helo seemed to materialize out of the sky just before it touched down on the *Blue Ridge's* flight deck.

As they made their way across the miles of ocean that separated the two ships, Ben occasionally looked out of the window to see a ship or boat or sea creature. The ride was smooth, but noisy. Even with earplugs, the sound of the engine inside the cabin of the H–3 was deafening.

Ben was busy looking out the open window nearest him when one of the crewmen tapped him on the shoulder. Facing aft, he turned to his left to see a young, enlisted woman's face.

"Sir, I thought you'd like to have a look," she shouted into his ear. She pointed toward the cockpit.

Ben turned the rest of the way around in his seat. The pilots had elected to leave the flight deck door open. He could see straight through the cockpit and beyond.

His eyes widened at the sight. The aircraft carrier, still two miles away, filled his field of vision. In the sea haze, the carrier resembled a large gray monolith lying on its side. The numeral 71, painted in white, figured prominently.

"Big son of a bitch, huh, Sir?" she asked.

"Yeah," Ben replied.

Years ago as a flight student, he'd made several arrested landings on *Kitty Hawk*. During the Persian Gulf War, he'd served aboard USS *Ranger*. However, this thing was a monster, almost twice the size of *Kitty Hawk*.

Ben remembered reading that at over a thousand feet long and displacing more than hundred thousand tons, she was the largest ship ever built at the time of her commissioning in 1995. The nuclear powered

Teddy Roosevelt was the at–sea home to three hundred, eighty–six officers; three thousand, one hundred eighty–four enlisted; and fifty tactical aircraft. *Big son of a bitch was right.*

The pilot brought the helicopter in over the ship's port side. The aircraft slid to the right until directly over the flight deck. It hovered there for a moment before settling aboard *Theodore Roosevelt* with a gentle bounce.

The rotors slowed and crewmen in yellow and white shirts surrounded the aircraft. The sounds of chains and other tackle gear penetrated the engine noise as they secured the helo to the deck.

The main cabin door slid open with a loud clang. If the noise inside the H–3 had been deafening during the flight, the noise on the flight deck was crushingly so. Not more than a few yards away, Ben recognized an F–18 Hornet and an S–3 Viking throttling up for launch.

An officer wearing a white safety helmet, goggles and vest tried in vain to shout above launching fighter aircraft. Ben pointed at his ears and shook his head. Both of the men turned at almost the same time to see the F–18 Hornet shoot down the catapult in a trail of fire and steam. A few moments later, the S–3 Viking followed the fighter into the sky. After the two aircraft launched, relative quiet made speaking possible.

"Commander McGuire?" the man shouted.

"Yes!"

"Come with me, Sir. The Air Boss is waiting for you!"

Ben nodded, gestured for the Senior Chief to follow, and climbed out of the aircraft.

The three figures walked briskly across the busy deck. Gusts of wind alternated cool and warm from the sea and the occasional jet engine. The smell of the air alternated, too. Each gasp of fresh ocean air usually announced the aroma of jet fuel or exhaust. They entered a superstructure door just as another aircraft throttled up for launch.

Their unnamed escort led the way up several ladders. Ben occasionally looked over his shoulder to make sure that Ericksen was still with them. His escort didn't offer the same courtesy.

By the time they got off the ladder well, the deck placard read 0–6 Level. The officer never slowed his pace. Ben had to take an extra step or two to keep up as he approached an open door. Ben held it for the Senior Chief, who uncharacteristically, had not uttered a word since climbing onboard the helicopter back on *Blue Ridge*.

The sign on the door read Primary Flight Control. Ben remembered this space from his few days as an aviator. The room, located well above the main deck, gave a breathtaking view of the flight deck below, and the ocean beyond. Several officers and men talked on radios or telephones, or watched the happenings on the deck below. Two of them sat in chairs. Their escort stopped in front of the one furthest from them. The back of his chair read AIR BOSS.

The man pulled off his white helmet and said, "Sir. He's here."

The officer to whom he reported wore khaki. Silver oak–leaf clusters twinkled in the light. *Good*, Ben thought. *We're the same rank*. However, Ben knew that didn't mean much. This guy was in charge of everything that flew off, around and onto that ship.

He was a former squadron commanding officer, probably a fighter squadron. Ben also knew that as far as he was concerned, he'd best be holding papers from God to get an audience with him. *And I am.*

A long moment or two passed before the Air Boss pulled his attention away from the flight deck. Ben waited, patiently. Finally, after what seemed an eternity, their eyes met. He looked Ben up and down like a piece of old cabbage in a rinky–dink supermarket. He seemed to focus in on the embroidered version of the warfare insignia above Ben's left breast pocket. He frowned.

"Skip Thorensen," he said as he extended his hand.

"Ben McGuire."

The other officer turned and looked at Ben with the same level of disgust. This guy was Black, and was also a commander. He looked familiar, but with the greeting he was getting, Ben decided to stick to business.

The Black officer didn't even nod as he returned his gaze to the flight operations below. Ben felt like he was suddenly in the wrong place or like he'd farted in church. He was a Surface Warfare Officer and he was on the most hallowed of Naval Aviator Ground.

"What can I do for you?" Thorensen finally asked.

"I'm here to start the NEO."

The sound of a launching jet pulled his attention toward the front of the ship.

Ben cleared his throat.

"And?" Thorensen replied.

"And, I understand that you're supposed to ready two helos and four SEALs to—"

"Listen, Shoe. This has gotta be some kind of fuck

up. There ain't no way in hell I'm turning two helicopters and their crews over to *you*."

Shoe was short for Black Shoe. Aviators usually called ship–drivers that name when they weren't listening. Trouble was, Ben was listening. *I haven't been called that in a long time.* "Is that right?" Ben replied.

"So what are you going to do now?" Thorensen asked. He grinned a sinister, yellow–toothed smile.

Ben looked around the space. Several of the others grinned as well.

Any other day in the Navy, being called Black Shoe wouldn't be such a bad thing. After all, he'd been called much worse in foreign languages. However, this guy was begging for a spanking. Ben's stomach churned.

"I'm going to make a phone call," Ben replied as he pulled out his cellular telephone.

"A what?" Thorensen asked.

The two aviators exchanged glances as Ben dialed the number for the Tactical Flag Operations Center aboard *Blue Ridge*. *I just hope to God the Navy will let me expense this call. I'll have to thank John when I get home.*

"Seventh Fleet. TFCC," the voice on the other end answered. Ben heard voices, radio calls, and the general goings–on in the background. The command center was as busy as usual.

"Yeah, this is Commander McGuire aboard *Teddy Roosevelt*. Put me through to Admiral Kiatkowski, please."

"One moment, Sir," the person on the other line replied. The line went silent during the transfer.

Ben shot Thorensen a glance. This time the aviator

looked a little less confident. His eyes widened when Ben winked at him.

"Yes, Commander. What is it?" the admiral asked.

"Sir, I'm over here on *Teddy Roosevelt*. It seems that your orders got a little scrambled in transmission. Anyway, I've got the Air Boss here and he'd like to okay this whole thing with you."

"Oh, sure. I understand. Put him on."

"One moment, Admiral."

Ben looked up at Thorensen. "It's for you."

The Air Boss reached for the little phone as if he were taking hold of a piece of delicate china. He moved it to his ear with the same amount of care.

Ben took another visual survey of the room. All of the smiles and grins had evaporated. Thorensen, in particular, winced as he put the phone to his ear.

"Commander Thorensen, Sir."

Ben and Ericksen exchanged gleeful glances. The Senior Chief even laughed aloud before slapping Ben on his back.

Thorensen wasn't getting the opportunity to say much more than: "Yes, Sir. I understand, Sir. I'll take care of it, Sir."

This went on for two or three minutes before the conversation started winding down. "Yes, Admiral. He's right here. Hold on, Sir."

Thorensen handed the telephone back to Ben. He still wasn't smiling.

"Yes, Admiral."

"I understand there's a storm moving in. Get going!"

"Aye, aye, Sir."

The line went dead.

Most of the noise and conversation in the space

had also disappeared during Thorensen's brief conversation with the Seventh Fleet Commander. It had yet to return.

"Who the hell are you?" he asked Ben.

"Just a guy trying to do his job."

The Air Boss took a deep breath and let it out in a huff. "Get two 60's ready for this guy—"

"Three," the Senior Chief interjected.

"What?" Thorensen asked.

"That'll be three helicopters and a squad of SEALs."

"But he said two. The orders said two—" Thorensen reminded Ben of a pleading child.

"That was before you pissed him off. Now, we'll take three."

"Listen, damn it—" Thorensen stood up on the pedestal of his chair.

"Sir. Can I borrow your phone?" the Senior Chief asked Ben.

Ben placed the cell phone in Ericksen's hand.

"Thanks, Commander." He turned back to the volcanic Air Boss. "Would you like to try for four, Sir?"

Thorensen's face was as red as the telephone on his console. He slowly seated himself and turned to the officer seated next to him. "Get three 60's ready for these guys."

"Thanks," Ben said in the most sincere tone he could muster.

"Yeah. Sure. Tell me, does he always speak for you?" he asked, motioning at Ericksen.

"Only when I'm pissed off. Don't worry, I'll get your birds back to you in one piece."

Thorensen shook his head as he pouted. He turned back around in his chair and returned his gaze to the flight deck.

I guess that's my cue.

CHAPTER TWENTY-THREE
WEDNESDAY, APRIL 14TH

Project Blue Flame Energy Laboratory
Senkaku, Japan
8:05 AM
11:05 PM, GMT

Marcia used her hand to shield her eyes from the blowing dust and sand as the laboratory's helicopter touched down a few yards away. As the sound of the rotors started to fade, so did most of the dust from the pad. However, the wind didn't die much.

She looked up to see a thick layer of fast-moving gray clouds. While the wind on the ground seemed to gust on occasion, the clouds well above her moved with all due haste toward the East. The sound of the two-person ground crew starting the fuel truck pulled her attention back down to earth. The helicopter required refueling for a return trip to the mainland.

Tristan sat on her left in the driver's seat of her Mule All-Terrain Vehicle. The little cars made getting around the small island easier. Since arriving, her son had so fallen in love with driving these small autos; she had hardly seen him for the last two days.

That was just as well. Since Deitrich and Yashita were off the island, most of the tasks associated with shutting down the facility had fallen to Doctor Loewen and her. With the first group of scientists leaving the island within the hour, everything was moving according to plan, except one. Loewen still struggled to find a rapid and safe reactor shutdown protocol.

Deitrich had at least called to check on the progress of things while he visited his ailing wife. Yashita, whatever hell he was raising, did so without so much as an e-mail.

"Go ahead, honey. Let's get over there," she instructed her son when she saw the two senior scientists and the technician climb out of the aircraft.

Tristan gunned the engine and burned a little rubber as he pulled away. Marcia smiled to herself. *It's been a while since I've seen him this happy. Maybe coming here was a good thing, after all.*

"Well, well. I see you've got yourself a chauffeur. Nice work, Doctor. I've been out here four years and haven't done nearly as well," Deitrich greeted them with a smile.

"Yes, it's hard to get good help way out here, but I seem to have persevered," she replied. They shook hands.

Tristan only grinned back.

"Climb in," she offered.

Yashita walked past the three of them without speaking. He continued until he got to another parked Mule near the hangar. He tossed a small bag into the seat next to him and drove off toward the lab complex.

"He was like that on the flight out, too. Almost two hours in the air and he only said two words, 'Good day'."

Marcia only smiled.

"What? You know something?" Deitrich asked as he stroked his beard.

"Climb in, I'll tell you about it on the way to the lab."

"Hey, Doc, you'll need to check out the gear I brought back when you get a chance," Tony Swinson called as he climbed into yet another ATV.

Deitrich nodded as he placed his two bags in the rear seat of the Mule and leaped in with a single bound. As soon as he was in place, Tristan put the idling ATV in gear and popped the accelerator again.

"Dear, you're going to toss Doctor Deitrich out of the back."

Tristan turned up his lip.

"Oh, no. Let him have fun. These little buggies are great. Huh, Tris?"

"Yeah. Great," her son replied in a put–upon tone.

"So what's up with Yashita?"

"Seems our colleague bullied his way into the Industry and Trade Minister's Office, gave him a piece of his mind about me 'just taking over' *his* lab."

"Whoa."

"Well, you know the Japanese. Protocol is everything. He got a formal dressing down from both the Minister and his boss. They told him to get his rear in gear and back out here!"

"Well, it's about time," Deitrich replied.

"I think it's a little late, Bob. I've been putting up

with him for too long. I wish they'd had the 'Come To Jesus' meeting years ago."

The small air complex was about two miles down a thin, winding dirt road from the lab and residence. It loomed ahead in the distance. The lab sat on the side of the island's only mountain, Mount Urabu. The two–story green– and sand–colored building blended into the lush jungle surrounding it like a beautiful painting. The one, and only, cooling tower blended in as well.

Loaded down as it was with three people, the Mule took the hill just fine, but at a slower pace than the ride down. On the way to meet the helicopter, Tristan had had his mother holding on with white–knuckle grips.

As they got higher in elevation, Marcia felt the wind rise. Her hair blew into her eyes several times. By the time they went through the gate surrounding the complex and the Logistics Area, she was using her hands to shield her face again.

"What's up with the weather?" Deitrich asked.

"There's a tropical storm forming about a hundred miles south of here."

"That going to slow us down?"

"Not if I can help it."

Tristan parked the Mule under a covered parking area next to ten more ATVs of varying shapes and sizes.

The Logistics Area filled the space in the neck of the I–shaped structure on the bottom floor. Administrative offices occupied the space above the Logistics Area. The larger side, or base, of the "I" held the lab. The fusion reactor, which they had worked so hard to perfect, was underground. They had buried it in the mountainside to hide it from the naked eye or overhead intelligence satellites. When the facility was used for safety testing, several floors of laboratory space occupied the area that now held the generator. U.S. Navy Engineers spent months gutting it for its new purpose.

The top, or other side of the building, was the residential area. The facility could house up to forty persons at one time. Currently, nineteen scientists were in residence at Blue Flame.

"Thanks for the ride," Deitrich said as he slapped Tristan on his back.

"Yeah, whatever," Tristan replied under his breath.

His comment and attitude drew an icy glance from his mother.

"You're welcome, Sir," her son said after receiving the non-verbal reprimand.

"Come on up when you get settled, Bob. We've still got a lot to do," she instructed.

"I'll be right there."

Marcia Hobson's Office
Project Blue Flame Energy Laboratory
9:10 AM

Marcia Hobson's office had a Government-issue feel to it. The metal desk, chairs, half-filled bookcase, and credenza, all gray, sat on thin, tightly-woven carpet. Hobson's chair backed up to a large plate-glass window. Bob looked out to see the tops of several palm trees rocking back and forth. Even with the onset of puffy, rain-laden clouds, the window gave the room ample light.

Marcia's guests faced the window, while she looked

across the desk at them. Sounds seemed to echo in the stark, roomy space as if in a small cave. She shifted her weight trying to get comfortable in the lightly–cushioned chair.

"The Navy should be here in the next few hours with helicopters to fly the remaining team members and some equipment off of the island," Marcia explained. "By the end of the day, all but a skeleton crew will be back in Japan."

"What about the reactor?" Deitrich asked. "That's not enough time to dismantle it."

"I know. I mentioned that to Washington. We still haven't found a way to rapidly shut it down. The five–day process is already running, though."

"I don't understand. If the Navy is coming to get us, who will mind the reactor?" Deitrich asked.

"You mean to destroy it," Yashita blurted out.

"I don't know that and neither do you. But just in case, make very sure that all of your notes are up to date so that we can rebuild it if we have to."

"Marcia, what's the buzz all about? Why all the cloak–and–dagger stuff? Is the military taking over our project?"

"No. They are not. I wish I could explain it all, Bob. But I'm under orders."

Deitrich shook his head. "I'm inclined to agree with Doctor Yashita, here. This is all very irregular."

Yashita turned and looked at his colleague. Astonishment filled his eyes so much that his mouth almost dropped open.

For that matter, so did Marcia's. *Now, do I have to deal with both of them?*

"I have instructions for both of you," she began. "Doctor Yashita, you will see to the computers. I want triple back–ups done. Make sure you account for all magnetic media per the Department of Defense Security Standards implemented two months ago. The LAN is in EMCON, so make your backups to the array. We'll hand–carry the disks with us when we leave."

"I suppose the computers will be destroyed, too."

She only answered him with a raised eyebrow.

Yashita started playing with his pen again.

"Doctor Deitrich. You will see to the reactor. Again, ensure your notes on modifications to the original design are up to date. You will also ensure that the implemented security guidelines are followed."

"I will protest this to my government," Yashita interjected.

"Doctor, you can protest to God in heaven above after we are off of this rock. But until then, do what I tell you. Both of you." Marcia was on her feet now, hands resting on hips.

The two men exchanged glances. After a long moment, they also stood and filed out of her office. Yashita slammed the door behind him.

The phone on her desk rang just as she was about to slam her fist down. "What?" she answered in a huff.

"Things not going well?" It was Langdon.

She took a deep breath. She knew that she had a reputation for being unflappable. Her career had blossomed by reinforcing that myth. "No, Sir. Things are going about as well as I expected."

"Good. This is a clear line, so I'll have to be brief and cryptic."

"I understand."

"I just got a call, your taxi is on its way."

"I understand, Sir."

"Good luck, Marcia. We're counting on you."

"Sir?"

"Yes?"

"About the, the new heater, if you get my drift. Can you tell me what—"

"Marcia. We're all playing this by ear. I promise. You'll know when I know."

"Do they know about the project?" she asked.

"No. And I'd like to keep it that way. Make sure your staff knows that."

"I think I understand, Sir. Bye."

"Goodbye."

She hung up the telephone and took a seat.

CHAPTER TWENTY–FOUR
WEDNESDAY, APRIL 14TH

Project Blue Flame Energy Laboratory
Reactor Control Room
Senkaku, Japan
10:15 AM
1:15 AM, GMT

"Okay, Doctor. So what's the real story?"
Swinson seemed to have appointed himself spokesman
for the seven scientists, the entire Reactor Control
Team, who stood or sat around the room. They were
there at Deitrich's request. Doctor Stanley Loewen
listened as the group quizzed their administrator.

"I've told you all that I know, Tony."

Besides himself and Deitrich, Dolores Shinozaki,
Tony Swinson, Professor Murray Rawlins, and Isako
Mutsuhiko, the medical technician, sat or stood in
attendance.

"Hey, where is Yashita?" Swinson asked.

"I told him we were meeting. He just looked at me
like I was speaking Greek," Rawlins replied.

"That guy is such a prick," Swinson interjected.

"So what's this all about, Bob?" Loewen asked.

"All Doctor Hobson will say is that the Secretary of Energy ordered her to shut down the project," Bob Deitrich said.

"Man, this is bull," Rawlins said. "We just got this son–of–a–bitch working right and they want us to turn it off?"

"So, how are we supposed to get back? I hear the helicopter is only going to make two more trips," Dolores asked.

"Well, that's the strange part," Deitrich replied. "The Navy's coming to fly us out."

Most of the scientists gasped, shook their heads, or simply cursed the news. "Are you kiddin' me?" one of them asked.

"I am not going to hand this over to DoD," Swinson said. "Anybody remember the Manhattan Project? That's how we got the A–bomb."

"You got that right. Who's going to run this thing when we leave? All those goons in the Navy know how to do is run a fission plant," Rawlins added. "Shit, that's easy."

"And if they scram this thing, they're going to get a big surprise," Dolores laughed.

Several of the scientists joined her delight at the prospect.

"Seriously, Doc," Swinson started. "Who's gonna run this thing?"

"Doctor Hobson wouldn't say." Deitrich shrugged.

"When are they coming?" Dolores asked.

"She said they'd be here in a few hours."

"No problem, then," Dolores said. "We'll just shut it down."

"What are you talking about?" Swinson snapped back. "It takes five days to shut down the reactor. Everybody knows that."

"Not any more. Stanley here figured out how to do it in just over six hours," she replied as she patted her boyfriend on his back. Dolores beamed as Stanley looked up to find the group both smiling and frowning at him.

"Stan? Is this true?" Deitrich asked.

"Yeah. I rewrote the simulation program. I think we can do it in about six—"

"You think?" Swinson cut him off. "What if you're wrong? It's a simulation, right?"

"He built the reactor! He knows what he's doing," Dolores shot back.

"Hey, look. Nobody really knows what will happen if we do something wrong. Didn't you once theorize that it could cause a black hole?"

"Yeah, but that was before—"

"Tony, Doctor Loewen knows this system better than anyone. He built most of it. If he says there's no chance of a black hole, then there's no chance." Deitrich's tone, like Swinson's, was razor sharp. "Besides, that's not the real issue here."

Tony Swinson deflated as Deitrich turned back toward him. "Stan, ordinarily I'd say, good work. But consider this: If the reactor is shut down, we lose a good reason for them letting us stay."

"I don't understand," he replied. "They're coming anyway."

"He's right, Doctor," Swinson added. "There's no way they're going to let some Navy guys stay here and run this thing. They'd blow it up in half an hour or less."

"If we can delay them long enough, maybe we can get word to somebody to stop this," Dolores added.

Loewen sighed. "So you want me to lie?"

"No, Doc," Swinson replied. "We just don't want you to tell them you've figured it out."

Stanley Loewen turned his gaze toward Deitrich. His friend, colleague, and supervisor showed no expression. He turned to Dolores who placed her hand on his shoulder.

"Stan, if the military gets this, they could turn it into a very terrible weapon."

"Like what? We've already got fusion bombs. I think you're being a little paranoid."

"Yeah, maybe," Swinson added. "But how do you feel about them just coming in and taking credit for all your work?"

After a long while, Loewen nodded.

CHAPTER TWENTY–FIVE
WEDNESDAY, APRIL 14TH

Aboard *Sea Horse Two One*
3,000 Feet Above Sea Level
1135 Hours
0235 Hours, GMT

Spending the night on the carrier had not been part of their plans. However, Ben's arrival and considerable influence had caught Thorensen and the carrier off guard. It took some doing to get three helos ready for the mission. Just over a day later, they were finally underway. Thinking about the ass chewing somebody was getting over this mess proved a less–than–adequate diversion. *I feel like shit.*

"Sir, there it is," Lieutenant Commander Paul Enright announced to Ben over the intercom system. The HH–60 pilot pointed out the left side of the front window.

Just in time. I was about to start looking for a barf bag.

Almost since taking off from *Teddy Roosevelt*, the

aircraft had danced all over the sky from building winds. They had been in and out of rain for most of the three–hour flight. In an effort to keep from losing his lunch, Ben had taken a seat in the flight deck doorway. Looking out seemed to help more than anything else. It also helped him to anticipate the bigger bumps. Two motion–sickness pills had only made him sleepy.

Enright flew the lead aircraft. Two more of the helicopters flew on each flank. The SEAL Team Leader, Lieutenant Junior Grade Dawes, and Senior Chief Ericksen rode with him. Young and very in–shape, Mister Dawes had a haggard, acne–scarred face. The dark–haired officer looked stern, serious, and not at all happy about being on this mission.

The other two birds carried three SEALs plus their three–person crews. In all, Ben was now responsible for fourteen people in addition to those on the island.

Enright was the helo squadron's Executive Officer. The Air Boss had sent him along as insurance on Ben's promise to get the birds and their people back in one piece.

"Let's give 'em a call," Ben suggested.

The pilot nodded and adjusted the frequency on his radio. "This is *Sea Horse Two One* to Blue Flame Lab. Do you read, over?" He released the transmit key and static filled the air.

"This is Blue Flame Lab, *Sea Horse*. Welcome to the East China Sea. We've been waiting on you," a woman's voice said over the radio.

"There're chicks on this island?" the copilot asked from the right seat. This kid was a junior grade lieutenant.

Ben only grinned at his youth.

"Request landing instructions, Blue Lab," Enright called after shaking his head at his copilot's comment.

"Helo pad is on the south tip of the island. Our Administrator is standing by for your arrival."

"Roger. We'll see you on the ground in about ten. *Sea Horse* flight out."

Ben went back to the main cabin area. "We're here," he said to Ericksen. The two of them stood and looked out as they approached the speck of dirt in the sea of blue.

Ben surveyed the island as they flew over. It wasn't very big, probably no more than about ten square miles. Now, it was little wonder that finding a chart for it had been a task all unto itself.

He spotted what he guessed to be the main laboratory complex and a small dirt road leading down to the air facility. Except for the buildings and a nuclear cooling tower, the island looked like one big jungle. Lush, dense vegetation seemed to run almost up to the shoreline. Dark–colored rocky outcroppings and high dunes guarded the beach, what there was of it.

LCDR Enright communicated landing instructions to the other two helicopters and led the way down. The closer they got to the ground, the more the wind seemed to bump the aircraft around. Ben had to grab a handhold when his balance finally gave way to the pitching deck.

"Wow," Enright said.

"What?" Ben asked as looked up.

"A tarmac. That's great!"

"Yeah. So?"

"Cuts down on crap flying into the engines."

Ben nodded.

The air facility also featured a single hangar. Several

large pallets and groups of steel drums guarded the area around it.

As they landed, Ben spotted some of the inhabitants approaching in small ATVs. They seemed to emerge from the greenery with a trail of dust and gray smoke.

Their air crewman, a young dark–haired enlisted man, pulled open the sliding door as soon as the flight crew took power from the rotors. Blustery air, laced with the smell of the sea, filled the cabin and Ben's nostrils. *Thank God.* He stepped down out of the helicopter.

The air crewman moved around the bird placing chocks against the wheels as Ben and the others stretched. A few yards away, the second of the helicopters touched down. The aircraft's rotor–wash blew dust and sand until her pilot started his engine shutdown.

"Sir," Senior Chief Ericksen said as he tapped Ben on his shoulder. He pointed at an approaching convoy of large four–wheeled go–carts.

"Let's go," Ben said to Ericksen and Dawes. All three crouched to avoid the still spinning helicopter rotors as they moved out to meet the approaching caravan.

The lead ATV carried four people. Even at fifty or so yards, he could tell the rider in the front–passenger seat was Black, as was the person driving. As they got closer, he could tell the passenger was female. At ten yards, just before they stopped, either his eyes lied to him or he was going into some sort of Dramamine–induced flashback.

"I can't believe it," he said more to himself than anyone else.

"What?" asked Ericksen.

The woman on the passenger–side of the ATV hopped out as it stopped in front of them. Her mouth dropped open and her eyes grew wide to match as she drew closer to Ben.

"Oh, my God. Of all the sailors in the flippin' Navy, I can't believe they sent *you*," she said. Her hands went to her hips as she scowled.

"You're Doctor Marcia Hobson? What happened? Did you finally find some guy with a lot of money to sucker into marrying you?"

With that, the person at the steering wheel of the ATV hopped out. "It's on now," the man, actually more like a boy, shouted. He rushed toward Ben with his fist up.

Ben shoved the kid away.

"Tristan!" Marcia shouted. "Tristan, stop it!"

When he took another swing, Ben grabbed the kid's arm and twisted it behind his back. He used it as leverage as he pushed the young man to the tarmac.

"Let him go, Ben. He's my son."

Ben's eyes grew wide with surprise. Immediately, he released the boy and stepped away.

Tristan got up slowly, grabbing at his shoulder. Marcia went over to him and checked him out. "Go wait in the ATV," she instructed.

The kid shot Ben a hate-filled glance.

"Go," she ordered.

He moved away, slowly.

"Sorry. I didn't know," Ben replied.

She folded her arms. "Yeah, I'm sorry, too."

The wind blew her hair around her face, but he could still see what had first attracted him to her more than twenty years before. "You look well," he eventually uttered.

"You, too."

Ben smiled. "Let's try this again. Hello, Marci." He put out his arms and they hugged.

"Hi, Benji."

"Benji?" Senior Chief Ericksen asked in a sarcasm–laced voice.

His words had the effect of a bucket of cold water. Ben cleared his throat as they gently pulled themselves apart. The other two people already in the ATV climbed out and started walking over.

"Senior Chief, this is Doctor Marcia Hobson. She's in charge here. We're old friends," Ben introduced.

"Nice to meet you, Ma'am," Ericksen said. They shook hands warmly.

"This is Lieutenant Junior Grade Dawes. He's the SEAL team leader."

They exchanged greetings as the last of the helicopters landed. When the noise and wind started to die, she introduced the members of her team.

"This is Doctor Deitrich and Doctor Yashita. They're the co–administrators of the lab."

The five men shook hands.

"What's your status, Marcia? We'd like to be fueled up and out of here in an hour or so. There's a storm building down south."

"It's already been designated Tropical Storm Shandra and its headed this way," she replied. "We're having some technical problems and aren't ready yet."

Ben looked up at the darkening sky. It looked really ugly to the south. "We need to report in," he eventually said to Ericksen.

Ericksen nodded in agreement.

"What kind of technical problems?" Ben asked.

"It has to do with our computer disk array. Probably nothing you'd understand," Yashita quipped.

"Doctor, tell me that you're not one of those Intelligencia guys who has nothing but disdain in his heart for the military."

He didn't answer.

"Oh, a Berkeley grad, eh?"

Marcia smiled, but only for a second. "Same old Ben."

"Well, Doc. As it happens today is your lucky day. Commander McGuire here, in his civilian life, is one of them high–dollar computer consultants," Ericksen interjected.

"Civilian life?" Marcia asked.

"I'm a Reservist now."

Her eyebrow went up. "They sent me a Reservist?"

"No," Ben replied. "They sent you two."

She exchanged nervous glances with Deitrich and Yashita.

"Commander McGuire, Sir?" Enright called as he approached.

"Yes?"

"You got a minute?"

Ben signaled him to come on over with a wave of his arm.

"This is Lieutenant Commander Enright. He's in charge of the aircraft," Ben introduced the officer as he arrived. Enright shook hands in a very brief manner with the three civilians.

"Sir, the winds are too high for us to take off. I think we're here until this thing blows by."

"Understood. Get these aircraft tied down and under cover as best you can. Set an integrity watch. We're headed up to the lab to solve some problems so that we can get out of here as soon as the weather breaks."

"Roger that." Enright turned and ran back toward his helicopter.

"Can you excuse me a second?" Ben said to Marcia and her colleagues.

"Sure," she replied as he pulled Ericksen away.

"Senior Chief. You and Mister Dawes here get the SEALs unloaded. We'll be going with Doctor Hobson and her team to help them get packed."

"Aye aye, Sir."

"So, Commander. Does Mrs. McGuire know you've got a chick in every obscure port in the world?" Ericksen asked. A wide, mischievous grin stretched across his face.

"She's an old friend, Senior Chief." Ben ensured that succinctness filled his voice.

"How old?"

"We dated in college."

The two men walked toward the ATVs as the SEALs assembled into ranks.

"*You* dated her?"

"What's the matter? Don't you think I can attract a beautiful woman? What about my wife?"

"Sir, I gotta be honest. A bunch of us thought that was just a fluke."

Ben gave Ericksen the finger.

"So, do you think she'd like me?"

"You? What's to like?" Ben laughed.

"I'm a nice guy. Kids and small animals love me."

Ben dug for words. Marcia was high–maintenance way back then. He didn't know if she had changed in the intervening years. One way or the other, he didn't want to get in the middle of anything. "Senior,

I haven't seen this woman in almost twenty years. All I can tell you is that she's a woman, a smart woman, with a lot of attitude. But you already knew that." He patted Ericksen on his shoulder. "That, and good luck."

"So you're not gonna help me? What kind of shipmate are ya?" he smiled.

"A smart one." Ben grinned and walked off toward Marcia and her son.

"So you're in charge of these guys?" Marcia asked as he arrived. Surprise and astonishment filled her voice and washed over her face.

"Yeah. Scary, huh?"

She smiled and shook her head again. Deitrich and Yashita only scowled back coolly.

CHAPTER TWENTY–SIX
WEDNESDAY, APRIL 14TH

Senkaku Island
Territory of Japan
12:35 PM
3:35 AM, GMT

With a sky full of thick, blowing clouds, darkness came on quickly. The sky grew so dark that Ben felt evening twilight was only moments away. The wind had picked up, too. He had to occasionally cover his face and eyes for protection from windborne twigs and leaves.

Towering palms sheltered the road. Ben reveled at the job someone had done in cutting through the heavy jungle growth. He looked up once or twice, as best he could with the whipping wind, to see a sliver of sky.

Ben rode with Marcia in the lead ATV. Her son, still favoring his shoulder, drove. Senior Chief Ericksen hiked with LTJG Dawes, the other three SEALs, and several aircrew members behind the caravan of three vehicles up the side of Mt. Urabu to the Lab Complex.

"So, how did you come to be in the middle of the East China Sea?" Ben asked.

"Well, this project came up and required me to do some travel. After the Secretary decided to shut the lab down, he sent me out here to see to it."

"Shut it down? Why are you shutting it down?"

Marcia turned in her seat to face him and an old, but familiar feeling came to him.

"I get it," he said. "If I don't know, I don't have a need to know."

"That's about the size of it," she replied.

"What kind of lab is this?" he asked as the large building and its fence loomed in the distance.

She gave him that look again.

Ben sighed. *This is getting frustrating.*

"Okay. What's the story with Deitrich and Yashita? They don't seem the happiest campers in Geek City."

"They've been here for…" she stopped herself. "They've been here for a while. They've put a lot of energy and time into this place and—"

"And they don't have a need to know, either," he finished the story for her.

She nodded.

"That puts you in a difficult spot. It's tough when a leader can't tell her folks what's going on."

She turned around again. Surprise, this time of a different nature, filled her eyes.

"I'm an information technology professional now. We know things," he said as he put his index finger to his temple.

She laughed. "Same old Ben."

"No, not really," he replied.

"So are you still married to that debutante I met during June Week?" Marcia asked.

His mind instantly reflected back to the awkward encounter, now more than twenty years in the past. He'd just asked his first wife, Katelyn, to marry him. Marcia happened along only seconds after Katelyn accepted.

"No. We divorced about two years ago."

She raised her eyebrow. "Wow. I thought you two were the very definition of what a couple was supposed to be."

"Yeah," he added. "So did I." All of his days with Katelyn O'Brien McGuire flashed through his head in just a few moments: the beginning, middle, and end.

"So you married again?" she asked.

"Yeah. About six months ago. Her name's Claire."

She nodded.

"And look at you. A big time scientist with the Energy Department."

"Well, Deitrich and Yashita would be the first to tell you that I'm no longer a scientist. But thanks for the compliment."

"You must be pretty high up in the food chain."

"I've done okay."

"Hobson. When did you get married?"

"Do you remember Derrick Hobson? He was in the class behind yours."

"Yeah. Big guy, played lacrosse. Is that who you married? Where is he now?"

"He died at Kafji during the Gulf War," she replied as she both looked at and touched the back of her son's neck.

Her words took away his breath.

We didn't lose many during that one. However, her words brought to mind the fact that losing one was, for some people, one too many. "He was a pretty good guy as I remember. Hell of a midshipman. I'm sorry for your loss," Ben replied.

The last few yards of their journey were completed in silence.

"We need to have a briefing as soon as possible," Ben said as they came to a stop.

"We've got some work going on. How about in a couple of hours in our lounge?" she asked.

"Sounds good."

National Military Command Center
Washington, D.C.
0001 Hours
0401 Hours, GMT

Captain Joe Rogers recollected the first time he had seen this room. He remembered thinking that one day something really big would happen and he'd be the guy monitoring, and possibly controlling, it all.

Now in the last two months of a two–year tour, he realized that it had been a year and a half of dull and banal administrivia with an occasional sprinkling of marginal excitement. However, he knew better than to ask for excitement. His career as a nuclear submariner had taught him better than to put a curse on himself as he typically got what he asked for.

The nineteen–year Naval officer sat back in his chair as he monitored both the movements of the people on his watch team as well as the several large screen displays arrayed around him. He tried to fight back a yawn, but it eventually won out.

"Keepin' you up, Sir?" Sergeant Martha Kelly asked with a smirk. Her West Texas drawl always made him smile. The first few months they worked together, he used to make her talk just to hear the accent.

"Kelly, it is wholly inappropriate for enlisted personnel to harass officers. Didn't they cover that in boot camp?"

"Well, Cap'n, like you always say, we're the Air Force. We don't really have a boot camp. We're just a bunch of corporate geeks in baby–blue uniforms."

"I said that?"

"Yes, Sir. On several occasions."

Kelly's tour was almost up, too. The senior Air Force non–com was headed back to some Air Force Base down in Texas. *Real* Bostonians like himself didn't often get to interact with many *real* Texans. Rogers knew he'd miss their banter.

"Yeah, I guess it does sound too wise for one of you guys to come up with."

"Shit, Sir. You got more pins than an Arkansas porcupine."

"Kelly, where do you come up with this stuff?"

"Daddy, mostly. 'Course, Ma's got a mouth on her, too."

"I'd love to meet 'em someday."

"Wouldn't do you no good, Sir. They'd confuse ya' and I'd get left in the middle tryin' to interpret."

Rogers grinned at the prospect of a Sunday sit–down dinner with the Kellys of Odessa, Texas. "Maybe so, but I gotta believe it'd be worth writing home about."

The red phone on his console rang. "NMCC Watch Officer, Captain Rogers," he answered.

"Sir, this is the NSA Watch. We're going to pump

some information over to your central display that's originated with National assets. Just a heads up."

"Thanks." Rogers put the phone back down.

"What's up?"

"Central screen's getting an update." His eyes were already on the geographic display of China's coastline.

"Tell you what. You get me a ride on that submarine you're going to and I'll see what I can do about gittin' you an audience with my Ma and Pa."

"It's a..." The update on the screen took over his entire brain. The ability to multi–task enough to carry on a side conversation left his brain like a fired torpedo leaves its tube.

"Holy shit," Kelly gasped.

"Yes, Ma'am." Rogers was already calling the Chairman of the Joint Chiefs.

McGuire Residence
Plano, Texas
12:32 AM
5:32 AM, GMT

Quiet, except for the sound of the air conditioner, filled the house. Claire couldn't hear any cars going by on the distant thoroughfare. *Everybody in the world is asleep, except for me, that is*.

She knew that wasn't so, but she still lay awake, tossing from one side to the other. Nearly an hour and a half had passed since she had awakened. The blue lights on her alarm clock seemed to illuminate the whole room. The covers on her bed were first too warm, so she kicked them off. Then the air became too cold, and she pulled them back up again.

Now even counting sheep failed. She got up to brew some herbal tea.

The microwave beeped, telling her that the water in the cup had come to a boil. After pulling it from the oven, she put a bag in and took a seat at the table. *I wonder what's on TV.*

She used the remote to switch on the set.

"This is *Headline News*. Again our breaking story: An unofficial source at the Pentagon has reported that the Chinese military has massed an invasion–sized force in the port of Shanghai. Chinese officials have declined to comment on the reason for the build–up. U.S. Navy units in the area have been placed on full alert and are moving to take up defensive positions around the Korean peninsula and Japan."

Claire jumped at the sound of her cup shattering on the stone tiles of the kitchen floor. "Oh, God."

Project Blue Flame
Residential Lounge
Senkaku Island, Japan
2:45 PM
5:45 PM, GMT

Ben's intro and briefing of the laboratory personnel had been short. His message had been simple: We're here to help. Pack what you can. As soon as the storm's over, we're out of here. The scientists and military personnel filed out of the room.

He and Enright were among the first to leave. They headed back down to the airfield to check on the helicopters. All three aircraft would have to remain outside, exposed to the elements during the coming storm. The hangar was too small to accommodate even one of them.

Ericksen stood on the other side of the room by the coffee makers. He watched as Doctor Hobson sat down on the couch and turned to stare out of the window. Ericksen, not usually the shy type, suddenly found himself without words or nerve. He cleared his throat to work up his courage.

On hearing the noise, she turned toward him. And smiled. *Man, she's cute. Well, here goes nothing.*

"So, can I get you a cup?" he asked from across the room.

"You know, that would be great. Thanks."

"Leaded or unleaded?" he asked as he picked up a cup.

She laughed. "Leaded."

"What's so funny?" He poured coffee from the brown–lipped decanter.

"My husband used to refer to it that way, too. I just haven't heard that in a while."

He walked over and handed her the Styrofoam cup of black liquid.

"Thank you." She smiled as she looked up.

"May I?" he asked as he gestured toward the empty end of the couch.

"Please."

Touchdown! He tried to suppress a toothy grin at the reception. "Commander McGuire says you're some kind of high–brow egghead."

She smiled again. "High–brow egghead. It's a little difficult for me to imagine Ben putting it quite that way. Of course, he *has* been in Texas for a while."

"Okay, Doc. You got me. I think he said high–energy nuclear scientist. In Amarillo, that translates to high–brow egg head," Ericksen joked back. "So, you're a brain, eh?"

"No, not really." Her voice fell off as she lowered her gaze. She tried to slink away from his compliment. After a while, her eyes came up to meet his.

Ericksen raised his brows.

"Okay, I'm a brain," she finally relented.

They both laughed.

"A SEAL, huh?"

"Yes, Ma'am."

"And a Reservist?"

"Yeah, I left active duty a little over a year ago."

"Got tired of it?"

"No, no. It's a great life."

"So?"

"My wife—"

"You're married," she interrupted. Her voice had a 'ah hah' quality to it.

"I was. She died six months ago." The memory of her last days weighed on him so much that he momentarily had trouble breathing. He forced himself to take a deep breath.

"I'm sorry. How?"

"Cervical cancer. She got it a few years ago and the doctors thought they had it beat. But it came back. I got out to spend time with her."

She sighed. "I know how you feel."

"Yeah, I heard. I was there, ya' know?"

"Really?"

"Yup. We were on the ground outside of Baghdad. I'd a given the hair off my ass for a crack at that som–bitch Saddam."

"I'll drink to that," she raised her coffee cup.

Ericksen raised his, too.

"So, what's Amarillo like?"

"Amarillo. It's nice, if you like long roads, starry nights, and clear, clean air."

"Out in the sticks, huh?" she asked with a smile.

"Now, I wouldn't exactly call Amarillo the sticks. But you can travel a good while before you find an opera or Broadway show," he grinned.

"A lot of country music I suppose?" she grinned as she asked the question.

"So you're a C&W fan, huh?

"Yes. Aren't you? I guess you must be a real *aficionado*, being from Texas?"

"Why, sure. Hell, everybody up there is a closet C&W *performer*. Even me."

"Really?" she asked. She took a sip from her cup.

"Oh, yes, Ma'am. As a matter of fact, I've written a few hit country songs in my free time."

"Really?" She sat erect. "You've written music professionally? What are some of the songs? Have I heard of any of them?"

"Well, let's see." Ericksen crossed his arms for effect. "There's 'I Keep Forgettin' I Forgot About You'."

She shook her head.

"How about 'I Don't Know Whether To Kill Myself Or Go Bowling'?"

She frowned. "Nope."

"Well, one of my all-time favorites is 'How Can I Miss You If You Won't Go Away'?"

She looked at him with doubt-filled eyes.

"And then there's 'Get Your Tongue Outta My Mouth 'Cause I'm Kissing You Goodbye'."

"You're yanking my chain. Aren't you?"

"And of course, there's the perennial favorite 'I Ain't

Gone To Bed With No Ugly Women, But I Sure Woke Up With A Few'."

"Okay, okay. I get the picture. You don't know jack about country music," she laughed.

"Hell, no. Just 'cause I got the accent, don't mean I'm tuning in to *Hee Haw*. I'm a Wynton Marsalis man."

"Really?"

"And, I play a mean tenor sax, if I do say so myself."

She smiled.

CHAPTER TWENTY–SEVEN
WEDNESDAY, APRIL 14TH

White House Briefing Room
Washington, D.C.
7:10 AM
11:10 AM, GMT

"**M**ister President, we only have this one piece of imagery to go by, but it appears that the Chinese Military is mobilizing a large portion of its Naval and Marine Forces," the thin dark–haired intelligence analyst explained. Her tone was respectful, no longer so tense. Energy Secretary Langdon knew her name now, Naomi Richardson. Her voice had a new air of confidence.

He looked on in silence with the other members of the National Security Council. The emergency session was in its tenth tense moment. State sat at attention in her chair while Defense jotted down notes. The whole gang was there, except the photographer.

"Tropical Storm Shandra is preventing the collection

of any more data. Infrared, radar, visual: they're all gonna have to wait until the storm moves out."

"Mister President," Defense Secretary Pete Wilson piped up. "We have detached USS *Pasadena* from the Ronin Blitz Exercise to try to get some intel. However, it will be several hours before she's in position," Richardson added.

"*Pasadena*. What makes her so special?" the Secretary of State's aide asked.

"She's a submarine."

"Oh."

"I have a question," the Vice President started. "Anyone got any idea why the Chinese would be doing this?"

Langdon exchanged a brief glance with the President. His boss then looked quickly away. *Still not giving up any secrets on this one.*

"Sir, there are no regularly scheduled exercises that we know of," Defense replied. "Sure, this could be a drill, but as you can see in this enhancement..." He used a remote control to change the view back a few slides. "Those are actual troops getting on actual ships. That costs a lot of money. Why do it if you're not really gonna use 'em?"

"CIA. Anything?" the Commander in Chief asked.

"No, Sir. Nothing. We haven't had any credible human intelligence resources there in years."

"Madam Secretary?" the President said to the Secretary of State.

"Mister President, they haven't had a lot to say to us lately. I can't even get their ambassador to meet me for lunch. I think the combination of the Cox Report and the bombing of their embassy did more damage to our relationship than we thought."

He reclined in his chair. He put up his hands in

frustration, "Let's keep watching it. Get the *Pasadena* down there as soon as we can."

"Yes, Sir," the Secretary of Defense and Chief of Naval Operations replied together.

"Now, what about our evacuation of that island?"

"Mister President, with all due respect, Sir, that's a little low on the agenda. We have a couple of other items to discuss first—" the National Security Advisor began.

"I set the agenda, Bill," the President interjected.

"Yes, Sir." NSA nodded at the CNO.

"We have a team on the island."

The President leaned forward. "And?"

"That's all we know, Sir."

The President sighed. He turned to Langdon and their eyes met for a long moment. "Ladies and gentlemen, though I cannot at this time tell you why, I believe the target of the Chinese operation might be the lab on Senkaku Island."

Langdon watched as the President's words caused the same effect as setting off a bomb in the room. After the expressions of astonishment started to settle in, they all stared at him, Langdon. He was on the inside now. Everyone in that room now knew that the President held *him* in his confidence and not them. *I guess I've got a seat at the big table now.*

"So, I need to know everything there is to know about the island. Let's reassemble here in six hours. By then, maybe we'll have a better idea of what the Chinese are up to." The President ended the meeting.

* * *

Doctor Stanley Loewen's Room
Project Blue Flame Laboratory
Senkaku Island, Japan
8:15 PM
11:15 AM, GMT

"Hell of a day, huh?" Loewen asked.

"I'll say."

He lay in her arms. The room, completely dark except for light leaking through the bottom of the door, shielded the worry on his face.

"Dolores, did you get a chance to talk to that Commander? He seems like a pretty good guy."

"Stanley, he's a military person. Those guys will make a weapon out of something we made. And I don't want that on my conscience."

"Dolores, I don't know—"

"Stanley, you know Bob. Don't you trust him?"

"Yeah, I guess."

"Then what?"

"Something about this feels wrong, Dolores."

She sat up in bed. "Change of subject?"

"Yeah, sure. What?"

"Tony Swinson's got a Japanese girlfriend."

"Swinson? He's married. How do you know?"

"I helped unload some of the supplies yesterday. One of the pilots happens to be a cousin of mine. She saw him the other day in Tokyo."

"Wow."

* * *

1st Information Warfare Brigade Headquarters
Beijing, China
2015 Hours
1215 Hours, GMT

"Sir, we're in!" Captain Qiu Maomao shouted from her workstation.

General Zhao, Colonel Pan, and Major Hong almost ran to her station.

Pan's strategy for gaining access into the Japanese Government networks had proven itself a worthy approach. After only an hour in the administrative and unclassified branches of the American Pacific Fleet's system, they found several dial–up numbers for Japanese Maritime Self Defense Force servers.

"You see, General. The Japanese are not observing the American EMCON environment," Pan explained.

They watched as the young Chinese PLA officer typed commands into her system. Her hands almost blurred against the keyboard.

"I have started downloading files from the island laboratory's main computer." Captain Qiu smiled openly as she conducted her work.

"How much data is there?" the General asked.

"Almost fifteen terabytes, Sir."

Zhao frowned. *That's a lot of information. We'll be detected before...*

"Damn," Qiu said, cutting off his thoughts.

"What?" Colonel Pan asked.

"I've lost my connection."

"Did they detect us?"

She didn't answer. Rather, she logged out of the Japanese server and logged in again. "Damn."

"What is it, Captain?" Colonel Pan asked.

"Sir, the server on the island has been disconnected from the network."

"What do you mean?" Zhao asked.

"Sir, it is as if someone cut the wire."

Zhao sighed. "Keep trying."

"General, if we do that, they will detect us."

"Do as I tell you, damn you!" Zhao shouted as he marched out of the room.

On his way through the door, the image of the Old Man sitting behind his desk flashed through his mind.

CHAPTER TWENTY–EIGHT
WEDNESDAY, APRIL 14TH

Marcia Hobson's Office
Project Blue Flame Lab
Senkaku Island, Japan
9:15 PM
12:15 PM, GMT

"Scramble on my mark. Ready, mark." With that, Ben turned the cipher key on the Secure Telephone Unit. At the same time, some two hundred miles away, Dave Ferguson did the same. Ben had brought the piece of communications gear so that the two officers could speak without the fear of electronic eavesdropping.

"How copy?" Dave asked from *Blue Ridge*.

"Loud and clear. How me?"

"Read you same. Send your report."

Ben exchanged brief glances with Marcia before speaking. "All aircraft and crews have landed safely. The storm worsened just as we touched down and will prevent a launch in the near–term. As it turns out, the civilians are experiencing some technical difficulties with their gear and were not ready, anyway. We will work to resolve their issues as soon as possible such that we can launch as soon as the weather clears."

"Roger. Copy all. Continue," Dave replied.

"One last item. It turns out that the head administrator and I are old friends. I anticipate no problems here. That ends my report."

"Can you elaborate on the technical problems?"

"Not at this time. I've been too busy trying to get the aircraft and crews secured for the storm. I'll get an update and contact you in six hours," Ben replied.

"Have you figured out what kind of lab it is yet?"

Ben was glad that Marcia couldn't hear the other side of the conversation. It probably would have put her more on edge than she already was.

"No. That's very closely–held information."

"Bunch of geeks, huh?"

"You said it, pal," Ben replied.

"You sound a little weirded out. Are you alone?"

"That's a negative," Ben replied.

"I understand. Are they being friendly at least?"

"Barely."

"Alarms going off yet?" Dave asked.

"No, not yet. But…"

"It doesn't feel right?" his friend of almost twenty years asked and in so doing read his mind.

"Exactly. We can discuss the intricacies of it later. I'm just glad I know some of the people out here," Ben replied.

"Very well. Good luck, buddy. Seventh Fleet out."

Ben hung up the phone and removed the cipher key. He placed it in his breast pocket for safekeeping.

"So that scrambles your transmission?" she asked.

"Yes. It's very effective."

"It's a good thing. All that probing he was doing could give somebody too much information." She smirked.

McGuire Residence
Plano, Texas
8:20 AM
1:20 PM, GMT

Claire opened one eye to see her alarm clock. "Oh, my God!" She should have been at work twenty minutes earlier. Her hand found the telephone on the stand next to the bed.

"Operations Department. Bill King," her boss answered.

"Bill. This is Claire. I've overslept. I guess I forgot to set my alarm. I…" her words came out in a staccato burst.

"Claire, relax. We heard the news. I figured you wouldn't be in today, anyway."

"Well, I would have called in," she replied.

"Don't worry about it. Have you heard from Ben?"

She paused. "No. I tried to send him an e–mail last night but I don't think I'll hear from him. He warned me that he might not be able to contact me if things got crazy."

"Well, things are certainly that," he sighed.

"I'll be there in a while. Just let me get a shower…"

"Claire, stay at home. Keep trying to e–mail him. You wouldn't really be here anyway."

"Are you sure?" she asked after a long moment.

"Hey, you're the hardest–working woman in the group. See you tomorrow?"

"Okay. Thanks, Boss."

"Not a problem. Good luck."

"Thanks. Bye."

"Bye."

She hung up the phone and lay back in the bed. After a long moment, she closed her eyes. "God, this bed feels good."

She rolled over and covered her head with the sheet and comforter. Claire took a deep breath and let herself go, trying to slip back into a slumber. She was almost there when the doorbell rang.

"Shit."

She got up, yanked her robe on and headed for the front door. The bell rang again before she could get there. "Okay, okay. I'm coming."

She got to the door and looked through the peephole. *Oh, great. Just what I need.* It was Katelyn McGuire. Claire closed her eyes and leaned against the door.

The bell rang again and Claire flashed open her eyes. She took a deep breath and opened the deadbolt.

"Katelyn. To what do I owe the pleasure?" she asked.

"I was watching the news when I got up this morning. I figured you were, too."

Ben's first wife was holding something behind her back.

"Yeah. It's been a long night. How did you know I was here?"

"I called your office. They told me you probably wouldn't be in today. I took a chance and drove by, spotted the car. And, well, here I am." She pulled a medium–sized bag from behind her. "I brought Starbucks and bagels."

Claire couldn't fight the smile forming on her face. Since their first meeting, this was the only time Katelyn had ever been the least bit nice. "Why are you doing this?"

"I've been through this before, Claire. Let me help you."

She nodded. "Thanks. Come on in."

Project Blue Flame Lab
Senkaku Island, Japan
10:20 AM
1:20 PM, GMT

He knew every square meter of the lab. Moreover, he'd known that this day might someday come. It was time to go to work doing his other job.

Communications on and off the island were possible through four channels: the phone line, a high frequency transceiver, the wide–area network, and a satellite telephone system. All four would have to be systematically disabled. The least–used systems would come down first.

McGuire Residence
Plano, Texas
8:25 AM
1:25 PM, GMT

Claire took a seat across from Katelyn as she emptied the bag of bagels and donuts. She caught herself staring at Ben's first wife, studying her face, hair and eyes. She was pretty. Her reddish brown hair was shorter now than in the photographs Claire had found of her. It took Katelyn looking up to break the trance.

"Something wrong?" she asked.

"No," Claire replied.

Claire removed the plastic cover from the coffee and its aroma filled the air. From the amount of rising steam, she knew it was still too hot to drink. The wrapping came off the bagels and the sweet odor of cinnamon and raisins joined in. She covered one in cream cheese and prepared to take a bite.

"This smells wonderful," Claire smiled. "Thanks so much for doing this."

"You're welcome," Katelyn replied.

Silence.

"How late do you normally sleep?" Katelyn finally asked.

Claire, a little confused at first, only peered back. Then she remembered she still was in her jammies. "Oh, no. Normally, I'm at work by now. I overslept. I stayed up watching the news last night and, well, you know." Her hands shook as she tugged at the collar.

"Oh."

More silence.

"I wonder what's on the news," Claire said as she picked up the remote. She fumbled at the buttons. *Why am I so nervous? She's in my house.*

"Claire?"

She kept pushing the button, but the television would not turn on. "Damn it."

"Claire," Katelyn called again. "It's okay. I already saw the news this morning. Nothing has changed."

Claire turned her gaze back to Katelyn. "Oh. Okay."

Is it because in all the time we've lived here, she's never come inside my house?

"I just thought I'd come over and let you know I'm worried, too."

She frowned at Katelyn's words. Something about them made her uncomfortable. "You still care about him, don't you?"

Katelyn smiled. "Not like I think you mean, Claire. Ben is the father of my children. I was deeply in love with him once. I will always care about him."

Claire nodded, remembering that he had said the same thing about his feelings for his ex–wife.

"I didn't lose Ben. We lost each other. It's more his fault than mine," she laughed. "But in the end, it really doesn't matter. Yes, to answer your question, I still care about him."

"I'm sorry," Claire replied.

"No, you're not," Katelyn laughed again. "If we were still married, you wouldn't have him."

Claire wanted to grin, but didn't know if it would be appropriate. *Hell, I don't know if this whole scene is appropriate.* "Just the same. I hope I never go through what you two went through," she finally said.

"That's for sure," Katelyn raised her white coffee cup in a toast. She followed up with a sip before waiting for Claire to raise hers, too.

She sighed. Time to change the subject. "What should I do to get some details? Ben left the number for the ombudsman."

"Ha," Katelyn laughed. "She's just a Navy wife, probably the CO's. If I know Ben, you know more than she does."

"Should I call the Navy?"

"No good there, either. Not unless you know the

Secretary of Defense or something. They won't tell us anything unless somebody is..." Katelyn stopped herself in mid–sentence. However, it didn't do any good. Claire knew what she was about to say.

"Killed."

Their eyes met. Katelyn nodded slowly.

Claire suddenly had the urge to cry again. The first one had come last night on finding out about the crisis. She turned her head away to fight it back. She was still looking away as the other woman spoke.

"Claire, Ben McGuire is charmed."

"What do you mean?"

"He's charmed. The guy has survived all kinds of near misses. I honestly think he could walk through hell and not even singe his shirt," she giggled. "It's like he was made for this life."

"I don't understand. He's been in this kind of mess before?" Claire finally took a drink from her cup. The brown fluid was perfectly brewed and now was at just the right temperature.

"He might be a computer consultant and big business man, now. But he will always be a Naval officer. That *Devon* thing proved that to me."

"*Devon* thing? Oh, you mean his ship. Boy, they were lucky to get out of that alive."

Katelyn nodded in agreement. "He likes saying that, but deep down, I know he's pretty proud of what he did."

All of a sudden, Claire felt like she'd walked into a room that she didn't belong in, or like she'd opened a gift for someone else. Here was Ben's ex–wife telling her something she didn't know about her husband. She took a deep breath, buried her pride and asked, "What are you talking about?"

"Ben, of course. He saved his ship."

Claire, despite her best effort to keep a cool veneer, didn't. "Ben saved his ship?"

"Oh, my God. You don't know?"

She shook her head.

"Ben, despite the fact he's an asshole for divorcing me, is a *bona fide*, all–American hero. I thought you knew."

"All I know is that he was on the *Devon*."

She sat back. "Have you got some time?"

"All you need." Claire's mind and heart were flooded with different feelings: anger, jealousy, pride, and dismay that he had not told her. *Boy, are you going to get it when you get home!*

Marcia Hobson's Office
Project Blue Flame Lab
12:30 AM
3:30 PM, GMT

The storm raged outside. Sheets of rain marched by the window. The lights from the Logistics Area gave just enough illumination to see the blowing palm trees and the occasional falling branch.

"It's getting rough out there," Marcia said to Ben.

"Yeah."

The office was dark with the exception of the desk lamp. She sat behind her desk while he occupied a guest chair. Both faced the window and the storm beyond. A half–empty bottle of red wine and two half–filled glasses stood between them.

"Texas," she said softly.

Ben smiled to himself. He knew what she was about to ask.

"Why Texas?"

"I went out for a training program with my new civilian job. I was only supposed to be there for three months. I never left."

"What's so great about it? I heard they really don't like Blacks down there. That's where that lynching thing happened, wasn't it?"

Ben let the comment roll around in his mind for a few moments. "Name me someplace in the United States of America that likes Black people," he shot back.

She sat in the dark for a long moment before answering. "*Touché.*"

Ben sat up in his chair. "Texas. They don't like Yankees too much. It's hot as hell in the summer. And the drivers, at least the ones in Dallas, love the left lane more than their mothers."

She giggled.

"But Texas isn't so bad. Most of the people are very nice. The living standard is extremely reasonable. And the weather is good most of the year. Hell, I can play golf practically year round. And Texans are really proud, sometimes more so than they should be, of *who* they are. I like that."

"You sound like a commercial."

"Yeah, maybe."

Silence.

"You know, I kept up with your career for a long time," she started again.

"Really?" This surprised him. After their last meeting, he was sure that Marcia had put him out of her thoughts forever.

"Sure. After that missile boat thing, I just knew you'd be an admiral by now."

"It takes a whole lot more to become an admiral than that," Ben replied. "But thanks for the compliment."

"So why'd you get out?" she asked.

"You can't believe the number of people who have asked me that question, on this trip alone."

"I can imagine."

Ben sat quietly for a long while. Up until that moment, he had only explained his actions to two people, Katelyn and his father. "I promised Katelyn children."

"I don't understand. Was staying in and having children mutually exclusive?"

"Over the year or so that I was on the *Devon* she got to witness three or four births. All of them occurred while the fathers were out at sea. She didn't want to go through it without me. And, I wasn't exactly sure I wanted a career of floating around for the rest of my life."

"But you were good at it."

"Yeah, but it seemed like such a waste. And I always thought I was missing out on something."

"I don't think I understand."

"Before the missile boat attack, life had been pretty dull. For thirty minutes, life got more exciting than most people can ever imagine. Then it got mundane again. It's like that most of the time: you sit around bored, waiting for bad stuff to happen. And when it does…holy shit! I guess I just wanted more out of my life.

"Are you getting it?"

"Yeah, most of the time. I like being a Reservist. I get the best of both worlds now."

"How does your wife feel about it?"

Ben sighed. "I think she'd like to see me out of this completely, but I also think she understands it's a big part of me."

"Well after the career you've had, I should think she should."

"She doesn't know about any of that," he replied as he sipped from the glass.

"What? Criminy, Ben! You were on the cover of *Time Magazine!* How can she not know?"

"She knows I was in the engagement, but that's about it. Claire met me when I was very much a civilian. I think it would be difficult for her to think of me in those terms. And it's not like I do it every day, now."

"Ben, your wife needs to know what you did."

"And she will, some day."

She shook her head in disbelief before taking a drink from her glass.

"So what happened after your husband died?"

Marcia rested her head on the back of her swivel chair. "Tristan and I moved back to Severna Park. I stayed with my folks for a while, then I went back to work."

"I'm really sorry about what I said. I can understand why Tristan tried to take my head off."

"He's a very angry little boy," she replied.

"He's not so little any more."

She nodded.

"Twenty years sure did go by fast. Didn't it?"

"Yeah." She smiled. "It seems like yesterday that you left me standing in Dahlgren Hall while you went to go meet the girl of your dreams."

Ben bowed his head. "Yeah, I guess that was bad form." He remembered leaving to go to the restroom.

On the way back, he met Katelyn O'Brien and his entire life changed.

"Bad form? You broke my heart."

"Wait a minute, now. I seem to remember a little incident not a year before when I caught my date to the Ring Dance sucking face with one of my classmates on the Dahlgren Hall dance floor."

She winced. "Oh, yeah."

Marcia, then Marcia Stone, had been two–timing: dating Ben and one of his classmates at the same time. After telling Ben she would be at a party with some of her girlfriends, she later showed up at the Brigade of Midshipman Social Center in the arms of one his classmates.

They both laughed. "We weren't supposed to be together, were we?"

The smile on his face evaporated. "No. I guess not."

"Claire. Is she a good woman?"

The thought of getting married again could not have been further from his plans. The idea of marrying someone of a different race, again, was even more unimaginable. Yet here he was, happy, truly happy, for the first time in his life. Claire had come out of nowhere, taking his heart in a whirlwind.

"She's great. I fell in love with her the minute I met her. She has a way about her, she's very cool."

"Cool?" she laughed.

"Yeah, cool. It takes a lot to piss her off. And, she gives everyone the benefit of the doubt. She's cool."

"She white?"

Ben frowned at the question. He should have seen it coming. Had he remembered Marcia's personality, he would have. "Yeah. So what?"

"Nothing. I was just curious."

He heard the edge in his own voice. He took a breath and let it, and the stress out. "Just don't give me a lecture like my mother did about finding someone in my own race."

"Well, it sure would have been nice if you'd given one of the sisters a shot."

"What makes you think I didn't?" he retorted.

She didn't answer at first. The sound of the rain and wind against the window filled the space between them.

"I dated around a little after Kate and I separated. I guess I wanted to see if I was missing anything. I *really* got around after the divorce."

"You always were a cad," she laughed.

"Yeah, well. You would have really thought so two years ago."

"Black girls?" she asked.

"You name it. White girls, Black girls, Asian girls, Latinas. I even met a couple from the Czech Republic."

"Geez, Ben. It's a wonder you didn't catch something."

"I didn't sleep with them," he protested.

She raised a doubt–filled eyebrow.

"Well, not all of 'em," he laughed.

"And?" she asked.

"The Black girls?" he added.

"Yeah."

"I don't know," he sighed. "Well, yeah, I do. I tried. I really tried. I went full out. I'd go to a club or party or bar and try. I got shut down so many times, it wasn't even funny."

"Really? You?"

"Oh, yeah. I remember one woman, real nice

looking, was sitting in this club one night. I went up to her and managed to get out, 'Hi.' She just put her hand up and turned her head."

She shook her head in disbelief.

"That was the worst of 'em. Everybody else did other things to make it apparent that they weren't interested: not return calls, give me fake phone numbers, you know."

"Hmm."

"I just got tired of trying so hard. You shouldn't have to make people like you."

"So what happened to your marriage? You guys seemed so happy. I hated that," she laughed.

Ben sighed. "We were, for a very long time."

She peered at him in the twilight.

"I guess we ran out of things to talk about. We grew apart and I did the typical guy thing and went looking for companionship someplace else."

"You? Mister Straight and Narrow?"

"Yeah. I was an asshole." He felt himself shrinking in stature with each word.

She shook her head in disbelief. "You *have* changed."

"Told ya so."

"No, I don't mean that. Everybody makes mistakes, Ben. Hell, you made them back then. Trouble is, you never felt guilty. I think you feel guilty now."

What can I say? I do.

"A piece of advice?" she offered.

"Sure."

"Let it go. You fucked up. A lot of people do. The night before Derrick left for the Gulf, we had a terrific argument. I never got the chance to say I was sorry.

It's not the mistakes we make, Ben. It's what we learn from them that counts."

Her words, even with a half–bottle of wine in him, made sense and hit home. He felt his own tears try to well up when he saw her wiping her face.

"Is that fruit from the font of wisdom created from the last twenty years?" he asked.

"Yes. And you should listen to it. The Energy Secretary does," she laughed.

He only smiled before standing. He walked over to her and picked up her hand. "Thanks for the advice. I'll try to follow it." He kissed the back of it. "It's good seeing you again."

"You, too."

"I've got to get some sleep. I recommend you get some, too."

"Is that fruit from your wisdom tree?"

"No, just the babblings of a drunken sailor."

She laughed. "Good night."

He let go of her hand and walked toward the door. "Good night." He shut it behind him.

Marcia put her head down on her desk after Ben left. The sounds of the storm and the wine began to work as she started drifting off to sleep. A knock at her door brought her back to consciousness.

She sat up in her chair and wiped her eyes. The bottle came off the desk and went into a drawer, along with the two glasses.

"Yes?" she answered.

The door opened and Bob Deitrich showed just his upper torso. She forced back a smile while her legs secretly twisted around each other under the desk.

"Got a minute?" he asked.

"You're still up? I'm surprised."

"I could say the same about you," he quipped.

Marcia's eyebrow went up. "What can I do for you, Bob?"

"I know you can't tell me everything, but please tell me that we're not turning over our work to the military."

"Of course not." She could hear the edge come off her voice. She could also feel the wine working. "Sit down, Bob."

He came in the rest of the way, shutting the door behind him. Deitrich sat in the chair where Ben had sat only a few minutes earlier. *Funny, tonight seems to be the night that all of the men I've ever felt anything about sit in that chair.*

"I only ask because you and that officer seem so close."

"Bob. He's here to help get us off the island. That's all. He doesn't even know what kind of research we're doing here."

"Really?"

"Yes, really. You've always trusted me before. Why can't you trust me now?" *Where is this pleading voice coming from? God, I'm way too drunk to be having this conversation, especially with him.*

"Well, that's the other reason I came by." Deitrich stood. He walked around the desk very slowly, like he was a cat creeping up on a small bird.

"Bob, I don't think..."

"I have to tell you this while I can. We'll be off of this island tomorrow and I know I won't have the opportunity or courage to say this..."

"Bob. Don't," she whispered.

He picked up both her hands and kissed them. Desire, hot and unabashed, flowed like lava from a volcano.

"I've adored you for five years," he said as he pulled her up from the chair.

I can't do this, she told herself.

He kissed her face, then her mouth.

She resisted at first and then kissed back, hard.

She gasped as his hand found her breast. "Oh, God," she heard herself mutter.

He pushed against her. She found herself climbing on top of her desk, all the time pulling him closer.

She happened to look down to see him reaching for the desk lamp. When she did, his wedding band caught her eye. She had seen the same stop sign for almost five years. The sight of it had the effect of putting out the fire raging inside her. "Stop, Bob," she heard herself say.

"But," he tried to kiss her again.

"I said, stop."

This time he put his hand back on her breast. He even pulled himself closer.

"Did you hear me? I said stop it," she ordered.

His face went from wearing an expression of surprise to one of anger in a slow, evolutionary second. "You little fucking tease."

"You're married and I'm your boss. This has gone too far as it is. I'm not going to let it go any further until at least one of those issues is resolved."

He pulled away. Then he turned and walked toward the door. "Is that why you did your little sailor boy and not me?"

"Bob, it's not like that."

"Sure. Whatever you say, Doctor."

He turned and stormed out, slamming the door behind him.

Marcia, tired and shaky, sighed as she started pulling her clothing back together.

CHAPTER TWENTY–NINE
WEDNESDAY, APRIL 14TH

Residential Lounge
Project Blue Flame Lab
8:05 AM
11:05 PM, GMT

"**H**owdy, Doc," Ericksen greeted Marcia as he entered the room. He flashed his best smile at her.

She barely raised her hand to wave back.

Now I wonder what that's all about.

The Residential Lounge doubled as a cafeteria. With eight tables and a food pick–up window, a body could chow down in a pretty comfortable setting. It reminded him of his high–school cafeteria; only the food was better, even if it was frozen. And, of course, the scenery had improved, too.

With all of their support crew back in Japan, there were no cooks. The kitchen's refrigerator, freezer and three microwave ovens were seeing a lot of action. Ericksen noticed a couple of people actually cooking, but they were the exception.

Marcia sat alone at the table furthest from the food window. Scientists and technicians ate at tables all around her. A few sat with their trays on their laps on the couch.

A few minutes later, Ericksen had his yogurt, toast, and coffee. He headed towards her.

"How's my favorite nuclear physicist today?" he greeted again.

She looked up at him with squinted eyes. As a matter of fact, she scowled.

"Doc, I've seen a lot of pissed off animals in my day, but you'd put the hair on the back of a grizzly on end. What's chapped your ass?"

"Chapped my what?" she asked. The scowl faded a bit.

"Chapped your ass? That's Texan for 'What's got you p.o.'d?'"

She shook her head and grinned, but only for a second.

"Nothing."

"Oh, bullshit." He gestured toward the open chair next to her with his head and elbow.

"Sure, sit down."

"So what's the matter? It's way too early for someone to have peed in your breakfast cereal already."

"I get tired of being treated like the anti–Christ," she whispered.

"Ah, cause you mean these folks here are too self–conscious and insecure to sit next to you?" he asked at the top of his voice. Ericksen looked around to ensure that an adequate number of them had overheard his comment. He looked back at Marcia to see her trying to lower her profile and head.

"Doc, if you go any lower in that chair, you're gonna be underneath the table in a minute."

"Well, I didn't expect you to just blurt out what we were talking about." She was whispering again.

Ericksen nodded that he understood. "Can I ask you a question?" He took a bite of his toast.

"Yeah, I guess," she replied. Her voice was unsure, full of trepidation.

"You ever lied to these people?" he asked as he chewed.

"No."

"About anything?"

"No, nothing."

"Do you treat any of 'em like crap?"

"Crap?"

"You know: yellin', screamin', cursin'." He gestured with his free hand. "Crap."

"No," she smiled.

"Then you ain't got nothin' to be embarrassed about. They oughta be bustin' their collective asses to have breakfast with you. Get my point?" He winked at her.

She smiled back, a little at first, then a big grin. "Yes. Yes, I do."

"Good. Can I get you some more coffee, Doc?"

"That would be very nice. Thank you," she replied.

"Good. I'm glad you said that 'cause my next step was gonna involve me singin' 'Sour Milk Don't Work Good for Your Cereal'."

"Is that another one of your original C&W songs?" she laughed.

Ericksen only smiled back as he gathered up their coffee mugs and stood.

On the way over to the coffee machine, he caught

the gaze of several of the other occupants. He either winked or made faces at them as he passed by their tables. While filling the cups, he noticed her son as he came into the room. Like him, Tristan made for his mom's table. He was standing in front of his mother when Ericksen returned with two steaming cups.

"Hey, Tristan. What's shakin'?"

Her son only glanced at him. Contempt filled his eyes.

"Tristan. Senior Chief Ericksen just spoke to you. Say something," she ordered.

The boy rolled his eyes and his head at the same time. He took a deep breath and sighed. "Hi," he mumbled.

"Excuse me," Ericksen said as he leaned in front of him to put Marcia's coffee in front of her. He sat back down at his tray.

"I'm sorry," Marcia said to Ericksen.

"Don't worry about it. Tristan's just bein' a teen-ager."

"Yeah, what would you know about it?" the kid snapped back.

"Why is it that every kid between the ages of eleven and twenty-one thinks that all adults skipped those ages while they were growin' up?" he asked Marcia with a rhetorical tone. He winked at the boy.

"Kiss my ass!" Tristan spat.

"Tristan! Now that's enough."

"Now, hold on, Doc. Don't go an' git yourself all riled," Ericksen said as he put his hand out and patted the air. "I got a deal for ol' Tristan here."

The two of them, mother and son, turned toward

Ericksen with the same wide–eyed look. *God, these two look just alike.*

"Tristan," Ericksen started as he dug into his pants pocket and came up with his wallet. "I was in Africa last year and some guy in Sudan told me to do the same thing." Ericksen pulled out a fifty–dollar bill. "If you can tell me the name of the capital of Sudan, this fifty's yours." He slapped it down on the table and looked up at the not–quite–yet man.

Tristan frowned for a long moment. Ericksen couldn't tell if he was confused or trying to come up with an answer. Still, the whole time, the kid never stopped staring back at him. *He's got guts. I'll give him that.*

"Whatever," he finally said.

"No, that's not the right answer," Ericksen said. "You wanna try again, this time for a hundred?" He put down another bill.

Tristan's eyes bulged. Then he frowned. He glared first at Ericksen, then at his mother. He turned on his heel and stormed out of the room.

"I'm sorry, Senior Chief. I don't know how to handle him sometimes. He's been this way for a long time. I don't know what I'm going to do." She held her head in her hands.

"Ah, Doc. He's just pissed. He'll grow out of it."

"Oh, yeah? What makes you so sure?"

"I used to be the same way. I lost my old man in 'Nam. I got pissed and stayed pissed as long as I could."

Her eyebrow went up.

"What got you over it?"

"Who says I'm over it?" he laughed back.

She didn't smile.

The grin on his face evaporated like water on a Texas road in the summer. "The SEALs. I learned how to," he used his hands to make little quotation marks in the air, "channel that aggression. I think they saved me."

She sighed. "Senior..."

"Darren," he interrupted.

She smiled and started again. "Darren. To be honest with you, I hope he never wants to do anything like that. The Service took my husband. It's not going to get my son, too."

"I know how you feel, Doc—"

"Marcia," she interrupted as she smiled.

He smiled back. "I know how you feel, Marcia. But that's his choice to make."

The frown on her face slowly softened. Ericksen's hands got suddenly sweaty. *Look at this, here. She's smilin' at me with those big ol' bedroom eyes.* He caught himself smiling back as hers started to slip away.

Her gaze was off him now. The same strained look on her face that he'd worked so hard to remove was back. Ericksen, out of instinct, turned around to see what had done such a good job of undoing his work.

Doctor Bob Deitrich approached the table. He already had a tray of food with him. "May I join you?" he asked as he arrived.

Marcia's gaze left the other physicist and came back to Ericksen. Her eyes screamed, *No!*

"Well, to tell you the truth Doc, we were just having a confidential discussion."

"Is that right?" he put down his tray and took a seat between them. "About what?"

Marcia folded her arms in silent protest.

"About flies," Ericksen replied.

Deitrich frowned. "Flies?" His East Coast accent played on Ericksen's ears like a sour note from his saxophone.

"Yeah, flies. You know anything about them?"

"Quite a bit actually. I have an undergraduate degree in Biology."

"Great." He shot Marcia a half grin as Deitrich took a sip from his coffee. "I was just askin' Doctor Hobson here if she knew why flies were like Yankees."

Deitrich looked up.

"No, Senior Chief. Why are flies like Yankees?" she asked.

"They both eat shit and bother people."

Deitrich frowned while she burst out in laughter.

Ericksen only smiled, partially at Deitrich, but openly at Marcia.

CHAPTER THIRTY
WEDNESDAY, APRIL 14TH

White House Briefing Room
Washington, D.C.
7:15 AM
11:15 AM, GMT

"**O**kay, talk to me."

"We lost contact with the island an hour ago," Langdon reported.

"Damn!" Turner replied. The Chief Executive crossed his arms and reclined into the folds of his chair. "What are we doing to re–establish communications?"

"We're trying to check all of the channels. We think our equipment is working fine. It's gotta be something on the island."

Turner sighed loudly. "Okay. Any more bad news?"

No one answered immediately. Only the sound of staffers writing in notepads filled the air.

"Mister President," Defense Secretary Wilson finally

began. "I'm afraid that we have made a slight miscalculation."

Turner frowned.

Energy Secretary Langdon, now seated at the 'big' table behind his own nameplate, watched the proceedings. This was his third meeting and now he felt like a full–fledged member.

With tensions between the U.S. and China escalating, the Chairman of the Joint Chiefs brought company to the day's gathering. The Service Chiefs, with the exception of the Chief of Naval Operations, sat along the back wall in the "cheap seats."

He glanced at Doug Miller. His aide beamed. Why shouldn't he? His boss, in less than a week, was now a member of the NSC. This naturally meant more exposure for him. Langdon mentally shook his head.

"The officer we placed in charge of the evacuation is a Reservist on two weeks of active duty. And while he's a Naval Academy grad, he was at the bottom of his class." Wilson, a Harvard graduate and Rhodes Scholar, had a reputation for never letting his guys forget his pedigree.

The President sat up in his chair.

Langdon noticed the CNO's face. The three–star admiral scowled at Wilson's words. Dissension was visiting the military side of the house.

"What's that got to do with anything?" General Marksee asked. Marksee and Wilson exchanged uncomfortable stares.

"We've been discussing some options for getting him replaced," the Secretary of Defense pressed.

"What do you mean?"

"Sir, we can put another officer, a real officer, on the island."

"Excuse me, Sir," the Chief of Naval Operations interrupted. "This officer is one of our best: reserve or active." Admiral James Hawkins sat at attention in his chair. The military head of the Navy was a burly man with silver hair and bushy eyebrows.

"Just the same, Mister President. It is my recommendation that we get someone else out there," Wilson added.

"So let me get this straight. We've got a major situation developing in the East China Sea and the best that we have is a Reservist with a dubious record running the whole thing?" The President leaned back in his chair as he played with a pen. He sighed, as he looked first at the Secretary of Defense and then the CNO. "What's it gonna take to get someone else out there?" he finally asked.

Hawkins sighed and bowed his head at the same time.

"Sir, we can put a man on the island with a submarine."

"A submarine?" the CNO snarled. Hawkins' head was back up now. He leaned across the table and pointed at the weather chart. "There's a tropical storm blowing out there. A sub can't surface during that."

The President turned back toward Wilson.

The Secretary of Defense sighed. "He's right," he said after a long moment.

The President grimaced. "Tell me about your man, Jamie."

The CNO nodded at Richardson and she advanced the projector a few slides until a Black naval officer in service dress blues appeared on the screen. He had a serious and, at the same time, wily expression. The decorations and ribbons on his chest looked almost as deep as the admiral's. His name and service number appeared at the bottom of the slide, "Aesop Benjamin McGuire."

"Sir, do you remember the USS *Robert B. Devon* incident in 1987?" Hawkins asked the president.

"Sure, sure. That was the Navy frigate that caught a missile in the Gulf of Sidra, right?"

"Yes, Sir. Well, there's a little more to the story than most people know."

The Secretary of Defense looked at his watch. "Is this gonna take long?"

Admiral Hawkins winced at his boss' comment, but kept going. "About two months into the deployment, the Weapons Officer broke his leg and got sent back to the States. Commander McGuire, then a lieutenant, took over for him."

"So he's a ship–driver?"

"Yes, Mister President. If I may continue, three weeks before the missile strike, the *Devon* had engine trouble. They put into port at Augusta Bay in Sicily for repairs. The ship ended up leaving port late. They had to bust their butts catching up with the rest of the Fleet."

Hawkins shifted in his seat. "The Sixth Fleet Commander gave the frigate permission to run like hell and make the best course possible in order to catch up. That 'best course' brought them within two miles of the Line of Death."

Langdon, like the rest of the people in the room, found himself riveted to each of the admiral's words. He also caught himself staring at McGuire's picture trying to imagine him as a much younger man.

"We think the Russians were feeding the Libyans intel. Bear in mind that this was after the air raid in which Khadifi's son was killed. We also think he sent some of his guys to get payback. The *Devon*, like all the reports state, *was* in international waters when two Osa–class patrol boats attacked. The first missile hit the bridge and killed five, including the ship's captain. The Executive Officer was badly injured and the Operations Officer panicked and lost it. McGuire, a very junior lieutenant, took command and engaged the two patrol boats. After evading a second missile, he destroyed one of the patrol boats and damaged the other. He withdrew and escaped, thereby saving the ship and the remainder of her crew."

"So why is this officer a Reservist now? I would have thought you guys would have put him on the fast track to his own command," General Marksee said.

"You're right. We did. This, at one time, was the most celebrated and decorated officer in the U.S. Fleet. He had his choice of orders and ships."

"So what happened?" the President asked.

"He went home one day after work, came back in the next day and resigned."

"Just like that?" Marksee asked.

"Just like that," he replied.

"Anything else?" the President asked.

"Yes, Sir. A few more things," he replied. Hawkins then opened a file folder on the desk in front of him. He read the rest. "Commander McGuire started out as a Naval Aviator. Just after he got his wings, McGuire failed his flight physical and transitioned into the Surface Warfare community. We already talked about him leaving the service. About a year and a half after leaving active duty, he was recalled for the Gulf War where he served aboard the Carrier

Group Flagship and was credited with directing successful attacks against three Iraqi patrol boats. He's an expert marksman. He's held command of three reserve units. Commander McGuire is a warrior, Sir. I'm not sure what all is at stake here, but he's been in harm's way before. He knows how to handle himself."

"What's he do as a civilian?" the President's Chief of Staff asked.

Hawkins used his finger to scan down the page. "He's an information technology consultant specializing in strategic planning and database systems. He has an MBA and an MS in Information Systems. By the way, he was at the top of his graduate school class." Hawkins and Wilson exchanged icy glances.

The President crossed his arms and leaned back in his chair. He turned toward Langdon. The Secretary wasn't sure if he was asking for his counsel or not. *What the hell? Why not?* "Sir, why don't we trust this guy? The admiral thinks he's got what it takes."

The President sighed. "What's the word on the storm?" he asked after a long moment.

Naomi Richardson fumbled through some of her papers. "Sir, it's building and has pretty much stalled."

He nodded his understanding. "By the time we get someone else on the island, this will all be over anyway. Pete, let's see what we can do to back up Commander McGuire."

"Yes, Sir."

"In the meantime, we need some eyes out there," Chief of Staff Nelson declared. "Ideas?"

"We have already directed the movement of a couple of satellites. But they won't be in position for another eight to ten hours," NSA Director Brewer replied.

"What about those high altitude RPVs we bought last year?" Defense Secretary Wilson asked.

Still seated in the rear of the room, the Air Force Chief of Staff cleared his throat before speaking. "We only had enough budget for five."

"High altitude RPV?" Langdon asked.

"Remotely Piloted Vehicle," General Shaffer replied. "It has about a thousand mile range."

"That's perfect," Nelson replied.

"Yes, Sir. But the weather has got to be clear as a bell to use it. Any kind of attenuation affects our ability to control them, especially at long distances."

"Can't you bounce the signal off a satellite?" Admiral Hawkins asked.

"Response time isn't there yet. We crashed two of 'em trying that. Besides, by the time we got one aloft it would be too cloudy to see anything anyway."

"What about a high altitude fly–over?" Naomi Richardson asked.

"Again, it'll be socked in by the time we get there. We wouldn't be able to see anything," the Air Force Chief of Staff replied.

"What am I paying you people for?" Turner asked.

Langdon couldn't tell if he were joking or not. With the way things were going, he guessed not.

Ministry of National Defense
Intelligence Directorate
Beijing, China
7:25 AM
11:25 PM, GMT

Mai adjusted her jacket as she stood. Her meeting with Minister Fong was in five minutes. She picked up her notebook and pen, tucking them under her arm. With her free hand, she checked the pocket for her cigarettes and lighter. She had just enough time for a smoke before the appointment.

She lit up and proceeded out of her office. She held the first drag, always the best, for a long while before blowing it out. Mai even closed her eyes for a long moment as she sauntered along.

When she opened them, she found a crowd of other Government personnel gathered ahead. "What's going on?" she asked one of the bystanders.

"They just arrested General Zhao for misuse of the People's property."

"Zhao Chin Lee?"

"Yes. Minister Fong had him arrested," the man said as Zhao walked by with two plain–clothed men as escorts.

Mai swallowed hard.

Zhao looked up for a moment and they exchanged glances. Mai lowered her head and eyes. Though not friends, they had met. She also knew he worked for Fong in some capacity with the fusion project. Once Zhao's entourage was past, she pressed her way through the gathering toward Fong's office.

Mai knew her master had high expectations. She also knew that failing him once was acceptable. How had Zhao, a Hero of the People, fallen? She tried to clear her mind of questions about the Army officer as she knocked on the door. *I need to worry about my own skin for now*.

"Come," she heard from the other side.

"Good morning, Minister—"

"What is your report?" he asked, cutting off her greeting. He sat at attention in his chair.

"The Task Force is on its timetable and almost ready. I will leave to join them soon."

"What of your asset on the island?"

"I received my final report from him last night before he cut off the island's communications—"

"Before he what?!" The Old Man leaned forward in his chair.

"Before he cut communications, Master," she replied in almost a whisper.

Fong slammed his fist on his desk. "What have you done?"

Mai's head went down instantly. She focused on the place where the floor met the side of the Minister's desk.

"Did you hear me? Answer, damn you!"

"I followed the plan, Master."

"What plan?"

She did not answer.

"I grow weary of repeating myself, Su Mai Lin!"

"I followed the plan I briefed you on two days ago, Minister."

Fong squinted as he seemed to focus on a set of papers on his desk. Then he reached for and rubbed his bald head. "Shit," he said more to himself than aloud.

"Did I fail you, Master?"

Fong sighed as he reclined in his heavy leather chair.

"No, my young friend. I failed myself," he replied. Fong reached for the phone and dialed several numbers.

"This is Deputy Minister Fong. It would appear that the report I received on the General was in error. Let him go with my apologies."

Mai waited in silence while Fong listened to the person on the other end.

"Yes, damn you. I'm sure. Send him home!" Fong put down the phone and turned in his chair toward his window.

Not knowing what to do or say, Mai stood still. She remained there in silence for what felt like an eternity.

"These are difficult times, Mai," he said without facing her.

"Yes, Minister."

"Continue with your plan."

"Yes, Minister."

"You may go."

CHAPTER THIRTY–ONE
THURSDAY, APRIL 15TH

Oval Office
The White House
Washington, D.C.
8:18 AM
12:18 AM, GMT

President Turner and George Nelson shared the couch while Jack Langdon sat across a small coffee table from them. Turner sat erect as he sipped coffee. Like Nelson, Langdon sat quietly waiting for their boss to speak.

Silence, except for occasional voices in the outer office, filled the air. President Turner placed his coffee cup on its saucer as he looked at Langdon.

"I've been considering a number of contingency options," he declared.

"Contingency, Sir?" Jack asked.

"In case we are not able to get the reactor shut down before the Chinese assault the island."

"So you think that's possible?" Nelson asked.

"Oh, yes," Turner replied as he reclined a bit.

"What contingencies are you considering?"

"Well, a conventional bombing attack would be ineffective," Turner replied.

"I agree. It wouldn't destroy enough of the facility to keep them from finding something."

"I should think that the radiation would keep most people away," Langdon offered.

"Most, but not them. They'd just send political prisoners in to pick through the rubble, radiation or not," Turner replied.

"What about a nuclear strike?" Nelson asked.

Turner picked up his cup and began sipping again.

Tactical Flag Command Center
USS *Blue Ridge* (LCC–19)
0930 Hours
0030 Hours, GMT

Commander Dave Ferguson had dutifully watched the clock tick away until it reached the time for Ben to call from the island. He was now fifteen minutes late. Just as he was about to make the call himself, the intercom on his watch console rang. The display showed the Chief of Staff's number.

"Great," he said aloud. Dave picked up the phone. "Battle Watch. Commander Ferguson, Ma'am."

"What's Commander McGuire's status?" The Captain's voice was crisp.

"Unknown, Captain. He hasn't called in yet."

Silence.

"Have you called him?"

"Just getting ready to do that, Ma'am."

"Well, get on with it. And when you get him on line reinforce the importance of timely reports."

"Yes, Ma'am."

The line went dead. *Shit. What a pain in the ass.*

Project Blue Flame Lab
Senkaku Island, Japan
9:55 AM
12:55 AM, GMT

"So let me get this straight. You've got a problem. I have the technical expertise to solve it and you're not going to let me in?"

Ben and Doctor Yashita had been going at it for almost ten minutes. Ben had shown up just after breakfast to get things going by solving their only remaining technical issue, the malfunctioning storage disk array.

"That is correct, Commander. This is a classified area."

"I have Top Secret Level Clearance," Ben interjected.

"That may be, but you do not have a need to know."

"To know what? I don't need to see your data to solve your disk array problem."

"I am sorry, Commander. But you may not enter," Yashita declared.

"Is there a something wrong here?" Marcia asked as she arrived at the door of the computer room. Ben had sent for her as soon as the doctor had denied him access the first time.

"Yes. Good of you to come, Doctor," Yashita replied. "I was just explaining to the Commander that he does not have authorized access to the computer room."

Her eyebrow went up. "I'm afraid he's right, Ben."

"Fine. Then get in there and solve the problem or we leave here without whatever you need," Ben replied.

"We can't leave without the data on those computers," Yashita insisted.

"Then let me in to see about fixing the damned thing!"

"No, I'm afraid that is impossible."

Ben held up his hands in frustration.

"I think I can resolve this," Marcia said.

The two men turned to her.

"We'll call Washington and get the Commander permission to enter the room." She looked at Yashita to seek his thoughts.

"That would be acceptable."

Then she turned toward Ben.

"Yeah, yeah. Whatever."

The two men turned to follow her. When the passageway narrowed to the point they had to walk in single–file, Ben stepped aside to let Yashita go first. The Asian raised his nose smugly as he walked by. Ben sneered behind Yashita's back.

The walk to Marcia's office took about two minutes. She pushed open the door and went around to her desk. She lifted the receiver to dial and immediately frowned at the phone.

"What's wrong?" Ben asked.

"Phone seems to be dead."

"Let me see," Ben said as he drew nearer.

He pressed several buttons, but no lights appeared.

Even the liquid quartz number display refused to show he had a line. "Where's your phone room?"

"It's also in a restricted area," she replied.

"Somebody tell me that we're not going to do the Senkaku Island version of 'Which came first, the chicken or the egg?' here."

Ben pulled out his cellular telephone and switched it on.

"That won't do you any good out here," Marcia said.

"Oh?" Ben still waited for the display to show a solid signal.

"The last coverage zone ends twenty miles north of here."

The Looking for Service message continued to flash at him. "Great." Ben put the device away and turned toward Marcia.

"Doctor Hobson. You can't allow—"

"I know, Doctor Yashita," she said cutting him off. "Let's go to the Radio Room."

She came out from behind the desk and led the way out of her office. This time Ben stepped in front of Yashita to cut him off. He smiled to himself.

The Radio Room was one floor below and adjacent to the Logistics Center. Marcia inserted her key and opened the door. She hit a light switch and several banks of fluorescent tubes flickered on.

Ben instantly recognized the gear. It was of Naval design, a URC–50 High Frequency Radio transmitter and an LST–6 Satellite Communications Terminal. "Where are you getting your electricity?" Ben asked.

"Why?"

"These systems soak up a lot of power. If we're running on generators—"

"It is not a concern," Yashita cut him short.

Marcia sat down in front of the console and flipped the toggle for power. Seconds later the sound of fans spinning up and blinking lights told him that power now flowed to the systems.

"We'll try the SATCOM first," she declared.

Marcia's comfort with the communications gear impressed Ben. Picturing her as something else other than the little groupie who used to hang out looking for midshipmen to date was difficult.

After letting the system warm up for a minute or two, she picked up the telephone receiver–like mouthpiece and pressed the transmit button. "DOE Operations, this is Blue Flame Laboratory. Over."

Static filled their ears when she released the button.

She checked the settings on the transceiver before trying it again. "DOE Operations, this is Blue Flame. Over."

Again. No response.

Ben frowned before walking out of the space. He walked quickly, almost running, to the lounge. Radioman Senior Chief Ericksen was sipping coffee with a few of the junior SEALs when Ben arrived. "Senior Chief, I need your help."

"Sir, you have the timing of a bad rash," he replied as they stood. "Excuse me," he said to them.

Ben started walking away even before the enlisted man was on his feet. "Sir? Wait up."

"Come on, Senior. This is important."

Ericksen started running to catch up. He and Ben reached the door to the Radio Room at almost the same time.

"Whoa. Nice gear," the Senior Chief said as he entered the space.

"Yeah, well there's only one problem. None of it works," Marcia replied.

"What about the HF radio?" Ben asked.

"I just tried it, too. No good."

"Senior," Ben said as he gestured toward the radios. "Senior Chief Ericksen is a Navy radioman."

"Well, I used to be anyway," Ericksen said as he started examining the gear. "I'll need some time to troubleshoot this stuff."

Ben nodded.

"I guess we will have to wait to figure out the access issue for the Computer Room," Yashita said. Ben was almost sure he was grinning when the sentence started.

"Yes," Marcia replied.

Ben checked his watch. "I don't know what the storm's doing. But I'll tell you this. Ready or not, when the weather clears, we're out of here. Computer or no computer." Ben exchanged glances with the two of them before marching out.

1st Information Warfare Brigade
Beijing, China
12:55 PM
4:55 AM, GMT

As soon as the People's Security Police released him, Zhao went home to change into a fresh uniform. Even though his incarceration as an enemy of the People had been brief, something about wearing a uniform soiled by the hands of prison guards bothered him. On his way out of the house, he had ordered his wife to burn the clothing before his return.

"General, are you all right, sir?" Colonel Pan asked

as Zhao entered the foyer of the headquarters building.

"Yes, Colonel," he replied as he strode past his second in command.

He heard Pan's rapid footsteps against the tile as the man hurried to catch up to him.

"Colonel," Zhao said in a hushed voice.

"Yes, General?"

"I want you to begin a new file," he whispered.

"Yes, General."

The door to Zhao's office loomed ahead. Administrative assistants and other low–level functionaries jumped to their feet as he blew through the area. Some even came to attention and saluted. Zhao simply nodded back at them.

He finally removed his hat when he reached his desk. He tossed the green hat with the ornate, gold–laden bill on one of the guest chairs. "Close the door, Pan," he ordered once the man crossed the doorway.

Zhao seated himself in an erect manner as the officer followed his order.

"I want you to begin a file on the Defense Ministry," he said aloud once the door was completely closed.

"General? Minister Fong's office?"

"Do you have a problem with that Colonel?"

He watched as Pan took a deep breath and let it out.

"No, sir."

"Will any of your personnel?"

Pan's eyes went from side to side as he processed his commander's query.

"No, my General. None of them will have a problem with it."

Zhao nodded slowly. He heard himself sigh as he reclined in his chair. It was good to be back. He knew the two hours he spent in Yanqing Prison would stay with him forever.

"Is there anything else, General?" Pan asked, bringing him back from the dark and damp depths of his nightmare.

"No, Colonel. That is all for now."

NMCC Operations Center
Washington, D.C.
0059 Hours
0459 Hours, GMT

Captain Joe Rogers studied the newest weather information with care. Shandra was breaking up. In about twelve hours, the weather would clear enough for some overhead intelligence. Not long after that, something else, although he wasn't quite sure what, would be happening, too.

He checked his watch. Someone else would be on duty then, unless he pulled a double watch. He frowned in thought. *Catherine's just going to have to understand*. Tonight was her birthday dinner.

Pacific Fleet Headquarters
Peoples' Republic of China
Shanghai Province
2:45 PM
6:45 AM, GMT

Mai Lin's helicopter landed right on schedule. She'd climbed out of the passenger cabin and taken two steps when a burly Chinese Marine officer saluted her with great deference. She returned the gesture with a simple nod of her head. They climbed into a waiting sedan.

Her hand was already in her shoulder–strapped purse digging out a cigarette. Smoking had not been allowed on the helicopter and the urge to satisfy that hunger ate at her like a blood–crazed shark.

"Is everything ready, Colonel?" she asked the officer as they drove off the airfield toward the docks.

Mai had worked with Colonel Li Ho Chang once before. The officer had so impressed her that she specifically requested him again. A tall, muscular man, Colonel Li sported a clean–shaven head.

"Everything is prepared. We are simply waiting for the weather to clear," he replied. Mai noticed that the officer even sat at attention.

She pulled deeply on the Western cigarette and then nodded as she looked outside at the ships and sailors making ready to go to sea. The entire port seemed busy. Vehicles of every shape and size: tanks, cars, trucks, cranes and tugs, all were in motion.

"The Fleet Commander, Admiral Xu, is waiting for you. He has many questions," the Colonel added.

"Yes, I suppose he does. It is not every day that he gets an order to mobilize his entire command."

She reclined deeper into the auto's seat as she relaxed, if only for a moment, with a good smoke.

CHAPTER THIRTY–TWO
THURSDAY, APRIL 15TH

USS *Pasadena* (SSN–752)
Periscope Depth
East China Sea
1615 Hours
0715 Hours, GMT

"**E**mergency Deep!" Lieutenant Paul Hansen
ordered as he pulled his eyes away from the periscope
sight. Hansen reached up to snap the hydraulic valve
to bring the scope down to the lowered position.

The already–alert watch team swung into action.

"Full dive on the bow planes and stern planes," the
Diving Officer ordered.

The helmsman controlled the bow planes while
two planesmen worked the sub's stern planes. These
enlisted men, charged with controlling the ship's
attitude, pushed forward on their yokes to place the
improved Los Angeles–class submarine in a dive. The
blunt nose of the matte–black boat plunged and
dipped as the bow planes cut into the water.

Commander Mark Laski grabbed hold of the periscope control valve for balance as he and the other men in the Control Room leaned back from the dive. All around him, men in blue coveralls stood at angles to the ship's deck. "I love this shit," Laski said to Hansen.

"Yes, Sir," the younger officer agreed.

The Chief of the Watch pushed open the control valves to flood the variable ballast tanks. The Helmsman ordered up a Full–Speed bell, and reported to the conning officer as the engineering watch acknowledged the order. The ship coursed through the ocean at just over eighteen knots, increasing speed quickly as the depth meter clicked past one hundred feet.

"Officer of the Deck, nice work. Stop your dive at one five zero feet," Laski ordered.

"Aye aye, Sir," Hansen replied. He turned toward the Diving Officer a few feet away. "Make your depth one five zero feet.

"Make my depth one five zero feet, aye."

Standing at the conning station with Lieutenant Hansen, Laski monitored the activity of his watch team as well as the ship's instruments. The depth meter indicated the ship passing one hundred forty feet.

The planesman started pulling back on the yoke to level off the ship. The Chief of the Watch, a senior enlisted man, adjusted the valves to trim the ship for level transit through the water.

Laski checked the depth gauge as Hansen reported his depth.

"One five zero feet, Captain. Slowing to Standard."

Laski nodded while Hansen ordered the lower

speed setting. "Good job, guys. Well done," Laski said to them all. He patted Hansen on the shoulder.

"Conn, Radio," a voice called over the ship's intercom system.

"Conn, aye," Hansen replied into the open microphone in control.

"Sir, Radio has traffic for the Commanding Officer," the voice said.

"Very well."

Laski nodded as he turned to head toward the Radio Room.

"Radio, Conn. The Captain is on his way."

Laski was in the second of his three–year tour. Based out of Pearl, *Pasadena* was a great boat. The three–hundred, sixty–two foot ship, with state–of–the–art computers and weapons systems, was one of the most technologically advanced ships in the world. With her eleven other officers and nearly one hundred enlisted men, the ship always buzzed with activity. Laski loved his role as Commanding Officer. *Pasadena* was a superb ship with an equally superb crew.

The radioman handed Laski the message as soon as he reached the space. "Thanks," he said to the much–younger enlisted man.

Laski read the message as he stood in the doorway. "Damn, and I thought this was going to be a boring week," he said aloud.

He leaned over and pressed the transmit button on the intercom system. "Conn, Radio. This is the Captain. Have the XO meet me in my cabin."

"Yes, Sir."

"We've got big doings."

"Aye, Sir."

Pacific Fleet Headquarters
Peoples' Republic of China
Shanghai Province
6:05 PM
10:05 AM, GMT

The setting sun gave all the lighter colored items an orange hue. Sunset was only moments away. Admiral Xu, the admiral in military command of the Task Force, stood next to Mai at the foot of the ship's brow. Like her, he waited in the rigid stance of attention.

Above them, the officers and crew manned the ship's rails. The entire crew of nearly four hundred men stood ready to receive their guest.

Mai shivered each time the wind gusted. Her wool suit did little to keep her warm. The pocket flaps on her black suit trembled, too. She watched her breath cloud just before the wind carried it away.

Mai spotted the black sedan as it turned to make its way down the pier towards the ship. Red flags fluttered on each side of the front of the vehicle. A pair of jeeps, each filled with four armed Marines, escorted the auto.

Two whistles sounded and the ship's company of personnel snapped salutes. Mai and Admiral Xu followed their lead as the sedan stopped in front of them.

Fong's aide, Yi Liu, jumped out of the far side of the automobile and ran around to open the door. Fong wore a mink hat and thick coat. Old and wrinkled hands pulled against the car's chassis as he climbed out.

"Mai Lin, is everything well?"

"Yes, Minister." She pulled her suit jacket tighter. "Minister, this is Admiral Xu Chao Hong."

The old man's eyes shifted briefly towards the naval officer. He turned back towards Mai before the admiral could speak.

"I came to see you off, Mai. Walk with me," he gestured with his arm towards the north end of the pier.

"Thank you, sir," Mai replied as she started walking.

He used his hand to gesture as he spoke. "No thanks are necessary, Mai. This is your moment, my young friend."

"I do not understand."

He did not respond. They walked in silence until they had a clear view of the bay. The large amphibious flagship bobbed slowly in the evening tide. The lines holding it in place made straining sounds each time it rose.

He looked into the distance for a long while. Mai turned seaward to see what he found so interesting. Finding nothing, she frowned and turned back towards her mentor.

"This is your moment of truth. And fortunately for you, this affair is to be played out on the world stage. You will be a hero of the people, for you will more than free us. Your success will be the triumph of China. Mai, if this endeavor is successful you will take my place in the Directorate. If not…"

Mai took in a deep breath. She forced down the urge to smile. She knew Fong would take a show of emotion as an insult. Maintaining an air of calm was paramount.

"Minister, I will not fail you."

Fong continued looking into the distance. He eventually reached for her hand and squeezed it.

PRC *Ship Yuting* (LST–0721)
Just Outside the Port of Shanghai, China
1905 Hours
1005 Hours, GMT

"Admiral, the last ship of the task force is now underway," the aide reported as he came to attention and saluted.

Admiral Xu nodded as he reclined in his Flag Bridge chair. He didn't allow the aide's report to pull his gaze from the seascape. His flagship, a relatively new amphibious tank landing ship, led the way out of port. Behind him, a destroyer, three frigates, and another amphibious troop carrier bobbed in the increasing wave action of the open ocean.

"What is the latest news of the tropical storm?"

"Sir, the meteorologist believes it will act to shield us from the Americans and the Japanese for the next two–and–a–half days."

Xu nodded. *I don't know what this is all about. But someone has at least been smart enough to plan it perfectly.* He checked his watch. Senkaku Island was just over twenty–five hours away. *What was this all about?*

"Dismissed, Captain. Return to the Combat Direction Center and await our orders. It is my guess that they will come soon."

"Yes, Admiral."

* * *

AIR BOSS'S Cabin
USS *Theodore Roosevelt* (CVN 71)
East China Sea
1535 Hours
1035 Hours, GMT

Commander Skip Thorensen entered and fell into his chair.

His assistant, Commander Jeff Robinson, couldn't help noticing the dazed expression on his boss' face. "What?"

"Remember that island we sent those three helos to the other day?"

"Yeah?"

"I just finished talking to the admiral. His staff is planning a strike on it right now."

"No shit? Cool."

"No, Jeff, not cool. It's a Special Weapons strike."

Robinson's jaw dropped. "What's on that island that—"

"I have no fuckin' idea."

"Shit. We're gonna drop a nuke. Son of a bitch."

"Yeah, son of a bitch."

"What about that team we sent?"

Thorensen didn't answer.

Doctor Deitrich's Office
Project Blue Flame
Senkaku Island, Japan
9:35 PM
12:35 PM, GMT

"How's the reactor, Stan?" Bob Deitrich asked in a hushed tone.

"Everything's fine. As far as anyone can tell, we're running on the fission system."

"Good work, Stan."

Loewen smiled at his boss' compliment.

Deitrich reclined into the folds of his thick leather chair. He put his hands together and interlocked his fingers and put them behind his head. "You know," Deitrich began. "I'll miss all of this."

Loewen sensed a frown growing on his face. "Are we going somewhere?"

Deitrich brought his hands down quickly as Loewen felt the weight of his gaze.

"I mean that sooner or later, they'll make us shut this down and move it to the States."

"Oh," Loewen replied. "I suppose you're right."

Deitrich's smile came back and he reclined in his chair again.

"What will you miss most?" Loewen seated himself in the guest chair across the desk from his boss.

"Riding on the beach. I'll miss those little morning jaunts on the ATV."

"And I thought you were going to say you'd miss the science," Loewen laughed.

Deitrich laughed, too. "Stan, you've got to learn to relax."

Loewen smirked. "I'll relax when I get the Nobel Prize."

"You've also got to learn to think bigger," Deitrich sighed.

Loewen smiled to himself. He looked around the office, first at Deitrich, then at some of the awards hanging on the wall, and finally at the telephone on his desk. "What do you think is up with the phones?"

"Probably the storm. Who knows? This place is

almost forty years old." Deitrich's voice suddenly took on an edge.

"I wonder if—"

"Geez, Stan. Don't you ever stop analyzing?" Deitrich asked in a huff as he cut him off.

Officers' Mess
PRC *Ship Yuting* (LST–0721)
2122 Hours
1322 Hours, GMT

"Officers. Attention," a male voice shouted above the conversations as Mai entered the room. The sound of dozens of chairs sliding across the floor announced a tense silence. Thick, gray smoke hung in the air. Burning cigarettes rested in ashtrays in front of almost every officer. Several long tables with chairs on each side filled the room. Almost a hundred officers, all dressed in blue dress uniforms, occupied the room.

Mai, wearing a single ponytail, took a long drag on a Western cigarette. When she slowly blew out the smoke, she watched hers mingle with the low–hanging haze. She nodded and the officers took their seats. "I am Deputy Assistant Minister Tu Mai Lin. This task force is at this very moment sailing into history."

Mai rested her hands on her hips as she paced back and forth in front of the gathering. Both Navy and Marine officers sat erect in their chairs as she spoke. "The Japanese and the Americans have built a facility from which they can easily spy on us." She watched a few of them shake their heads in disbelief.

"The Americans, they are demons. But we will not treat them as such. We have preceded them by almost a thousand years of civilization and culture. Our mission is to show them our strength as we did a few years ago at the Taiwan Straits. They will tremble in fear when our warships approach their shores, they will run like cowards in the night when our Marines storm their beaches."

One of the officers stood and shouted, "Long live Mother China!"

The rest of them joined the cheer and applauded with zeal.

"Are you with me, Comrades?" she shouted.

"Yes, Minister," Admiral Xu Chao Hong replied for the officers in his command. "We will show the Americans and Japanese the sharpened edge of our resolve," he added over the growing bedlam.

Mai nodded as she smiled.

CHAPTER THIRTY–THREE
THURSDAY, APRIL 15TH

Project Blue Flame
Senkaku Island, Japan
11:55 PM
2:55 PM, GMT

Two fluorescent light fixtures cast uneven shadows in the switching room. Relatively small, it wasn't much bigger than a broom closet. However, the little room acted as the electronic focal point for the island's communications system. Several junction boxes, all labeled with white plastic plates, lined the equally gray walls.

Ericksen used a cordless screwdriver to remove the access panel to the private branch exchange, or PBX, unit. "Hmm," he said. "Wires, wires, wires."

With some assistance from Doctor Hobson, Ericksen found schematics for almost every system on the island, including the telephone and satellite communications systems. He spent almost three hours tracing wire–runs to find the main switching room and this box of components.

The PBX unit served as a gathering and switching point for the facility's telephone lines. Ericksen decided to start troubleshooting the phone lines there. Starting with the phone system seemed as good an idea as any.

Circuit cards rested in parallel slots while bundles of multi–colored wires surrounded them. Dust covered the interior of the gray metal box containing the PBX's components. He examined the circuitry carefully.

Black soot covered one of the cards. It stood out like an ink–stain on a white sheet. "Well, this could be easier than I thought."

He turned around to open the fuse box. A couple of seconds later, Ericksen flipped a switch to power off the unit.

He used his screwdriver to remove the single threaded fastener holding the burned card in place. When the screw came loose, he carefully grabbed it and pulled it. "We don't want to drop that in there."

He pulled at the card with both hands and it came out with a jerk. He examined it closely. Dark charring covered several components in the middle of the card. He touched a capacitor and it fell apart into tiny black specks.

"Shit. That thing got hot."

He checked out the silver product number on the card. His next stop was a spare parts cabinet on the other side of the lab complex. "Hope we've got a replacement."

He checked out the cards in the slots adjacent to the burned component. They looked singed but intact.

"I guess I'd better pull these, too." He picked up the screwdriver.

Doctor Stanley Loewen's Room
Project Blue Flame Laboratory
Senkaku Island, Japan
12:40 AM
3:40 PM, GMT

Aside from the light seeping in beneath the door, darkness filled the expanse of Stan's apartment–like room. He sat in a lounger in the middle of the small living area, sipping his second beer. The buzz had just started and it wasn't helping. *What the hell are you doing here, Stan?* This all felt really bizarre.

In all the years he had worked with Bob Deitrich in one capacity or the other, the man had never broken a rule. Rather, he was as by the book as they came. Now all of a sudden he was not only disobeying orders, but also leading others in doing so.

A knock at the door pulled Loewen from his thoughts. He looked across the dark space towards it. Rather than get up, he took another gulp.

"Stan," he heard Dolores call.

He finally stood, but did so too quickly. His head spun so he plopped back down.

She knocked again as he regained his bearings.

"Coming," he replied.

This time Loewen stood with more deliberate effort. The buzz had grown, but he retained a tad more control. He took his steps towards the door with care.

He opened the door to find Dolores in her bathrobe. "Hi," she said.

"Hey."

"Busy?"

"No, just having a drink," he replied.

She looked around him with curious eyes. "In the dark?"

Stan looked over his shoulder at the dark cavern that doubled as his living area. "I guess I was doing some thinking, too," he replied as he turned his gaze back towards her.

She untied her robe and let it fall open.

Stan smiled when he saw the exposed flesh of her nakedness.

"I was talking to Bob. He said you looked a little stressed when you left his office. I was hoping I could help," she sighed.

Stan grinned as she stepped forward and brushed past him. He closed the door and she slipped into the darkness with him.

Project Blue Flame
Senkaku Island, Japan
1:15 AM
4:15 PM, GMT

Ericksen placed the last of the three replacement cards in the PBX. Without bothering to replace the unit cover, he flipped the power switch and walked over to a wall–mounted telephone.

"Shit," he said more to the PBX box than himself. No dial tone.

He scratched his head. "Well, that would have been way too easy."

* * *

Residential Lounge
Project Blue Flame Lab
2:02 AM
5:02 PM, GMT

"Well, Senior. How's it going?" Commander McGuire asked Ericksen as he poured himself a cup of black coffee.

"It's going about as well as it was the last time you asked, sir." *Officers, they're all alike, even the good ones.*

"What's next, then?"

Ericksen held up the metal pitcher, offering McGuire some.

He shook his head and Ericksen placed the container back on the burner. "Well, I've been working on the phone system for several hours now. I've checked everything I know how to: replaced a few burned circuit cards and switches, and done a few loop back tests. I'm moving on to the radios. That's my specialty anyway."

"So why did you start with the phones?"

"I thought it'd be easier. Troubleshooting a radio is pretty complicated, especially without an electronics technician. Phone systems are pretty modular."

McGuire nodded. "You look beat."

"Thanks, Sir. You look pretty sexy yourself."

He smiled. "Stay after it, Senior."

"Aye, sir."

* * *

Radio Room
Project Blue Flame Lab
Senkaku Island, Japan
2:35 AM
5:35 PM, GMT

Ericksen rubbed his eyes with his knuckles. As his vision cleared he rolled his arm to see his watch. *I'm gonna give this a little while longer. But I've got to get some sleep.*

He'd been at it several hours now. Worse yet, he had made no significant progress. Despite replacing several radio and telephone system components, they still couldn't reach the world off the island.

Ericksen had just removed the nineteenth access panel of the day. This one covered the innards of the HF Radio's power supply.

The sound of the door to the space opening caught his attention and gaze. He turned to find Marcia Hobson, carrying a full coffee cup, entering the room.

"I thought this might help," she said with a smile.

"Thanks, Doc," he replied as he reached for the cup.

"Marcia. Right?" she laughed.

"Right. Thanks, Marcia."

She placed the cup in his hand. As she loosened her grip on it, however, he clasped his hands around hers. He used his thumb to stroke the back of her hand as if he were brushing drops of water off a rose petal.

Ericksen looked up to see Marcia's brown eyes. They were wide, full of life, and fear. They reminded him of a two full moons on a clear Texas night. *You're moving too fast, Son. She's not ready for this yet. Not here, anyway.*

Ericksen gently pulled the cup from her hand. "Thank you."

She sighed and let the air out slowly. Then Marcia cleared her throat. "You're welcome."

Ericksen smiled as he took a sip. "Good coffee."

"I'm glad you like it, Senior..." she caught herself. "Darren."

Silence.

"How's it coming?"

"It's not."

She frowned. "Time to start worrying yet?"

"No," he lied. "There's probably a good reason for this. I'm just not a good enough technician to find it."

She smiled. "I doubt that."

He smiled back.

"Well, I'm going to get out of here and let you get back to work," she declared.

"You don't have to go," he said just above a whisper.

She stared back at him. For a long while, neither spoke. "Yes, I do," she replied. "See you in a while? Maybe we can have breakfast again?"

"I look forward to it."

She eased towards the door. "See you at breakfast."

Ericksen didn't respond. He simply followed after her with his eyes.

"Wow," he said to himself. "Talk about thunder and lightnin'..."

He took several more sips of coffee before returning to work. Ericksen had to consciously push her face and smile from his mind as he began checking wire connections against the system's schematic.

As he reached to examine the next bundle of cables, something caught his gaze. He dug through the wire wraps to get at it.

"Well, I'll be damned."

Ben McGuire's Room
Project Blue Flame Lab
Senkaku, Japan
7:00 AM
10:00 PM, GMT

The knock at the door caused Ben to awaken with a start. He fumbled around for the lamp next to his bed before finally turning it on.

"Come in," he said as the light blinded him into consciousness. He checked his watch as his vision cleared.

"Sorry, Sir," Senior Chief Ericksen said as he entered. "I figured I wasn't gettin' any sleep, so why should you?"

Ben half–smiled in response. Still dressed in his cammies, less the boots, he sat up. "What's going on?"

"I can't find anything wrong, Sir."

"What?"

"They're not working, that's for sure. That just means that whatever is wrong is going to be difficult to find for anyone but an electronics technician."

"So we're completely cut off?"

"Yes, Sir."

"Why didn't you guys bring one of those satellite phones with you?"

"What are you talking about, Sir?"

"You know. Like in that Steven Segal movie?"

"Sir, you've got to stop believing what you see in the movies. Those things cost about five grand a month. When was the last time you saw the government spend that kind of cash?"

Ben frowned. "What do you think the chances are that the phones, radio and satcom would all go out at the same time?"

"About slim and none. We've got a saboteur."

Ben nodded in agreement.

"Look at this," Ericksen said as he placed a Mont Blanc pen on the desk in front of McGuire.

"Where did you find this?"

"Among the wires in one of the cabinets."

"Do you think that the person who wrecked the equipment left it?"

"Oh, yeah. But why would somebody who's smart enough to do a perfect job of fucking up the radios make a dumb move like this?"

Ben picked up the pen and examined it.

"Let's look at what we know. We can't trust anybody on this island except us."

"What about your friend?" Ericksen asked.

Ben stood and paced as best as he could in the small space. "I haven't seen her in twenty years. Until I know who the bad guy is, she's just as guilty as all of 'em."

"What do we do next?"

"We weed out our traitor." Ben picked up the pen. "There's one more person we can probably trust."

"The guy that owns that pen?"

"Yep. But he can't know it. We've gotta grill the poor bastard who belongs to this."

"I'll put my guys on alert."

"We're going to do more than that. We're going to search their quarters and turn this place upside down."

"Man, are these eggheads gonna be pissed."

"I'll have Marcia call a meeting. While they're in the lounge, have the SEALs search the place."

"I'll take care of it."

So much for the milk run.

CHAPTER THIRTY-FOUR
FRIDAY, APRIL 16TH

USS *Pasadena* (SSN–752)
East China Sea
Near the Coast of China
Periscope Depth
1005 Hours
0205 Hours, GMT

Laski had the conn, or control of his ship. The depth gauge read sixty feet as he surveyed the Chinese Fleet. *Pasadena* was roughly two hundred miles off the Chinese mainland, headed east.

"Well, well. What do we have here?" Laski said more to himself than his crew. He spied a Russian–built Soveremny–class destroyer in company with several frigates and other amphibious warships. "That wasn't supposed to be ready until Christmas," he said as he took a digital picture of the ship.

In the last hour, Laski had snapped almost a hundred photographs. Once complete, they would transmit the entire package to the Commander of the Submarine Forces Pacific Fleet.

"How we doing, XO?" he asked Lieutenant Commander Art Sandoval.

"One more to go, Sir. The LST is near the center of the screen. Approximate bearing—one nine zero, Sir."

Laski nodded as he turned the periscope toward the general bearing of the amphibious tank landing ship. "Ah, yes. There she is: zero nine three degrees, relative."

Laski pulled away from the periscope and lowered it. "Helm, left standard rudder. Come left, steer course zero six five."

"Aye, Sir. My rudder is left one five degrees, coming to zero six five."

"Sonar, conn. Range to target?"

"Conn, sonar. Target is twelve hundred yards."

"Conn, aye."

At eight knots relative closure rate, Laski estimated they'd be there in four and a half minutes. He watched the clock tick off the time. At three minutes, he ordered the submarine to assume the same course as the Chinese formation. Moving around them was pretty easy. The task force was in a hurry, doing about fourteen knots and making lots of noise.

"Helm, right standard rudder. Steady on one one zero, true."

"Aye, Sir. Sir, my rudder is right fifteen degrees, coming to course one one zero, true."

Once the ship was steady on course, Laski raised the periscope. They were in the wake of the Chinese LST. "XO, its hull number is 7211."

"Aye, Captain." Sandoval punched the information

into the computer. "Sir, it's the *Yuting*. Three thousand, seven hundred seventy tons displacement. She carries two hundred fifty troops, ten tanks, two helicopters, and four amphibious transports." The computer displayed a graphic of the ship from several angles.

As he listened, Laski studied the ship in the periscope. Troops moved back and forth, a platoon of marines worked out on the flight deck. Of all the personnel, suddenly one stuck out more than the others.

"XO?" Laski asked without taking his face away from the eyepiece.

"Sir?"

"Are the Chinese letting women into their maritime forces?"

"Not that I know of, Sir. Why?"

Laski changed the magnification on the periscope and got a digital telephoto image of what appeared to be the Chinese task force's only female member. "Oh, there's a woman smoking a cigarette out on the fantail of the ship."

"Conn, Sonar. Submerged machinery noise, close aboard, starboard side."

The words went through Laski like bullets. He yanked down the periscope. Making a minimal amount of noise suddenly became very important. "Diving Officer, make your depth three hundred feet slowly." The last thing Laski wanted was the hull–popping noise from a rapid descent.

"Aye, Sir. Make my depth three hundred feet, slowly."

"Helm, come left, steer zero six five."

"Aye, Sir. Coming left to zero six five."

"Chief of the Watch, pass the word for quiet on the decks. Use the messenger." Again, silence was of the highest priority. The intercom system would surely broadcast noise into the surrounding water. Passing the word by mouth, while not as efficient, was much quieter.

"Aye, Sir."

"Sonar, conn. What is it?"

"I make it as a Han, Sir."

"One of the nuclear attack boats," Sandoval added.

"Is he changing course to follow us?"

"Negative, Sir. He's maintaining course and speed," the sonar technician replied.

The *Pasadena's* commanding officer sighed heavily. "I think we've got enough, XO. Let's get the hell out of here. I think we've used enough of our luck supply today."

Residential Lounge
Project Blue Flame Lab
Senkaku, Japan
4:15 PM
7:15 AM, GMT

"Is this everyone?" Ben asked Marcia, watching the noisy throng that had gathered at his official request. The team of ten scientists and technicians sat on chairs, the floor and even tables. A few leaned against walls. An interesting–looking lot, some wore neckties that didn't match their shirts. Most wore white coats and thick, horned–rimmed glasses. It reminded Ben of a scene from *Revenge of the Nerds*. He mentally squared his shoulders. *I wonder what they're really doing here.*

"Yes. Now can you tell me why we're here?" she asked.

"In a minute, Marcia. In a minute."

Ben walked to the front of the room. A large white dry–eraser board and a podium set it apart from the rest of the space. Lieutenant Junior Grade Dawes and Senior Chief Ericksen took up positions at one doorway while two other SEALs, complete with rifles, stood in the other.

"May I have your attention," Ben began. The room settled down and Ben felt the weight of the room's collective gaze. *Here we go.*

"We have a saboteur among us."

"What?" Marcia said aloud. The rest of the group expressed varying forms of doubt as well. Expletives of one form or another laced most of their comments. A few of them were even directed at the military in general and at Ben specifically.

"Okay, I can see you don't believe me. Your telephone lines are down."

"You've got to do better than that, sailor–boy," somebody shouted.

"Your HF radios and satellite communications systems are offline as well."

The room grew quiet.

"These are all relatively high–tech systems with fairly good reliability. You're smart people. You do the math. What are the chances that all three would go down within a six–hour period?"

Ben tried to scan as many faces for reactions as he could. However, there were too many of them. He focused in on Marcia. She wore an expression of bewilderment, surprise and anxiety.

"Do you have any idea who it is?" a young Asian woman asked.

Ben exchanged glances with Ericksen. The Senior Chief nodded that he was ready.

"As a matter of fact we do." He dug into his camouflage pants pocket and pulled out the expensive black ink pen. "We found this in one of the circuit cabinets in the radio room," Ben explained as he held it up for all to see.

Almost as if on cue, they all turned toward Yashita. The Asian scientist's eyes grew wide with surprise. All color seemed to leave his face.

"Doctor. Is this your pen?" Ben asked.

"Yes, but—"

Before he could finish speaking, Ericksen and Dawes put their hands on him. Yashita pulled away and the Lieutenant grabbed his lab coat and threw the man to the floor. A few of the women screamed. Most of the group simply pulled away from the melee.

Ben watched as Dawes and Ericksen put a plastic wire–wrap around the man's wrists. "I tell you, I haven't done anything!" Yashita protested. Once he was secured, they roughly pulled him to his feet.

Ben moved toward the SEALs and their prisoner. "What will you do with him?" Marcia asked as Ben walked by.

"Take this piece of shit back to the Radio Room and interrogate him," he replied. Ben pulled away and she went to follow.

"Sorry, Ma'am," Petty Officer Jackson, one of the other SEALs, said as he used his body to block her way.

"Ben?" she called.

"Sorry, Marcia. This is Navy business. You'll have to wait here."

Petty Officer Lind, another of Dawes' men, took up his position on the other side of the protesting scientist as they moved him down the corridor. Dawes and Ben stopped a few feet down the way. "Remember, try to keep them in one area," he instructed.

"Aye, Sir."

"If someone has to leave the area, let 'em go, but not without an escort."

"Yes, Sir."

Ben turned toward the Radio Room.

Tactical Flag Command Center
USS *Blue Ridge* (LCC–19)
1630 Hours
0730 Hours, GMT

"Ma'am, I've tried them on every circuit I know of," Dave explained to Captain Nation.

The Chief of Staff had just finished chewing the other half of his ass for not yet making contact with Ben.

"That is unacceptable, Commander."

"Yes, Ma'am. I agree. Now what?"

"Do I have to come down there and do it myself?"

"Captain, it would be my distinct pleasure to have you come down so that I could assist you personally," Dave replied. *Who the hell does she think she's dealing with?*

The telephone line went silent while tempers on both ends cooled.

"Keep trying," she finally said.

"Yes, Ma'am."

"Commander?"

"Yes, Captain?"

"I know he's a friend of yours. And that's the only reason I'm not going to put your ass in the brig. Don't let that happen again."

Dave sighed. "Yes, Ma'am."

Silence. "What are your thoughts?" she finally asked.

"There's only one way he'd not make contact, and that's if he couldn't. Something's not right."

Residential Lounge
Project Blue Flame Lab
Senkaku, Japan
4:30 PM
7:30 AM, GMT

Loewen fought the urge, but couldn't help himself. *I have to know.*

"Excuse me," he said to Dolores. Loewen stood very quietly. When he did, he noticed one of the SEALs watching him. When Loewen smiled, the man did not return the gesture. He crept over other members of the team to where Bob stood looking out of a window.

"Hi, Stan. Having fun yet?" Deitrich snickered. "That's usually your line, isn't it?"

Loewen tried to force a smile, but it didn't work. "No, Bob. I'm not. Was it you?"

Deitrich didn't answer. He kept staring out of the window.

"My God. Why?"

"Stanley, you're such a fool."

Radio Room
Project Blue Flame Lab
4:35 PM
7:35 AM, GMT

When Ben arrived in the Radio Room, Yashita was still protesting his innocence. His lab coat, glasses, and shirt all looked like they had gone through a shredder. Ericksen and one of the junior SEALs, Petty Officer Lind, stood on either side of him.

Lind, a Second Class Engineman, stood five feet, six inches. Blond, he owned one of those perfectly sculpted surfer's bodies. Like his teammates, the kid looked chiseled and fit.

"Doctor. I just have one question for you," Ben said as he closed the door to the room.

Yashita turned his anger toward Ben. The doctor had reverted to his native Japanese. The only thing Ben could make out was *kokojin*. He shrugged off the insult. He'd been called worse than 'chocolate boy' over the years.

"Doctor. Shut the fuck up," Ericksen ordered.

Yashita fell quiet.

Ben took out the pen again. He held it up to the man's face. "When was the last time you saw this?"

"Almost two days ago. I remember having it in Doctor Hobson's office and then, it was gone."

"Are you saying she took it?" Ericksen asked.

"No. I had it when I left her office."

"Was anyone else with you in the office?"

"Yes. Doctor Hobson was meeting with Doctor Deitrich and me."

Ben knew about the pen. A few carefully phrased

questions let him know that everyone on the island knew how Yashita prized it. Still, it was the only thread he had any hope of pulling. His head told him 'no', but his gut won out. He nodded at the young SEAL.

Lind unsheathed his knife and cut Doctor Yashita's hands free.

The scientist frowned. "I don't understand."

"Doctor, I could be wrong, but I don't think you're our man."

"But the other room. You arrested me—"

"We had to make it look good. Right now, the real saboteur is feeling pretty safe."

Yashita nodded that he understood.

"We still need your help, Sir," Ben said as he held out his hand for the man to shake it.

Yashita exchanged glances with Ben and Ericksen. He put his hand in Ben's. "What do I do?"

"I need to know who, other than yourself, has access to the Computer Room."

"No one."

"Really?" Ben replied.

"We went to the two–person security procedure about a year ago. I have the only access key, but even I must take someone into the room with me if I go."

Ben noticed Ericksen frowning in thought. "Senior. What is it?"

"I'm not sure, but I could swear I saw someone coming out of the Computer Room last night."

"Who?"

"I'm not sure. I'm not even sure I saw anyone. I heard a door shut, I asked who was there and no one answered. I walked down the corridor but didn't see anyone. I thought it was the wind."

Ben's eyes found Yashita's. "I need access to your Computer Room."

"Impossible," he replied.

"Look. I don't know what you people are doing here. And frankly I don't really fucking care. But for whatever reason, someone is trying to keep us from communicating with the outside world. Now doesn't that strike you as a little weird?"

Yashita's eyes slowly lost their sternness. "Let's go," he finally said.

CHAPTER THIRTY-FIVE
FRIDAY, APRIL 16TH

Computer Room
Project Blue Flame Lab
Senkaku Island, Japan
6:15 PM
9:15 AM, GMT

Ben and Doctor Yashita sat in front of the terminals for the laboratory's UNIX servers. Ben had surveyed the space and found nothing visibly wrong with the computers. He now, under the scrutiny of Doctor Yashita, ran a few diagnostic routines designed to help him figure out what was running out in the server's memory cache. Senior Chief Ericksen and Lind stood watch on the other side of the door.

Fortunately, he had more than a passing familiarity with the hardware. Xenon 9000s were standard issue in most companies. Not the top of the line, but not the bottom either. The fact that the Government had spent that kind of money for three of these babies impressed him.

A knock at the door interrupted the session. Ben stood and went to the door.

"Sir," Ericksen began as soon as the door opened wide enough for the men to see each other.

"Yeah?"

My guys have torn this place apart like an Oklahoma tornado. Nothin'."

Ben nodded. "This guy's smart, Senior. I'm not surprised. He's not gonna make it easy on us."

The SEAL nodded in agreement.

"I'll be out as soon as I can. Stay sharp."

"Aye, Sir."

Ben closed the door and returned to his chair at the main console. He typed in the Finger command. The computer started searching the root directory of the entire file system. He was out to detect any jobs running on the server. *Bingo.*

"Look at this. Somebody's got a data stream going."

"A what?" Doctor Yashita's voice held strain.

This is the trouble with novice System Administrators. They don't have a clue as to how to look for the hard problems. "A data stream. Someone is pulling information down from your server and running some sort of compression program."

"Why?"

"You're getting your back up, Doctor. It's just that someone else is doing it for you. That's why you can't get enough system resources to start up your own."

Ben tapped on the keys again.

"What are you doing now?"

"Trying to find out who's doing this."

"How will you do that?"

"Simple. We'll just look at their log–in."

The screen blinked and came back with five aster-isks.

"Shit. He's smarter than I thought," Ben said as he stroked his chin. He closed his eyes for a long while in thought. "Let's try this."

He worked the computer keyboard again. Next, he used the History command. With it, Ben could find out every Unix command the person executing the file export had run. He would use it to trace it back to his IP, or Internet Protocol, address. A series of numbers separated by periods came back. "I've got you, you bastard! Doctor. Who has the IP address of 101.10.208.91?"

Residential Lounge
6:18 PM

Marcia sat on a couch next to her son. It seemed like a millennium had passed since Ben and his men yanked Doctor Yashita from the room. "I can't believe he's a saboteur," she said aloud but more to herself than anyone else.

"Well, he sure acted like he was guilty of something," Tristan said.

"I must go to my office," Deitrich said to Lieutenant Dawes.

She watched as Dawes eyed the man carefully. "Why?"

"First of all, I'm not your prisoner here."

"Doctor, I'm not going to have a debate with you. Commander McGuire wants you in here for your safety and that's the way it's gotta be unless you've got some sort of emergency."

"Well, as it happens, I do."

"Oh yeah? What is it?"

Dawes put his hands on his hips.

"I left a simulation running on my computer. If I don't check it, I could lose a lot of work."

"I'm sorry, Doctor. But—"

"Doctor Hobson. Will you tell this Neanderthal that if I have to start this simulation over again it may delay us getting off the island?!"

This was the first time he had actually spoken to her since their near–tryst the night before. Despite his attempt to sit with her at breakfast, Marcia felt Deitrich had been treating her as if she had the plague. Now he wanted her to intercede on his behalf. *What nerve.*

"I don't understand. What kind of simulation?" Dawes asked them both.

"I'm afraid that's classified," Marcia replied. "But he's right. If he doesn't finish, it could keep us here a little longer, or at a minimum, make our departure precipitous."

"Woo, Doctor. Don't use big words like that. We might lose him," Deitrich quipped.

Dawes shot him a stern glance. The two men locked in a staring contest until Marcia cleared her throat.

Dawes called one of his men over. "Petty Officer Jackson. Escort this," he paused, "*gentleman* to his office."

"Yes, Sir," the young Black man replied. Like the rest of them, he was lean and lethal.

"How long is this going to take?"

"About twenty minutes," Deitrich replied.

"He's got five," Dawes said to the enlisted man. "If he resists you in any way, put a bullet in his leg."

Quartermaster First Class Jackson smiled at his

senior's instructions and Dawes smiled at Deitrich. "But make sure you wait exactly five minutes and one second before you shoot him. I wouldn't want the bullet in his leg to be labeled, 'precipitous'."

Deitrich scowled at the Navy officer one last time before he stormed off down the passageway. Jackson took large and hurried steps to catch up with him.

Tactical Flag Command Center
USS *Blue Ridge* (LCC–19)
1820 Hours
9:20 AM, GMT

Captain Nation sat, arms folded, looking at the geographic displays in front of her. Overhead satellites as well as electronic intelligence placed roughly a third of the Chinese Pacific Fleet within fifty miles of Senkaku Island.

The U.S. Fleet and the Japanese Maritime Self–Defense Force were about one hundred and fifty miles out, but the Americans were on the wrong side of the storm. Nation estimated that before the weather would clear enough for them to launch aircraft, the Chinese would be within striking distance of the island.

Readiness reports, requests for information, and orders poured in and out of the Seventh Fleet Commander's afloat headquarters. All around her, men and women labored to be at the maximum level of readiness when the storm broke.

The ship was still taking the occasional heavy roll causing things on desks to slide, sometimes even to crash on the floor. The smell of seasickness, along with coffee, filled the air. As much as she was at home at sea, Nation was more than ready for things to settle down. At least then she could get some work done.

"Coffee refill, Ma'am?" she heard Ferguson ask. His voice had the effect of pulling her back from her musings.

"Yes, please."

He poured the Captain a fresh cup and then took his seat next to her. Since intruding on his watch, Nation had not interfered or coached. She simply sat and listened. The Reservists ran a professional watch, she decided. Very detail—oriented, they didn't miss anything.

"I know what kind of war fighter your friend is. What kind of diplomat is he?"

Ferguson reclined in his chair. "Well, Ma'am. I think there's good news and bad news for that question."

Her eyebrow went up.

"He's a consultant. And from what I hear, a really good one. I know he's a shit—hot analyst. So if there's a way to do the consulting thing and save their asses, he will."

"And the bad news?"

"He absolutely hates Asia. He hates the food, can't stand the culture, and it's hard to get him to go out of his way to be open to it."

"Great."

"Ma'am?"

"Yes, Commander." Nation sat up in her chair as she prepared to take her leave.

"I have one question." Ferguson lowered his voice to barely a whisper.

"I think I know what you're about to ask."

He nodded. "Why would the Chinese pick now to

invade that island? It's been there forever. What's on that island that they want?"

"That's exactly what the admiral asked the CNO."

Ferguson's raised eyebrows told her he expected an answer.

"When I know, I'll tell you," she replied.

"Does the admiral even know?"

She stood. "No, Commander. I don't think he does. And I'll bet the CNO doesn't either."

CHAPTER THIRTY–SIX
FRIDAY, APRIL 16TH

Doctor Robert Deitrich's Office
Project Blue Flame Lab
Senkaku Island, Japan
6:22 PM
9:22 AM, GMT

Deitrich checked his watch as he unlocked and entered his office. The young SEAL stayed at the door. "The clock's running, Sir," he declared.

"Yes, yes. Of course it is," he replied. The scientist made his way around his desk and took a seat at his computer. *Good. It's done.* He smiled to himself.

"Have you ever stopped to think how much more fulfilling your life would be doing something else?" Deitrich asked the enlisted man as he pressed a button on the external, high–capacity storage disk drive. The disk popped out after making a whirring noise.

"Yeah, whatever. Hurry up." The sailor seemed to be splitting his attention between his work and the passageway. He kept looking in the office for a second or two and then at the hallway. Deitrich slipped the disk into his lab coat pocket.

He opened another program and checked it, too. The Building Security System wasn't as aesthetically pleasing to look at as the other applications on his desktop, but it worked just fine. He checked the timer on it against his watch. He minimized the window. Deitrich quietly slid open a desk drawer.

"Are you sure that I can't interest you in some kind of internship program? I have to believe it's a lot better than jumping out of airplanes and boats and such."

This time the SEAL didn't even respond. He glanced at his watch and then back out into the hallway. Deitrich took the pistol Tu Lin had given him from the drawer and placed it in the other pocket without a sound. "I'm done here," he declared.

"Good. Let's go." Jackson used his index finger to indicate his desire for him to move faster.

Residential Lounge
6:25 PM

Stanley Loewen started wringing his hands seconds after Bob Deitrich left the room. He had sweated through his shirt and lab coat in just a few moments. A trickle of sweat started its way down his temple and he wiped it away. *So much for the Loewen cool today.*

"Stanley, what's the matter with you?" Dolores asked for the tenth or eleventh time.

He sat next to her after his brief exchange with Deitrich.

He didn't answer this time. *Come on, Stanley. Think. There's got to be some way out of this.*

He watched the SEALs with their assault rifles move back and forth. *Shit.*

"Stanley?"

"Dolores, we...I'm..." The reappearance of Bob Deitrich at the door took away his words.

Deitrich thanked the Navy enlisted man for his company as if he were thanking a dinner date. He smiled at Doctor Hobson and then walked toward Loewen, who squirmed lower in his seat as Deitrich drew nearer.

"May I join you?" he asked.

When Loewen didn't speak, Dolores answered for him. "Sure, Doctor."

Deitrich plopped down on the sofa and landed right next to him.

Loewen turned toward him when he felt a hard metal object poking at his ribs. *A gun. He's got a gun on me.*

Deitrich smiled and, as if he knew exactly what Loewen was thinking, nodded his head.

CHAPTER THIRTY–SEVEN
FRIDAY, APRIL 16TH

Residential Lounge
Project Blue Flame Lab
6:30 PM
9:30 AM, GMT

Ben, Ericksen, Lind, and Yashita charged into the room. Ericksen and Lind had their weapons drawn. The commotion they caused frightened the others; it even alarmed Dawes and the two remaining SEAL enlisted men.

"Doctor Deitrich," Ben called. Deitrich was seated on a couch next to two others. His back was toward Ben and the SEALs.

The scientist didn't respond.

"Doctor Deitrich, please stand up," Ben said.

"What's going on, Commander?" Dawes asked him. The officer moved his hand down to unsnap his holster.

"As you wish, Commander," Deitrich replied. He stood and slid a pistol from his pocket. In almost the same motion, he yanked Loewen to his feet by his hair.

Ericksen, Dawes, Jackson, and Lind pulled their weapons. All of them sighted in on Deitrich. Ben, unarmed, stood between Ericksen and Dawes.

One of the people who had been sitting with him, an Asian woman, screamed. She fell to the floor and crawled away. The other civilians cried out as they huddled on the floor.

"Well, I can see you're a lot smarter than I gave you credit for," Deitrich sneered.

"Get out of here," Ben ordered the civilians. He and the SEALs parted just enough to let most of them pass. Marcia and her son moved toward the door.

"No, Doctor Hobson. You and your little son stay put," Doctor Deitrich ordered.

"No. They leave. Now!" Ben shouted. He put his hand on her and pulled her toward the door. Deitrich in turn pulled the hammer back on the pistol he held against Loewen's head.

Ben released her.

"What do you want with her?"

"I think she knows what I want."

Ben exchanged brief glances with Marcia, and then with Ericksen. The Senior Chief moved slowly to stand beside Marcia's son.

"You can't think that I want anything to do with you, especially now, Bob," she said. Marcia turned toward him. Tristan stood at her right.

"Oh, sure. Let a little mess like this stand in the way of a good thing," Deitrich laughed as if he had been drinking all night.

"This guy is nuts," Ben whispered to Marcia.

"I heard that, Commander."

"Come on, Doctor. Where are you gonna go?" Ericksen asked.

"See, now that goes to show you that you don't know everything," he quipped.

"Put the gun down," Ben said.

"Lind? Have you got the shot?" Dawes asked.

"No, Sir," the young petty officer replied. He held his rifle up to his face. It was square against his cheek and his finger was on the trigger. "The civilian's big head is in the way."

"Something else you don't know, Commander?"

"What's that?"

"What a little fucking tease your friend Doctor Hobson is."

Tristan growled in a low, subdued tone. Veins in the teenager's forehead bulged.

"Easy, kid," Ericksen said to him. He put his hand on Tristan's shoulder but the youth jerked it away.

"Oh, but that's right. You two go way back. Did you get any? Did she tease you? Or did she let you fuck her the way I want to?"

From the point at which Tristan rumbled like a lion working up his anger, everything started moving in slow motion. The teenager took one step toward Deitrich and the fanatical scientist fired his pistol. Ericksen jumped in front of Tristan and he cried out in pain as the bullet hit. Blood splattered as the enlisted man fell to the floor.

Deitrich cowered behind Loewen as he backed the two of them toward the door. Petty Officer Jackson dove for the floor. He managed to keep his weapon up and pointed in Deitrich's direction.

"Hold your fire! Hold your fire!" Ben moved slightly.

During the pandemonium, Marcia tackled her son, shielding him with her body. Tristan poked his head up to look around like a prairie dog after a thunderstorm.

Deitrich pushed the door open with his foot and backed out. He still used Loewen to protect himself. The heavy, fire safety–glass door swung shut.

Dawes and Lind rushed to the door. "Sir, he's punching in code!" the SEAL officer shouted. A second later, the sound of magnetic clicks filled their ears. "He's locked us in!"

"Damn!" Ben shouted. Deitrich had escaped the room without any harm.

Ericksen, on the other hand, had a hole in his chest the size of a fist. His blood was everywhere. Ben almost threw up at the sight.

"Damn it, Senior!" Ben said as he held one of the sofa pillows to the wound. It rapidly soaked through with blood.

"Couldn't let him shoot the kid," he gasped.

"Yeah, I know," Ben acknowledged.

"Did you get him?"

"Not yet," he replied.

"Well, what the hell are you waitin' on? Shit, Sir. Would you quit actin' like a fuckin' officer for five minutes and go get that som–bitch 'fore he hurts one of my boys?" His breaths got shallower with each word. He managed to put his bloody pistol in Ben's hand.

The urge to throw up was gone now. Something else, more primal, replaced it. "Aye, aye. Senior."

Ben stood. "Take care of him," he said to Marcia.

She only nodded as she took Ben's place at his side.

Ben flipped off the safety and turned toward the

three SEALs. He rushed to the door where Dawes stood.

"What now?" Dawes asked. "He's engaged the magnetic locks."

Ben looked up toward the ceiling. "If I remember, the magnetic panels are about three to five inches from the top of the door on the middle. Right?"

"Yes, Sir. I think that's right."

Ben looked at Dawes and gestured toward the door. "Petty officer Jackson, take out the lock."

"Aye, Sir." The enlisted man took aim and fired two bursts of machine gun fire toward the top of the door.

Plaster, wood, and sparks flew. The door crept partially open to reveal the corridor beyond. Ben looked down to find a foot of someone's body. The door obscured the rest of the figure. He pointed at it to make sure Dawes saw it, too.

"DeSilva," Dawes said to the other SEAL.

"Sir?"

"Stay with the civilians."

"Aye, Sir."

Weapons ready, they pushed open the door and moved out in a crouch. Lind and Jackson took up positions behind them.

Once in the corridor Ben saw the foot belonged to Loewen. As he got closer, Ben checked him for wounds. There were none. He felt for a pulse. The SEALs kept watch while he checked out the scientist.

"Dead?" Dawes asked.

"No. He's breathing. I think he's just out cold."

Ben examined him closer. He turned the unconscious man's head to the right to see a splash of blood near the base of his skull. "Looks like Deitrich hit him with the gun."

Ben turned his gaze down the corridor. "Marcia!" he shouted.

"Yes?" she responded from the lounge.

"Get your people together in one spot. We're going after Deitrich."

"Okay."

"And get your medic. Loewen's out here. It looks like Deitrich tried to cave in his head."

"Will do."

"Let's go," Dawes said to Ben.

He nodded.

They swept the corridor as they moved toward the building's exit. Dawes and Lind watched front, while he and Jackson covered their flank and rear.

A few feet short of the door, Ben heard the engine to one of the ATVs starting. He and Dawes sprinted as fast as they dared toward two swinging doors that led to the Logistics Area and the ATV lot beyond.

They found these doors locked, too. This time, both Lind and Jackson opened up with their rifles. A few seconds and tens of rounds later, the doors swung freely.

Ben kicked open his side of the door first. As it swung out of the way, he saw Deitrich pulling away on one of the four-wheel ATVs.

All four men raised their weapons and fired. Deitrich turned around in his seat and fired back. They dropped as bullets hit the wall and doors behind and around them. Several more shattered the glass windows in the outer doors.

Ben scrambled to his feet first. He ran out into the rain to an ATV and started looking for the starter. Left, right, left again. Nothing. "Hey, somebody help me here!" he finally shouted.

Jackson got to him first. "I used to ride bikes, Sir." He looked it over and pointed at a little red button on the edge of the right handlebar.

Ben pushed it and let out a triumphant, "Yee, hah!" as the vehicle roared to life. "Shit hot!" he shouted. He gunned the throttle, spun out and killed the engine all at once. "Damn!"

He started it again and this time eased the throttle up. He kicked it into gear and burned rubber as he took off after Deitrich. Ben heard other ATVs starting as the wind filled his ears.

The ride jarred him. Rain partially blinded him. The wet seat and handgrips brought a new meaning to slick. Once or twice, it nearly tossed him off. Riding a bucking horse had to be easier.

The worst of the storm had moved on, but the wind still howled and rain still poured. Ben squinted and blinked to clear his vision as he pressed the pursuit. Letting go to wipe his face was simply not an option.

Deitrich headed toward the air facility. Knowing that road was well traveled, Ben figured he could barrel along without too much trouble.

He was wrong. Ben holstered his weapon to get a better grip on the vehicle.

The steep downhill grade and wet surface made it treacherous. The road down the mountain was stair–stepped, steep drop, flat, and then another drop. He slowed down after the first drop. As he came to the next stair, he saw Deitrich near the bottom.

Ericksen's words echoed in his ears. *Stop being an officer*. Ben swung the ATV off the little road. The grade was much steeper, but it was all downhill now. Ben ducked tree limbs and branches as he powered the vehicle along. He looked for Deitrich out of the corner of his eye. He was only about a hundred yards away now. At the bottom, Ben pulled out his pistol.

Ben's first shot seemed to awaken Deitrich. Even from seventy or so yards, Ben saw him jump in fright. He must have barely missed him. Ben fired again as mud, leaves, and jungle grass flew in his face.

The air facility loomed in the distance. Ben knew the helo crews would be out prepping the helicopters and he didn't want them to be surprised. He'd have to waste a few shots from his pistol to warn them. *I wonder how many I have left.* Ben raised his weapon and fired two more shots when he was within sight of the helicopters.

The aircrews dropped to the wet tarmac as Deitrich and Ben sped by. Deitrich fired at Ben but he ducked and pressed the throttle to full. Ben followed the scientist off the facility toward the ocean.

Dunes laced the approaches to the beach. Some were only three or four feet high; others were twice that height. Deitrich and his ATV took the first one. Man and machine sailed through the air together, as if they had done it a hundred times. Ben was sure they had.

Ben's first Senkaku sand dune loomed ahead and he slid his pistol back in his pocket. He felt the incline and applied more power. The ATV lost ground, and he twisted the throttle for more gas. The front of the craft fell back. Ben stood up and leaned forward. He stopped on the top of the dune.

"I've had enough of this shit," he said aloud.

Deitrich was about twenty yards ahead and pulling away. Ben swiped his face with his sleeve. He pulled out his pistol and checked the remaining ammo. *Damn. Only one more bullet.* He slammed the magazine back into the stock and loaded the round into the chamber.

Deitrich had fallen into a rhythm. Every six to eight seconds, he and the ATV topped a dune. Ben pulled the pistol up and took aim. Down, then up, then down. When he started up again, Ben squeezed the trigger.

A split second later, Ben saw the blood splatter as Deitrich rolled away from the machine. The scientist's body and his ATV fell below the crest of the dunes. He slammed his ATV into park and jumped off. On foot, he traversed about half a dozen dunes before cresting the one where his target lay.

As Ben approached, Deitrich scrambled for his gun. The weapon lay about six feet away and beyond his reach. Ben made it down the hill before Deitrich could get to it. "No, no. I don't think so." Ben picked it up for him.

Deitrich lay on his stomach. Ben could clearly see that the bullet had struck him near the middle of the right shoulder blade. Ben knelt next to him and touched the area with his index finger. The scientist cried out in pain.

It felt like gravel inside, like a beanbag chair. Ben was sure that it would take a lot of physical therapy before he'd be able to use it again, if ever. Either way, he knew he didn't care.

"So. Are you going to kill me now?"

"Oh, no, Doctor. You've got way too much to tell me."

"I'm not going to tell you anything, Commander. I'll die first."

The sound of more ATVs pulled Ben's attention up toward the dune crest. Dawes and Jackson had arrived. "Nice shot, Commander!" Jackson exclaimed with a big grin.

Ben grinned back, but only for half a second. He turned his attention back to Deitrich. "See, now. With all that education you've got, I thought you knew that there are things worse than death."

Deitrich looked up as Ben stood. He put the toe of his boot right on top of the wound and pressed gently. Deitrich cried out in pain.

"Gentlemen. Doctor Deitrich and I need a few moments."

Dawes smiled and signaled Jackson to vacate the area.

CHAPTER THIRTY–EIGHT
FRIDAY, APRIL 16TH

White House Briefing Room
Washington, D.C.
6:20 AM
10:20 AM, GMT

"**M**ister President," the Chairman of the Joint Chiefs began. He sat next to his boss at the big table. "The storm is blowing out. By morning it should be possible to put planes in the air."

He nodded his head while looking at the Chairman's presentation on the big screen. The Chairman's directness and candor had always impressed Langdon. The General had never made any bones about his dislike of the President, most of his cabinet, or their politics. He did his job, stayed clear of reporters seeking dirt, and kept his mouth shut except in the interests of his troops.

The cabinet members passed the photos taken from the USS *Pasadena* around the table, one at a time.

"Who is this woman?" the President asked. He studied the photo over the rim of his glasses.

"Su Mai Lin, a.k.a. Tu Mai Lin," the CIA Director replied. "She was one of their top operatives here in the U.S. She disappeared about twelve years ago. We think she's still in the game, but don't know in what capacity."

"She was here in the States?" Langdon asked. "Why didn't you arrest her?"

"We could never get anything on her until after she disappeared," the FBI Director replied. "We picked up some of her cohorts, but the trail ended with them. One of them even committed suicide while in custody to keep from talking."

The President continued examining the photo.

"General, how long before you could be ready to launch an operation to push them off the island? That's presuming of course that they mean to take it."

"What are we doing here, Mister President?" General Marksee asked.

"What do you mean?" the Chief of Staff replied.

"I mean that I am not going to order our forces into action until I know what we're doing," the career Army officer replied. "That little island is a speck in the middle of the ocean. It has no tactical or strategic significance. Why would the Chinese risk a war with us over this? No disrespect intended, Sir. But this is bullshit."

"You're way out of line!" Chief of Staff Reynolds barked.

The President's eyes grew wide. Langdon couldn't tell whether he was angry or surprised at Marksee's words. The President lowered his head for a moment.

When he brought it up again, he turned toward his Chief of Staff. "The General's right."

Reynolds settled into the folds of his chair.

"I'd like for all non–Cabinet members to clear the room, please. And no one speaks to the press."

Almost half of the people in the room stood and filed out. Langdon fought back the urge to smile as Miller packed up and stood. He knew the staffer would be asking what went on for the rest of their time together. The sound of closing notebooks and rustling papers filled the air for the next few moments.

It all seemed to stop with the closing of the big wooden door to the room. President Turner held everyone's attention. "We have a situation of great potential danger. The General's comments are especially appropriate as I am considering the use of a nuclear device to prevent technology, very important and dangerous technology, from falling into the wrong hands."

The Cabinet all leaned forward in their chairs. At the phrase 'nuclear device', some mouths dropped open.

"Doctor Langdon," President Turner continued. "Why don't you tell us how this all started?"

Langdon nodded. "Almost six years ago one of the projects we funded at M.I.T. produced some rather interesting results," the Energy Secretary began.

Tactical Flag Command Center
USS *Blue Ridge* (LCC–19)
1945 Hours
10:45 AM, GMT

Dave, even when he wasn't on watch, spent most

of his time in TFCC now. The relieving Battle Watch Captain, Commander Steve "Groucho" Marx, had his assistant leave his seat at the main console to make room for Ferguson. He studied the large screen displays.

Now rather than show the entire Seventh Fleet area of responsibility, the three screens showed different sections of the East China Sea from China to Okinawa. Intelligence estimates of the size and position of the Chinese Naval Forces were displayed in red, while American and Japanese units appeared in blue. Dave happened to look up at one of the smaller television monitors in time to see a CNN reporter. The caption at the bottom of the screen read "USS *Theodore Roosevelt* in the East China Sea."

"Can we turn that up?" Dave asked. He had to fight the urge to grab the remote control.

"Yeah. I'll do you one better." Groucho instructed the enlisted watch supervisor to re–tune one of the large screen monitors. Seconds later the center screen displayed the reporter.

"I'm standing on the flight deck of the *Roosevelt*. There is definitely an air of excitement here that this reporter hasn't seen since the Gulf War. No one is saying anything about what is in the planning. Just like in the Gulf War, tight–lipped military officials are avoiding any statements that could provide us any real information. The most that anyone in uniform will say is that they are aghast that we would actually go to blows over such a little piece of land. All we know right now is that the American and Japanese Navies are working together for the first time ever. And over my shoulder, beyond that cloudy horizon, the Chinese Navy waits. This is Mike Castle, aboard the aircraft carrier *Teddy Roosevelt.*"

"That's an understatement," Dave said to Groucho. "What in the hell are we thinking about?"

Residential Lounge
Project Blue Flame Lab
Senkaku Island, Japan
7:59 PM
10:59 AM, GMT

Marcia held Ericksen's hand as the medical technician tended to him. In the almost hour and a half since Deitrich shot him, Ericksen had yet to stop bleeding. Tiny beads of sweat shone on the forehead of the young Japanese woman working on him.

Marcia tried to look into Isako Mutsuhiko's eyes for some indication of how things were going. The blood–soaked pad on Ericksen's chest told the story. The medical technician finally looked up at her. She didn't have to shake her head. Ericksen's fate was written in her eyes.

"Bad news. Huh, Doc?" Ericksen asked as he tightened the grip on her hand.

"What are you talking about, Darren? I—"

"Shit, Doc," he said cutting her off. "Don't piss down my back and tell me it's raining." He smiled. Then he squeezed her hand. "It's okay."

She forced a smile.

Ericksen coughed a few times and blood trickled from the side of his mouth.

Tears welled up in the corners of her eyes.

"Kid?"

290

Marcia turned her gaze toward her son. He sat on the floor next to her.

"Yeah?" he answered.

"You mean, 'Yes, Sir.' Right?" Ericksen asked.

Tristan lowered his head for a second. "Yes, Sir," he replied.

"Quit being so tough on your mom. She needs your help."

Tristan swallowed hard. Marcia saw tears in his eyes. "Omdurman," Tristan said softly.

"What?" Ericksen gasped out.

"Omdurman. That's the capital of Sudan."

Ericksen smiled. It looked forced. "Reach in my pocket." He pointed at the side of his uniform.

Tristan did as he asked. A few moments later, he pulled out a wad of bills.

Ericksen smiled again. "You know, Doc. My wife always said that this Navy shit would be the death of me. I'll let her know that she was right after all."

The light in his eyes faded as his hold on her hand got tighter for a brief moment and then gently slipped away. Marcia wept openly.

"Ma. He saved my life, didn't he?"

She only nodded her head. Marcia eventually buried her head in her son's shoulder as he put his arms around her.

PRC *Ship Yuting* (LST–0721)
East China Sea, Five Miles from Senkaku
8:01 PM
11:01 AM, GMT

The amphibious warfare ship tossed in the still–choppy sea as if it were an empty rowboat. The nearly two hundred soldiers and their equipment didn't seem to make much difference. Mai held onto the edge of a desk as she spoke to Deputy Minister Fong via secure telephone. She longed for the package of saltines back in her cabin as her stomach gurgled its discontent.

"We will land in another hour and a half," she reported.

"Have you made contact with him yet?"

"No. We've made several attempts, but have had no response. I'm sure he's run into difficulty."

"What will you do?"

"We will take the laboratory if necessary."

"Very good. Keep me informed," he instructed.

"Yes, Minister."

She left the Communications Center for her crackers.

CHAPTER THIRTY–NINE
FRIDAY, APRIL 16TH

Residential Lounge
Senkaku Island, Japan
Project Blue Flame Laboratory
8:35 PM
11:35 AM, GMT

Ben, the three SEALs, and Deitrich entered the lounge. Marcia, sitting on the floor by Ericksen, caught Ben's attention immediately.

"No," he said, mostly to himself.

He brought his gaze up to meet Marcia's. She shook her head. Tears filled her eyes.

Ben sighed as he walked over and knelt beside them.

Ericksen looked almost asleep. Except for the still–bloody wound, he looked peaceful. "Goodbye, Senior," Ben said just above a whisper.

Ben turned to Marcia. "I need to talk to you."

She nodded and stood.

"Are you the doctor?" Ben asked a white–coated Japanese woman at Ericksen's feet.

"I'm a medical technician. Yes, Sir."

"I want that piece of shit ready to travel," he said, pointing at Deitrich. "He's got a bullet in his right shoulder."

"I'll take a look at him," she replied.

"Lind and Jackson, take the good doctor here down to the clinic. If he does anything to make trouble, convince him to stop."

"Yes, Sir," Lind replied for the two of them. They put their hands on Deitrich and stood him up. He cried out in pain. Petty Officers Jackson and Lind herded Deitrich out while the med–tech followed behind.

"Mister Dawes. Go get that bag he told us about," Ben ordered.

"Aye. Aye, Sir." The officer turned and headed toward the residences.

"Come on." Ben took Marcia by the arm and led her out of the room.

They walked quickly, arriving at the Radio Room in just a minute or so. Ben pushed open the door and let her go in first. He closed the door behind them.

"Listen," Ben started. "I know you've got your reasons for keeping what you've been doing here a secret. But I need you to understand that a Chinese military task force is on their way, if they're not here already. They're coming to get whatever you have."

"Oh, my God." Her mouth dropped open.

"What the hell is this place for?" he pleaded.

Marcia sat down at the console. She buried her face in her hands. "What do you know about nuclear fusion?" she finally sighed.

"Ah, energy created when atoms are put together versus splitting. It's how the sun works."

"Right. We've perfected fusion," she replied.

"I didn't think that was possible."

"We've been running on power from a fusion reactor for almost a month now."

"Holy shit. No wonder they want it," he replied.

"One of their spies broke into an office in Tokyo. We thought they'd just step up their spying activities. I don't think anyone ever figured they'd try something like this," she said.

"With this island so close, it's pretty tempting." Ben sighed. "Shit. This is worse than I thought."

"What do we do now?"

A knock at the door interrupted them.

"Come in," Ben said.

LTJG Dawes opened it. "Sorry for the interruption, Sir. We found the bag. It had a radio in it, just like he said. He's being called."

"That's what I thought."

"Come on," Ben said to them as he led the way out of the room.

A few minutes later, Ben was back in the lounge sitting in front of the transceiver.

"Chinese Task Force, Chinese Task Force. This is the Seventh Fleet Task Element Commander on Senkaku Island," he said into the microphone.

Only static filled the air when he released the transmit button. The remaining scientists and the SEAL Team all gathered around to hear Ben's transmission.

"Chinese Task Force, Chinese Task Force. This is the Seventh Fleet Task Element Commander on Senkaku Island," he called again.

"American, this is the Chinese Task Force. Where is Doctor Deitrich?" a female voice asked.

Ben pressed the button. "Doctor Deitrich is indisposed. I will be making contact with you."

Again, static filled their ears. This time it lasted nearly two minutes. It felt like a lifetime had passed before the voice returned.

"You know the location of the designated meeting place?"

"Yes," Ben replied.

"I trust that you understand that we are prepared to do whatever it takes to get what we've come for?"

Ben took a breath as he examined Ericksen's covered body. "I understand. We don't want any trouble."

"That is good. We will be there at the appointed hour."

The line went dead and Ben put down the microphone.

"We can't leave," Marcia said.

"The hell we can't," Dawes replied.

"The 'technical problem' we told you about—" Marcia started.

"Yeah?"

"It wasn't the back–ups. We can't shut the reactor down."

"What do you mean? Just shove the rods in and turn off the lights," Ben replied. "I don't remember much of my Naval Engineering class, but that much I do."

"It's not that simple," Loewen said from the other side of the room.

Everyone turned toward him. He was sitting up

now. An Asian woman helped him hold a wad of bandages to the back of his head.

"This is a fusion reactor, Commander," he said.

"Yeah, if we shut it down, it could start a black hole, right here," another technician added.

Ben exchanged a serious glance with Dawes.

"What? Like on *Star Trek*? Give me a break," the Navy commando replied.

"He's right," Loewen said as he stood.

"Who? Dawes or Mister Doom and Gloom over here?" Ben asked as he gestured toward the technician.

"Your officer is correct. The black hole story was invented by Doctor Deitrich to keep this thing running until help came."

"I guess we know now which help he was waiting on."

"Hey, I still believe Deitrich," the technician said.

"Tony," Loewen started. "There is no chance of a black hole—"

"How do you know? Because of your simulation?" Tony interjected.

"Simulation?" Ben asked.

"I wrote the computer program which simulates the fusion reaction. Everything we've done so far has been validated by the simulation, except a rapid shut down."

"So what you're telling me is that we can't just blow this thing up?" Ben asked.

"That's right," Tony added.

"Well, not exactly," Loewen interjected.

Ben shook his head. "Has anyone ever explained the concept of a straight answer to you people?"

Loewen sat down and held the bandage to the back of his head. "Look, the reactor has two main points of failure: electron–neutrino regulation and loss of magnetic containment."

"Electron what?" Dawes asked.

"Electron–neutrino. Too many of them and the reactor will produce too much energy, too few and the reaction will shut down."

"Well, that sounds good to me," Ben replied.

"Again, it's not that simple. We don't know how long it would take the reactor to over–pressurize. It could be a few minutes to as much as an hour," the female Asian attending Loewen added. She was close enough for Ben to read her nametag now: Shinozaki.

"What about the other thing? The magneto container?" Ben asked.

"Magnetic containment, Sir," Dawes corrected.

Loewen smiled for a second before continuing. "The stuff making the energy is a super hot gaseous liquid called plasma—"

"How hot?" Dawes asked.

"About ten million degrees Celsius," Marcia replied.

Ben's eyebrow went up.

"It's held inside the chamber by a magnetic field. If that magnetic field fails—"

"It would melt everything around it," Ben finished the sentence for him.

"That's right, Commander. Everything around it, above it and under it. And that's what worries me."

"Why?"

"All of these islands are of volcanic origin. That means they're porous as hell and there are underground vents all over."

"Yeah, so?"

"The water table starts pretty high out here, at about thirty feet. This mountain, if you wanna call it that, is only about a hundred feet above sea–level," Loewen explained.

"Steam explosion," Ben interjected.

"Very good, Commander. With the sea at an average temperature of seventy–five or eighty degrees and the hot plasma, it would be a major steam explosion."

"How major?"

"It could destroy this island."

"Won't it restart the volcano?" another of the technicians asked. This was a different guy; his nametag read Rawlins.

"No, I don't think so," Loewen replied. "It's been extinct for over a million years. Out here, the Zone of Subduction moves at about ten centimeters per year—"

"Doc. Slow down," Ben interjected. "The what?"

"Zone of Subduction. It's a convergent plate boundary that forms where an oceanic plate sinks beneath another plate. The place where volcanic activity normally takes place."

"Okay. So it moves?"

"Yeah, they all move. Out here, they move westward. So, the zone is probably over a hundred kilometers from here. We won't set off the volcano. But we will get a pretty good fizzle and pop."

"Fizzle and pop?" Dawes asked.

"A major explosion but one smaller than something needed to create a major seismic event."

Ben exchanged glances, first with Marcia and then Dawes. He thought about the prospect of the secrets of the fusion work falling into the hands of the Chinese. *God, I hate guessing.* "Not much choice, here," he said mostly to himself.

Finally, he turned to Yashita. "Doctor, please find

me a laptop that's got one of those high capacity drives, and a disk that looks like this one," Ben said as he held up the one he'd taken from Deitrich.

"Are you going to give it to them?" Yashita snapped back.

"Doctor, I'm gonna do whatever I have to do to get us off this island in one piece. If I have to use this to buy us some time, then I will." He and the Asian exchanged stern glances.

"Doctor Yashita," Marcia said as she put her hand on his shoulder. "We've already had too many people injured and killed. Please, do as he asks."

Yashita sighed and eventually nodded.

"Lieutenant?"

"Yes, Sir."

"Get some charges. I've got a demolition job for you."

"Aye aye, sir."

"Doctor Loewen, do you have a PC with a C compiler on it?"

"Yeah, why?"

"I've got a little work to do, myself."

CHAPTER FORTY
SATURDAY, APRIL 17TH

Senkaku Island, Japan
6:00 AM
9:00 PM, GMT

Darkness still commanded most of the early morning sky. The sun, still well below the horizon, didn't have many clouds to reflect its rays. The storm, now well to the southeast, had taken most of the sky–cover with it.

Thanks to Deitrich, Ben waited in the designated place, a small clearing just a half–mile from the ocean at the edge of the jungle. A small fire provided some light and a signal to let the Chinese know everything was safe for them to meet.

"Commander McGuire," Dawes called over the PRC–90 radio.

Ben walked over from his work to pick up the walkie–talkie. "McGuire, here."

"Sir. There are three landing craft coming ashore. All of them are filled with troops." Dawes and two of his men watched the goings–on from concealed positions.

"Roger. What's the status of the scientists?"

"Sir, they're all at the air facility. The pilots say we can be in the air in five minutes."

"Understood. As soon as they start leaving, I want to be out of here."

"Roger that, Commander. Standing by. Out."

Ben put the radio down and returned to building a fire. He and Deitrich waited, one probably more patiently than the other. Hands still bound, the scientist sat on the ground not far from Ben.

"Whatever you're planning won't succeed," Deitrich warned.

"I'm not planning anything, Doctor. I've got people I'm responsible for. Unlike you, I take that responsibility pretty seriously."

"They've been here for over a thousand years. No matter what we do, they'll win. There's more of them and they're smarter than we are."

Ben looked at him as he flipped more logs onto the fire. The storm had knocked down plenty of tree limbs, but finding anything dry enough to burn had been next to impossible. Consequently, there was a lot of smoke. However, it would have to do. He wanted to ensure the shore party wouldn't have any trouble finding them. "Is that why you sold out your country?"

Deitrich shifted in his place by the fire.

"What? No answer?"

Ben turned back toward his setup. A laptop computer connected to a portable storage device and power supply lay on the sand in front of him. He powered up the system.

"Commander, do not respond. They're about a hundred yards from you," Dawes said over the radio. His voice was hushed. "We've got you on night scope. This is my last transmission."

Ben nodded so that Dawes could see him. He rolled down the sleeves of his uniform and buttoned them. He searched the still–dark grove with sharp eyes. A long, thoughtful moment passed before anything happened. He sighed to push away his nerves. When he breathed in, the smell of a lighted cigarette invaded his nostrils.

"She's here," Deitrich said from behind him.

The bushes rustled all around him just before eight camouflaged soldiers emerged. All wore varying hues of green face paint and helmets. They pointed the business end of their AK–47 rifles at Ben, then at Deitrich, and then at Ben again.

Ben instinctively put his hands up. He scanned their faces. Their eyes were wide open. Ben knew that one stupid move could cost him his life. *Shit, I can't believe I'm in the middle of this.* His mind turned momentarily to Claire, Adam and Vanessa. *God, get me out of this in one piece and I'll be in church every Sunday for the rest of my life.*

"Are you armed?" a woman's voice asked.

Ben, his hands still up, glanced around for her. She was in front of him somewhere, but he still couldn't see her. "No. I'm unarmed."

She said something in Chinese and one of the soldiers moved forward. When he was about a foot away, the man lowered his rifle and patted Ben down. When he was done, he turned and shouted something back. A few moments later, an Asian woman, also dressed in forest cammies, stepped into view.

Her long, dark hair was pulled back into a single ponytail. She was older than Ben had expected. Even at ten or twelve yards, the crow's feet around her eyes showed clearly.

Her lips seemed to crinkle into a perfect shape around a lighted cigarette before she pulled it away from her mouth. Deitrich sat up when he saw her face. She looked at him, too, then turned to Ben. "You may put your hands down," she said. Then she tossed the cigarette to the ground without moving to mash it out with her foot.

Saying something about Smokey the Bear came into Ben's mind, but only for a second. He lowered his arms. "I see you two know each other."

"What is wrong with him?" she asked.

"I shot him."

The woman looked at him in disbelief. She turned her gaze toward Deitrich, but only for a second, and then back toward Ben. "What is your name?"

"Commander Ben McGuire, United States Navy."

She said something to one of the troops and he walked over and cut Deitrich's hands free. He didn't move from his seat. Ben suspected he was too weak to do so. Else, he would be looking for a little revenge.

"A pleasure to make your acquaintance, Commander. Has he told you what we came here to get?" she asked.

All business. "Yes. I have it here." Ben, aware of the guns still trained on him, carefully reached into his pocket and pulled out the storage disk. He held it up for her to see.

She took out a small pistol and pointed it at him. "Be careful, Commander."

Ben held his free hand up. "Lady, I just want to get off this rock in one piece."

"How do I know it is genuine?"

Ben gestured toward the computer and disk–drive set up. "I figured you'd ask that."

"Proceed," she directed.

Okay, Ben. Don't fuck this up. He walked very slowly to the computer and knelt in front of it. He placed the disk in the drive. He pulled up a listing of the disk's contents and turned the machine to face her.

She came closer and peered at the display. She looked at Deitrich. "Is this what you gathered?"

Ben then turned the display toward him.

He examined it. "Yes."

Ben placed the laptop back on the ground. He logged off the storage disk and was ready to take it out of the storage drive. *Okay. First, the distraction.* "You realize, of course, that I have people in the jungle?"

He watched as her eyes went up and toward the thicket behind him.

"I thought as much. How many of your famed Navy SEALs are out there? Ten? Twenty?" she asked.

"Enough," he replied.

"Surely, you can't expect to beat us?"

"No, they're an insurance policy. You kill me, they'll kill you and destroy the disk."

"I understand. There'll be no reason for that. We have what we want." She put out her hand.

Ben slowly placed the disk in it.

She examined it for a long moment. "Thank you, Commander. Is there any chance you could take Doctor Deitrich's place? You seem well–suited for this work."

Ben forced a smile. "Lady, not for all the tea in China." He let the grin dissipate. "Now, get off my island."

She shouted orders to the soldiers and they retreated to the edge of the clearing. She pulled her gaze from him and turned it back to Deitrich. "Goodbye, Robert." She pulled out a cigarette from one of the pockets in her camouflage uniform and put it in her mouth unlighted.

"Tu Lin. Please, take me with you. I can help you make sense of the data," he pleaded. He managed to struggle to his feet.

"What will happen to him?" she asked Ben.

"He's a spy and a traitor. On top of that, he killed one of my men. If he goes to jail for the rest of his life, he'll be lucky. Personally, I'd like to shoot the bastard, again."

She turned back toward Deitrich.

"I'm sorry, Robert. You are a man without integrity, without honor. There is no place for someone like you in my country." She lit her cigarette and drew at it hard and deep. The woman took one last look at them both and turned to walk to the soldiers.

Deitrich staggered in her direction. "Tu Lin. Please!"

She turned to face him. For a moment, Ben thought she'd changed her mind. Her eyes seemed to fill with tears. It even looked like she was about to put out her hand to him. Instead, she nodded at the soldier nearest her. The man raised his rifle and fired a single shot.

Deitrich's chest exploded. Stunned, Ben stared at the body and slowly turned his gaze back toward her.

"My name is Su Mai Lin. I am a loyal member of the Communist Party. And you, you ridiculous man, were my stooge! You knew too much to live," she shouted at Deitrich's still body.

Ben swallowed hard. *I guess I'm next.* He felt his heart trying to pound its way out of his chest.

"Until we meet again, Commander," she said.

"By the way," Ben called.

"Yes?" She turned back around to face him.

"Don't go up to the laboratory. It's wired to explode."

"Come now, Commander. Your government spent a great deal of money building it. You mean for me to believe that you would destroy it so easily?" She laughed. "You don't have the authority or the courage." She laughed again. "And more importantly, you don't have the firepower. You Americans are all alike: so full of yourselves."

Ben sighed as she turned to walk away. "You've been warned."

Her laughter lingered after she and the soldiers disappeared into the bushes.

Ben stayed put for a long while. He felt frozen in place, occasionally glancing down at the shock that still covered Deitrich's face. Soon, only the crackling of the fire filled his ears.

"Commander. Are you there?" Dawes called. His voice cut through the relative silence.

Ben coaxed himself to turn toward the radio.

"Sir," Dawes called. They're climbing back into their landing craft."

Ben went for the radio. "Get going. I'll meet you at the rendezvous point." Ben checked his watch. "We've got forty minutes."

"Roger. On our way, Sir."

Ben hoisted Deitrich's body into the back of the Mule ATV. He climbed in, started the vehicle, and buried the accelerator. The fire and computer disappeared from the side–mounted rear–view mirrors as he drove into the early morning darkness.

CHAPTER FORTY–ONE
SATURDAY, APRIL 17TH

PRC *Ship Yuting* (LST–0721)
East China Sea
0605 Hours
2105 Hours, GMT

The landing craft rocked in the choppy seas as it approached the *Yuting's* stern. Deputy Assistant Minister Su Mai Lin stood, holding on to a rail, near the helmsman. The occasional large wave made the troop–laden craft roll heavily in the seas.

As the landing craft carrying her and her Marine escort neared the ship, the ship's well deck became more cavernous. The sea's action against the landing craft lessened as well.

The *Yuting's* well deck exposed two levels, the main deck and one above. The higher elevation had cranes and other lifting equipment for loading out landing craft with heavier equipment. The main deck featured cleats and fenders to dock the craft while water filled the bay. She looked up at the main deck to see Colonel Li and the ship's captain waiting for her.

Sailors received lines from the Marines as the craft neared the dock. After the first one was secure and the boat was alongside, she bounded up the ladder to receive their greeting.

Both men saluted. "Welcome back, Deputy Minister," the older Navy captain said. "I trust all went well?"

"Very well, Captain. You may prepare to take the island." Mai did not attempt to hide her happiness. She smiled openly at the two officers.

"Yes, Ma'am." He snapped his salute into place and wheeled around.

"Colonel. Your men performed superbly. Please express my congratulations to them with promotions as you see appropriate," she added.

"Yes, Ma'am. I'll be in the Combat Direction Center if you need me." He saluted in much the same manner and marched away as well.

Mai took one last look back at the landing craft full of Marines and saluted. A little confused on what to do, some returned the gesture while others bowed, saluted, or did nothing at all. She headed for her stateroom.

The walk up three decks went quickly. All along the way, crewmen greeted Mai Lin and then stood to the side to let her pass. She decided she liked the Navy. The service had a regal nature about it. It, more than the Army or Air Force, knew how to treat a person of her importance.

As she passed a young sailor, her thoughts turned to Deitrich. The young man walking by reminded her of him somehow. Perhaps it was his age, he couldn't have been more than twenty. When she first took the scientist to her bed, he had just celebrated his twentieth birthday.

Mai entered her room and when she saw her computer and disk drive, all thoughts of her former lover and stooge left her mind. *Singularity of purpose*, she thought. *That is why we will win and they will lose. Westerners are all the same. They let the welfare of a few get in the way of the larger picture.* She switched on the two machines.

Senkaku Island, Japan
0610 Hours
2110 Hours, GMT

The Mule ATV, weighed down by Ben, two SEALs and Bob Deitrich's body, labored against the rain–soaked ground. The wheels occasionally lost traction in the loose soil. The gasoline–powered engine strained loudly as it waddled through a muddy area. Ben calculated the lab's air facility was only about a half–mile away.

"Good thing we don't have that far to go. I don't think this piece of shit's gonna make it," QM1 Jackson commented from the back.

"Gecko Leader, this is Gecko Four," the radio screeched. GM3 DeSilva was calling from the air facility.

Dawes keyed the mike on his radio set. "Leader. Go."

"Leader, Four. I have two platoons of Chi–Com Marines coming ashore about two klicks from the air facility."

"It's starting," Ben said.

"Four, we're enroute to your position. Should be there in about two minutes."

"Four copies two minutes. Hurry, I wouldn't want you to miss the party."

"Gecko Leader copies," Dawes said as he ended the transmission.

Ben took his eyes off the trail ahead of him for a moment to turn toward Dawes.

"Not to worry, Commander. We're as ready as we can be."

"It's the 'as can be' part that worries me, Lieutenant."

Senkaku Island
0615 Hours
2115 Hours, GMT

The little ATV trudged on through the muck until the top of the CH–47 hangar loomed above the trees. Once on flat ground, Ben floored the accelerator and aimed straight toward the three Navy helicopters. The rotors on the birds were already turning.

"Let's go, gentlemen," Ben shouted above the engine noise as he brought the cart to a stop at the nearest helicopter. Ben hopped out to his left. Dawes and Jackson went to the right.

The two SEALs hoisted Deitrich's body out of the ATV and carried it toward the helicopter's open door.

"Sorry, man. This one's full," the helicopter's crewman said.

Ben looked up to see all of the available space filled with people and gray colored cases. "What's in those?" he shouted.

"Some sort of scientific gear. They insisted on bringing it."

"Is it worth leaving one of their guys here?" Ben shouted to them.

None of the scientists answered at first. They exchanged nervous glances with each other. Then the one named Tony spoke. "Yes, I'm afraid it is."

"Where the hell is Senior Chief Ericksen's body? You bastards might leave your own behind, but we don't!" Dawes chin jutted forward aggressively.

"Lieutenant! He's on the other helo. No worries," the air crewman replied.

Dawes nodded.

"Put him over there," Ben said to Jackson and his Team Leader.

As the two men carried Deitrich's body away from the helicopter's door, the sound of popping metal preceded that of firecrackers.

"They're fucking shooting at us!" Dawes screamed as he hit the deck.

Too soon. I didn't think they'd figure it out this soon. Shit!

A bullet shattered the cabin window in the helo's door. Plexiglas flew everywhere.

No choice. I'm screwed. "Launch! Launch now!" Ben jabbed his hand at the air crewman. "Tell the other birds to get the hell out of here!"

"But what about you?"

Ben answered the young flyer by pulling the helicopter's sliding door shut.

The SH–60's engines whined as the pilot throttled them up. The rotors whipped up so much dust and dirt that Ben and the two SEALS squinted their eyes almost completely shut. They stayed on the ground until the noise and man–made wind faded. The sound of the Chinese troops shooting at the departing aircraft continued.

"Come on, Sir. We can't stay here," Dawes said, grabbing Ben by the scruff of his jacket and pulling him to his feet.

The three men ran in a crouch toward the cover of several storage drums on the southwest side of the helo pad. GM3 DeSilva gave covering fire as they joined him.

"Hell of a mess you started here, shipmate," Jackson said as he brought his weapon up and joined the fray.

"Hey, I didn't start it. You know me, man: Make love, not war!"

Ben used his 9mm pistol to take out two Chinese marines. "Now?" he asked Dawes.

"Not yet, Sir. Wait 'til they start advancing," DeSilva interjected.

Ben nodded as he aimed and squeezed off another round. Just over seventy–five yards away, he spotted another enemy soldier's head explode with a red mist before he fell.

He swallowed hard, realizing that he'd just ended the lives of three men.

CHAPTER FORTY–TWO
SATURDAY, APRIL 17TH

Senkaku Island, Japan
0618 Hours
2118 Hours, GMT

I'm out," Ben shouted above the gunfire. The receiver of his pistol locked open after it spent the last cartridge.

Dawes pulled himself down behind the cover of the pallets. He opened his holster and pulled out his pistol. "Here, enjoy."

Bullets whizzed by overhead. Some ricocheted off their cover. The SEALs went up two at a time, squeezed off short bursts of fire and pulled back down for cover.

Dawes timed his rise with Jackson. Ben pulled back the receiver to load a round in the chamber and turned to rise. As he got in position, Dawes fell back, his shoulder spurting blood onto Ben's face.

"Oh, God," Ben said. None of the others stopped. The concept of his own mortality overwhelmed him.

"Sir," Jackson called.

Ben couldn't speak. Instead, he looked up at the enlisted man.

"Now, Sir?" he asked Ben.

Ben looked to Dawes for an answer. The whites of the SEAL's eyes started showing. *Move, Ben. Help him. He's going into shock.*

"Yes," Ben said almost in a whisper as he nodded. He bent to help Dawes.

Ben knelt over the SEAL. As Ben put his hand over the bullet hole, he saw Jackson and Lind grab two of the little green handles and give them a twist.

The air, already deafening with gunfire, got even louder. Two explosions knocked Ben forward and he almost fell on top of the wounded SEAL.

Jackson and Lind moved to another set of Claymore detonators and triggered them. This time, Ben braced for the shock. He looked up to see smoke and debris falling back to earth.

Jackson stuck his head up for a look. "They're pulling back!" he shouted.

Lind and DeSilva came back up and fired on the retreating enemy Marines. "Look at 'em run!" Lind shouted.

"Cease fire," Dawes said in a hoarse tone.

Ben repeated the order for him. "Cease fire, cease fire."

"Save it. They'll be back," Dawes said. "Help me up, Sir."

Ben, his hands soaked in Dawes' blood, pulled him so that his back rested against the pallets.

"Hell of a party, huh, Sir?"

Ben could only manage a nod.

Combat Direction Center
PRC *Ship Yuting* (LST–0721)
0618 Hours
2118 Hours, GMT

"That bastard!" Mai said aloud as she stormed into the darkened and smoke–filled space. *I should have shot him when I had the chance. When we take the island, I will personally shoot Commander Ben McGuire.* Blue lights cast eerie hues and shadows. Mai, coming from complete daylight, paused a second to allow her vision to adjust.

Navy and Marine personnel either huddled around consoles or communicated on radios. A few enlisted personnel stood at clear glass status boards, updating them with white grease pencils and cloths.

The room buzzed with excitement. Speakers carried radio communications from the troops and other ships in the company. Messengers, technicians, soldiers and sailors, all moved back and forth with a sense of purpose.

A short enlisted man almost knocked her down as he sped by with a hand full of papers. "Be careful, you," Mai shouted after the man. He didn't stop. *He obviously does not know who I am.*

"Colonel Li!" she shouted from across the room. The burly Marine officer stood with several of his junior officers in front of a large bulkhead–mounted chart of the island. Red marks near the helicopter base stood out, even across a darkened space.

"Yes, Deputy Minister?"

"What's going on?" She walked over to him.

"We have engaged the Americans in combat, Minister."

"Where?" she asked as her gaze left him and moved to the map.

"Here at their air base. We estimate they have a company–sized unit of approximately forty men defending—"

"And how many defending the laboratory?" she asked, cutting off his report.

The officer's face went blank. He looked to his left and right for input from his officers, but they gave none. Instead, they lowered their heads.

"Colonel. Break off this attack. I do not care to capture the air base. Our objective is the laboratory. I think you will find it lightly guarded."

"Yes, Deputy Minister. Immediately," he turned toward his officers.

Their heads were back up now, eyes wide with attention. He nodded and they scattered, almost like children, to radios.

"Damn you, Commander McGuire. Damn you and your entire country," she muttered.

USS *Theodore Roosevelt*
0620 Hours
2120 Hours, GMT

"Sir, the E–2 is reporting in," a female petty officer said.

Skip Thorensen and several of the senior aviator–types huddled in the back of the Combat Information Center. Electronic status boards and radar sweeps kept the occupants busy. Relatively quiet, except for the occasional radio call, the place was almost boring this morning.

"I've been waiting on this," he said to them. He pulled away and walked over to the radio operator's console. "What's up?"

"Sir, they've already checked into the link. Their updates are in the computer," she said as she pointed at the Joint Maritime Command Information System (JMCIS) computer screen in front of her.

Radar and sonar contacts from ships all over the Fleet washed through a computer processor for representation and information. The information was then disseminated via its own secure communication link.

Friendly contacts appeared as green circles of one type or another: complete circles for ships, top–halves for aircraft and bottom–halves for submarines. Unknown contacts had a yellow square motif while known hostiles appeared as red diamonds.

The E–2 Hawkeye Early Warning aircraft appeared on her screen as a green, half–circular icon. Course, altitude and speed appeared next to it. The Chinese Task Force, still over one hundred fifty miles away from the *Roosevelt* Carrier Battle Group, showed up as red diamonds. The last known position of the submerged contact reported by the *Pasadena* appeared in red as the lower half of a diamond.

"Are those the helos?" Thorensen asked about two green half–circles just over a hundred and twenty miles away.

"Yes, Sir. Their IFF is squawking loud and clear."

"Where's the other helicopter?"

"Sorry, Sir, no data on that one yet," the woman

replied. "But look at this. They're bustin' ass, Sir. Doin' a hundred and sixty knots or better."

Thorensen studied the contacts. She was right. The helos wouldn't be in communications range for another half hour or so. *That's too long.*

He had just looked out on the flight deck. The wind was still gusting up to thirty knots. "Nuts. I can't believe they launched those helos in this."

"Maybe the weather on that side of the storm is better now," CDR Jeff Robinson replied.

Thorensen frowned. He didn't know Ben. However, he knew Enright. For him to take off and fly like hell in weather like this meant something was wrong.

"Jeff, get the F–18 pilots up."

"We can't launch in this," the officer protested.

"We might not have a choice. Do it, Jeff. Do it now."

Robinson's hand was already on the telephone receiver.

"Shit," Thorensen said. He picked up his phone to call the captain.

Senkaku Island, Japan
0627 Hours
2127 Hours, GMT

Ben checked his watch.

"How much more time?" Dawes asked. The SEAL's watch was attached to an incapacitated left arm. Ben had used one of their field medical kits to bandage and sling the arm. Though he knew it wouldn't make any difference in just over five minutes.

"Three minutes, forty seconds to go."

Ben sat on the tarmac next to Dawes. The three enlisted SEALs kept vigil, their rifles ready to go again.

Ben sighed. "Well, this is certainly not the way this was supposed to end." He forced a smile.

Dawes leaned to his left. "Can you reach in my pocket for me?" He used his good hand to point at the pouch near the bottom of his blouse.

Ben did as the officer asked. He found a silver cylinder about four inches long.

"Open it," Dawes said.

Ben gave it a twist and it opened with a pop. He lifted the top to find a cigar.

"Thanks. I've been saving this for a special occasion." Dawes lifted it out and placed the end of it between his teeth. In one solid bite, he pulled off the tip and spat it to the ground. "There's a lighter in there, too, Sir."

Ben smiled and reached in again. He pulled out the butane lighter and flicked it on for him.

After one or two strong draws, rolling it at the same time, Dawes had it going. "It's a Macanudo from Havana. This is my last one."

Ben smiled at the officer's delight. "Never could develop a taste for those."

"Oh, no? You ever try a Cuban?"

"Can't say that I have."

"Here, give it a pull," Dawes offered.

Ben examined the cigar before placing it in his mouth. He pulled at it, taking it in deeply. A second later he was trying to cough up a lung. He gave it back to Dawes.

The others, and to a certain extent himself, all got a good laugh at his expense.

"I don't think I've ever seen a green and Black commander," Jackson laughed.

"Yeah, me neither," Ben wheezed.

As oxygen finally filled his lungs again, Ben reached into his own pocket. He pulled out his wallet and turned to the picture of Claire, his children, and himself. He remembered taking it as if it had just happened. They had all been in Sears, buying tents and camping equipment, when Vanessa got the idea.

"Nice looking family, Sir," Lieutenant Dawes said.

Ben found himself choking back a tear. "Thanks."

"Hey, Sir?" Jackson called.

Ben looked up to see the enlisted man peering through binoculars. Both Ben and Dawes answered at the same time.

"You're not gonna believe this. They're leaving."

Ben didn't move. It didn't make any difference. He checked his watch again. Two minutes.

"They're not leaving," DeSilva said. "They're headed up to the lab."

"Just like you said they would, Sir," Dawes added.

"It's what I would have done. That's what they came here to get. There was no way that disk would have satisfied them."

Ben turned his attention back to the picture. Her last words to him at the airport came to mind. He laughed, "Now I get it. Meet me wearing your new coat, huh?"

"Wake up down there!" the PRC–90 radio crackled. It lay on its side by one of the Claymore igniters.

Ben and Dawes exchanged the same wide–eyed, open–mouthed glance. Ben leaned over the SEAL and picked up the transceiver.

"Unit calling, say again," Ben said. His heart

pounded at the thought, maybe he was already dead and this was to be his torment.

The SH–60 helicopter roared by overhead. The helicopter couldn't have been any higher than about fifteen or twenty feet. Ben's heart cheered with the three enlisted men. He batted away a tear as he helped Dawes to his feet.

"And you were worried," Lind said to Jackson.

"Me? You! I wasn't worried," his shipmate replied.

"Come on, fellas, we're not out of this yet. We've got to get off this island."

The rotor–wash temporarily blinded Ben with dust, but it didn't slow him down. Dawes moved as quickly he could. The cabin door slid open to greet them. They hoisted Dawes in first and then the remaining four men, with Ben last. The helicopter started rising even before the air crewman slammed the door shut.

"Nice of you to make it," Marcia said as he looked up to see her. She and Loewen, smiling widely, sat on the deck as far back in the aircraft as they could.

The bird lifted off slowly at first. It gained speed slowly, very slowly. Ben looked forward, into the cockpit, to see the sea below him. LCDR Enright had the aircraft pitched over, presumably using the rotor to climb as well as get them out of the area as quickly as possible.

"This thing's pretty heavy, even with all the shit we stripped out of her," the air crewman said.

Ben checked his watch.

"Forty–five seconds to go," Loewen said.

"Why did you come back? This was damned stupid. You've got a kid," Ben shouted at Marcia.

"Hey, it was my kid's idea!"

"And I wouldn't have missed this for the world," Loewen added.

"Where are the other two aircraft?" Ben asked the air crewman.

"By now, halfway to the ship, Sir."

Ben shook his head. He turned to Jackson. "You still have Doctor Deitrich's radio?"

"Yes, Sir."

He reached into a pocket and pulled out the compact communication device. "Chinese Task Force, this is the Seventh Fleet Element Commander, over."

"Yes, Commander?" a voice answered. It was the woman. He noted her voice had sort of a hissing, snake–like quality. "I've been expecting your call."

"I warned you not to go to the lab. God help you."

Combat Direction Center
PRC *Ship Yuting* (LST–0721)
0629 Hours
2129 Hours, GMT

"What is he talking about?" Colonel Li asked.

"He's bluffing," she replied.

"Deputy Minister, I think—"

"No! You do not! I do. Follow orders or be relieved, Colonel."

"Deputy Minister, there is no reason for him to bluff about destroying the lab. That is what I would do," the Colonel replied.

She paused and took a breath. Mai sighed heavily. "Perhaps you are correct, Colonel. Call your men."

"Thank you, Deputy Minister." Colonel Li turned toward the radio.

Mai pulled out her Makarov pistol, walked to the

officer and squeezed the trigger. The sound of a single gunshot to Colonel Li Ho Chang's head shattered the silence in the space.

"I will have no more talk of thinking like Americans," Mai declared.

Aboard *Sea Horse One*
Five Miles North of Senkaku Island
5000 Feet Above Sea Level
0630 Hours
2130 Hours, GMT

"There it goes!" Loewen shouted. He peered out of one of the cabin windows.

Ben dropped the radio and looked up to see the spectacle. The scientist took up most of the small window, about a foot and a half square. Ben and Marcia crowded in from either side.

The top of the building seemed to evaporate right in front of them. A tall column of black smoke rose out of the structure. A wall of fire seemed to move out from the lab, down the mountain and to the sea. The water near the beach turned into white steam when the wall touched it.

"The pilot had better get some altitude," Loewen said. "This is gonna be bigger than I thought."

The air crewman used his intercom to pass on the physicist's advice. Seconds later, the aircraft's pitch changed and they rose faster. "Eight thousand feet," the airman reported.

Ben continued to watch. He estimated the small island was just over four miles away now, but he clearly saw steam shooting out of the ground. White, black, and brown ribbons of gas spewed in all directions. Then, the color got darker.

The small mountain on which the lab had once existed began to crumble. It came apart in small boulders first, then large. They rolled, taking out trees and splashing into the ocean.

Senkaku Island died a traumatic death. One, gigantic earth–laden explosion boiled up. In wide–eyed horror, Ben watched the shockwave move across the water. As it touched the Chinese ships, two exploded. Others belched fire and smoke.

"Tell Commander Enright to step on it!" As the shockwave got closer, the effect it had on the sea dissipated, but Ben could still see it coming.

"Everybody hold on to something!" Loewen shouted.

A second later the helicopter danced all over the sky. It pitched first, then rolled, almost to a ninety–degree angle. Ben glanced toward the cockpit. He didn't know if it was up, down, or what. Enright struggled with the stick and collective to get control.

Suddenly, an old feeling came back. They were weightless. That meant they were falling. "God help us!" Ben braced himself.

He felt himself slowly getting heavier. Light came from the windows, too. Everything started to settle as the drone of the engines filled the space.

Ben unclenched his body and relaxed. He looked out of the windows back toward the island. Smoke obscured the entire landmass. Smoke and fire also rose from the now dark specks surrounding the island.

"Doctor Loewen," Ben said.

"Yes, Commander?"

"That was one hell of a fizzle and pop."

PRC *Ship Yuting* (LST–07211)
East China Sea
0845 Hours
2345 Hours, GMT

Now under arrest, Mai stood on the bridge next to
Admiral Xu. Beijing had just placed him in charge of
the operation. He nodded as he listened, as if the
person on the other end of the ship–to–shore telephone could see him.

Smoke filled the air around her. Damage control
crews were still putting out fires. Down on the main
deck, medics worked on injured and dying crewmen
and Marines. Rows of men, some covered in white
sheets, littered the metal deck.

She looked out toward the other ships, or what was
left of them. Two had sunk. Their new Russian–built
Soveremny–class destroyer was fully ablaze. The rest
of the fleet had suffered similar damage. On her way
to the bridge, she'd overheard one of the Marine
officers discussing losses. More than four hundred of
his men had been on the island when the laboratory
exploded. In mere moments, the entire operation had
gone from singular success to profound failure.

She caught herself staring at the island as she puffed
on the last of the American cigarettes she'd bought
in Tokyo. Smoke rose from the area where the laboratory used to be.

I wonder if his body is still there. Memories of their
time together, both long ago and most recently,
flashed through her mind.

Her attention came back to the ship's bridge as the
admiral ended his call. His gaze fell upon her and she

knew, even before he spoke, that her fate had been sealed. She took a deep breath of smoke and let it out so very slowly.

"Deputy Minister Fong has just resigned citing a long illness with cancer," he announced.

She felt the life go out of her with the rest of the cigarette smoke. She let the butt drop to the deck.

"You may retire to your cabin until we reach Mother China," he said as he unholstered his pistol.

Mai made herself take the steps toward him. *Maybe if I had not killed Robert this would not be happening. Perhaps we will be together, after all.* She pulled the pistol from him slowly.

"Deputy Assistant Minister Su will need an escort to her cabin," the admiral said.

Two marines, two of those who had gone with her to the island, came to stand next to her. She took one last look around, one last look at the island, before leading the way down to her stateroom.

National Military Command Center
Washington, D.C.
1946 Hours
2346 Hours, GMT

Captain Joe Rogers' wildest dreams had come true. The United States and China were a stone's throw from exchanging blows. There was only one place he'd rather be than at NMCC, in command of his Ballistic Missile submarine.

Sergeant Kelly stepped up onto the watch platform and winked. "Having fun, Sir?"

Rogers only smiled. She'd heard him bitch about his boring job too many times over the last two years.

Everyone in the center was hoping. All of the large monitors were up now, displaying various renderings of the island in the East China Sea that had grabbed the world's attention. Charts, electronic images, and even naval early warning aircraft data all ended up on the screens. America's Navy was ready for war, and so were her commanders.

Noticeably missing was any satellite data. The Air Force Space Command had promised coverage starting two hours earlier. "Your boys are late," he said to Kelly.

She glanced up at the large display screens. "Yeah, well. It's hard to get good help these days."

"There's gonna be hell to pay if we don't start seeing some overhead data soon." Rogers sighed as he loosened the tie on his service dress blue uniform.

He examined his empty coffee cup. The air in the center had a bite to it today. He stood.

"Can I get you something, Captain?" Kelly asked.

"Nah. I need to stretch anyway."

Rogers picked up his cup at almost the same time one of his phones rang. "NMCC Watch. Captain Rogers."

"Sir, Major Wilson, Space Command here."

"Well, it's about damned time. Welcome to the war. Where's my satellite coverage?"

"Sir, ah. We ran into a little technical problem—"

"Hey, I'm not interested in fucking excuses," Rogers snapped as he cut off the younger officer.

The line went silent for a long while.

"Well?" Rogers asked.

"Sir, we're pumping the info through now. But..." the Air Force junior officer paused.

"Yes?"

"There's not much to see."

Just as Rogers was about to grill the kid a little more, one of the screens in front of him blinked. The blank, midnight blue screen switched on and a picture of the island appeared.

"Oh, my God," Rogers uttered.

A huge smoke–filled hole now took the place of where the mountain once stood. Several ships appeared to be on fire, evidenced by smoke. There was no longer an island to fight over. There wasn't even much of a fleet to fight.

White House Briefing Room
Washington, D.C.
7:50 PM
11:50 PM, GMT

"Sir," Naomi Richardson said as she put down her phone, eyes wide with excitement. The President sat up, as did the rest of the gathering.

"Yes?" Turner replied.

"They've just landed on the ship!"

Turner brought his gaze to Langdon. He looked anxious. His eyes were as wide as headlights.

"Jimmy," he said to Admiral Hawkins. "Call 'em. Get Doctor Hobson on the phone."

"Yes, Sir." Hawkins picked up the nearest phone and started dialing.

A few seconds later he instructed the person on the other end to connect him to the USS *Theodore Roosevelt*. "I'm on hold, Sir," he said after a long silent moment.

"Yes, yes. This is Admiral Hawkins. Who is this?"

Silence.

"Wait a moment," he said.

Hawkins took the phone from his ear and pressed a button to turn on the speaker. "Doctor. Can you hear me?"

"Yes," a female voice said from a gray box in the center of the table.

Turner nodded at Langdon.

"Marcia? This is Jack Langdon."

"Yes, Sir?" Her voice was low, shallow and raspy. She was tired.

"Marcia, were you able to get all of the project information off of the island?"

"Yes, Sir. We have it all."

The room breathed a collective sigh. Someone even tried to start a round of applause. A stern glance from Chief of Staff Reynolds put an end to that.

"What about the Chinese?" Langdon asked.

"We never saw them, Sir. Commander McGuire met with them. He got us off the island."

Hawkins smiled at her words. He even shot Secretary of Defense Wilson a prideful smile. Langdon smiled, too.

"Not so fast. Ask if they got anything," Turner ordered.

"Marcia, did the Chinese get any information?"

The line went quiet.

"Marcia? Did you hear my last question?"

"Yes, Sir. I'm told that Commander McGuire had to give them a disk with critical information on it to secure our safety."

Wham! The table shook as President Turner's fist hit the table. Everyone in the room jumped with a start. "Damn it!" Turner said under his breath. "I knew we shouldn't have sent a reservist. Damn."

"Sir? Who's there with you?"

Langdon didn't answer at first. He looked at his boss for guidance. Turner didn't do anything at first. He sat there with his head down. He finally looked up and nodded.

"The President and most of the Cabinet. This whole thing has got a lot of people interested."

"Sir, please tell them that Commander McGuire did everything he could. Two people were killed out here. There wasn't another choice."

"I'll tell him," he eventually replied.

He turned back toward Turner. "Anything else?"

The President shook his head. "No. That's quite enough."

"Marcia?"

"Yes, Sir?

"Is Tristan okay?"

"Yes, Sir. He's fine."

"I'm glad. I'm glad you're okay. Who did we lose?"

"Doctor Robert Deitrich and one of…" She paused. It even sounded like she gulped. "And one of the SEALs."

Langdon shook his head at the news. "See you in a few days."

"Yes, Sir."

The line went dead with a push of a button.

"You'll have to pardon me for being a little less than Presidential, but *shit*!" Turner said as he stood and stormed out of the room.

Nelson came to his feet, albeit in a more dignified manner, and followed in his boss' wake.

CHAPTER FORTY–THREE
SUNDAY, APRIL 18TH

Flight Deck
USS *Theodore Roosevelt* (CVN–71)
1301 Hours
0401 Hours, GMT

Ben's orders from the Seventh Fleet Commander were as clear as they were brief, "Get back over here for debriefing, ASAP." With that in mind, he bid Lieutenant Dawes, Doctor Yashita, the rest of the SEALs, and even the Air Boss farewell. Marcia and her son walked with him.

"Don't be such a stranger," Marcia said as she hugged him.

"Same to you." He put his hand on her head to pull her even closer.

She allowed the hug, but as she withdrew, Ben saw her wipe a tear.

"Tristan. You take care of yourself," Ben said as he extended his hand to the young man.

"Yes, Sir. I will, Sir. You do the same."

"Ya'll come on down to Texas sometime," Ben said in his best Texas drawl.

Marcia smiled. "We will. Darren told me about this place just outside of Amarillo called the Palo Duro Canyon. I promised him we'd see it sometime."

They exchanged smiles as they shook hands. "I'm sorry for your loss, Marcia. Both of them."

She nodded as the fight to keep tears from rolling down her face continued.

Ben waved as he walked out of the superstructure door toward a waiting helicopter.

The others would be aboard the ship another day. They planned to disembark in Japan for flights home.

Flight Deck
USS *Blue Ridge* (LCC–19)
1335 Hours
0435 Hours, GMT

When the rotors finally stopped turning, the air crewman slid open the main cabin door with a loud clang. Even as he landed, Ben spotted the contingent of Seventh Fleet Reservists waiting for him on the flight deck. They applauded as he stepped from the helicopter. Dave Ferguson stood in front of the gathering with their Commanding Officer.

Ben didn't know how to feel. The attention both embarrassed and pleased him. Nervous, he finally let out a smile. Their CO, Captain Anders, was the first to reach him as he walked toward the doorway.

"Welcome back, Ben. Excellent work!"

"Thanks, Sir." The two men shook hands.

Everyone in the group took turns patting him on the back, exchanging smiles and handshakes. As good as it was to be back, Ben couldn't help thinking about Senior Chief Ericksen. At one point, he even thought he saw his face in the throng.

"I've gotten a shit load of e–mails from your wife. Whatever you're gonna tell her, you'd better make it a good story that you can remember," Dave laughed.

"How many e–mails?"

"About fifteen or twenty. Don't worry, I saved them all for you."

Ben nodded.

"You all right?" he asked.

Ben looked off into the distance. The line where the sea met the sky was clearly visible today. The sun, high overhead, cast small shadows. The sapphire–blue sky made it a perfect day. It only reminded him that Senior Chief Ericksen wasn't around to see it or anymore like it. He swallowed hard.

"It got rough out there, Dave. Shit, I—"

"Stop it."

"But, I—"

"I said to fuckin' stop it. You did what you could. That's all any of us can ever do."

"I hate to break this up, but Ben's gotta go see the admiral and Chief of Staff," Anders interrupted.

Shit.

Anders put his arm around him. "Not to worry, kid. Everybody is pretty pleased with the job you did."

"Yes, Sir. Thanks."

He looked around the group, and then at Dave. "I'm sorry about the Senior Chief. I wish that we all could have made it, but—" Tears welled.

"Let it go, Ben," Anders ordered.

He took a deep breath as he lowered his head.

"Let's get this meeting with the admiral over?"

"Aye aye, Sir."

Anders took the lead and Ben followed him forward and down to the Zero One Level.

Admiral's Cabin
USS *Blue Ridge* (LCC–19)
1350 Hours
0450 Hours, GMT

"Commander McGuire reporting as ordered, Sir," Ben stated from the position of attention.

Admiral Kiatkowski and Captain Nation were seated, he behind his desk and she in one of his guest chairs. Captain Anders stood behind Ben by the door.

"Stand at ease, Ben," the admiral said as he leaned forward.

Ben relaxed his stance, but only a bit.

"Rough couple of days, huh?" he asked.

"Yes, Sir."

"Eager to get home?"

"Yes, Sir." He nodded.

"We only found out the real reason for all this rigmarole a few hours ago. I take it that you're fully aware of what we're talking about?" Captain Nation asked.

Ben frowned. "What rigmarole is that, Ma'am?" *Sure, I know. However, it's supposed to be classified at the highest level possible. She's testing me again. Always with the tests.*

Nation smiled back at him.

I guess I passed, again.

"Very good, Commander," the admiral said.

"It's too bad that the Chinese got the disk. I know that you did a good job of getting everybody off that rock in one piece, even with that Deitrich fellow, but it would have been nice not to have lost that much information."

Ben reached into his lower camouflage pants pocket. He pulled out an eggshell gray disk and handed it to Captain Nation. "You mean this disk?"

Their eyes almost popped from their respective high-ranking sockets. "Is this…" she barely asked.

"Yes, Ma'am. I gave the Chinese agent a disk with a virus on it. It oughta eat itself and just about any computer they put it in. I switched 'em just before handing it over."

"The boys in Washington are going nuts right now. Why didn't you just give it to one of the scientists once you got to the carrier?" Captain Nation asked.

"Ma'am, the Energy Department seems to have a security problem. I couldn't be sure any of them could be trusted."

Smiles, wide-open smiles, replaced the expressions of surprise. Anders patted him on his back, again. Nation handed the disk over to her boss who handled it like a fragile jewel.

"Commander, do you realize what you've done?"

"Yes, Ma'am. I do. And I'd like a favor or two," he replied.

The admiral took his attention from the disk to listen to him.

"Yes, what is it, Commander?" she asked.

"Senior Chief Ericksen gave his life to make sure we got out of there with that disk. I'd like for him to have a burial at Arlington."

The admiral nodded. "I'll see what I can do."

"And?"

Ben dug into his other pocket and pulled out his

cellular phone. "I made a really expensive phone call while I was out here. Do you think the Navy could reimburse me?"

The admiral started laughing, a little at first, and then uncontrollably. Nation and Anders soon joined in. Ben, in the midst of all the humor, finally found it difficult to keep his composure. He grinned at his seniors' delight.

CHAPTER FORTY–FOUR
FRIDAY, APRIL 23RD

Office of the Secretary
Department of Energy
Washington, D.C.
3:00 PM
7:00 PM, GMT

"With this promotion, Marcia, you're now a major player here in Washington," Langdon said as he shook her hand.

"Thank you, Sir." She seated herself in the guest chair.

"The really good news is that Doug and you are peers now."

"That's good news?" she smiled.

"Ah, you can handle him. Especially when he finds out you're gonna be his new boss."

"I don't understand. You just told me that we were peers."

"For the time being. I'll be announcing my retirement next week. I've recommended to the President that he name you as my successor."

Marcia almost fell from her chair.

"Sir, I don't know what to say—"

"Say you'll take the job."

She sat quietly for a long moment. "Of course I will."

"And say that you'll get this agency straightened out. I didn't do such a great job here, Marcia. With the stuff we've let get out, the world isn't as safe as it used to be." He stood and turned his back to her as he looked out of his window at the street below.

"You've done a good job, Sir."

Langdon wheeled around. "But not as good as the one you'll do, Marcia."

She smiled at the compliment.

"May I ask you for a favor?"

"If I can," she replied. She sat up and opened her notebook.

"No, no. You won't need that."

She slowly put her pen and pad away.

"Tell me about Ben McGuire."

She looked up at him. "Why?"

"Like you, he's going places, Marcia."

She nodded. "I would agree. He's something else."

1st Information Warfare Brigade
Beijing, China
0305 Hours
1905 Hours, GMT

"General," Colonel Pan said as he stood outside Zhao's office door. "I thought you'd like to see this."

Zhao, who had been looking over other documents, signaled the man to enter with a nod of his head.

Pan walked over and handed three stapled documents to his commander.

Zhao's eyebrows went up at the news. "So, that's why the Deputy Minister let me go." He read on.

Zhao, until his arrest, had resisted using his organization's skills against fellow countrymen. However, Deputy Minister Fong's actions had changed all that.

"Have you got electronic copies of these?"

"Yes, General."

"Are they properly backed up and safe–guarded?"

"Of course, General."

Zhao nodded. "Very good, Colonel. Thank you."

Pan came to attention, pivoted, and marched out of Zhao's office.

Zhao's gaze followed after the younger officer for a while before he let it fall to the pages documenting the fall of Fong Du So and his aide, Su Mai Lin. Obtaining the information in itself had been easy, easier than getting into the Japanese and American networks during the last operation.

He thought further. Now he was in a position to know what was going on in the world that might affect his country. He was also in a role that would allow him to know, and possibly affect, what was going on *inside* his country.

Zhao had spent almost five years abroad, studying in the West. As he explained to Fong, not all of that time was spent studying computer systems. He had also spent some time trying to understand his potential adversaries by studying their history and literature.

Zhao pulled out one of the books he'd obtained

340

during his time away from China. He turned to a page he had marked in Francis Bacon's *Meditations Sacrae and Human Philosophy*. Years before, almost prophetically, he had circled a line that read, "For knowledge, too, is itself power."

"How true, Sir Francis. How true."

The McGuire Residence
Plano, Texas
3:15 PM
8:15 PM, GMT

Ben had only been home for a few hours. Most of that time, he'd spent with Claire, getting reacquainted. Jet lag tugged at him, but he pushed himself to climb out of bed.

"Where're you going?" she asked. A dreamy tone filled her voice. She lay on her side, facing him, underneath the tossed covers of their bed.

He sat on the edge, wiping his face with his hands in an effort to fully awaken. "To finish unpacking. And then, I'm gonna sleep and sleep."

"No, you're not," she replied.

He turned to see a mischievous glint in her eyes.

Ben smiled and leaned to kiss his wife. "I missed you. More than I ever thought I could miss anyone."

"Me, too."

"I gotta tell ya', meeting me in the airport with nothing on but your coat was absolutely the best way to welcome me home."

"I just hope the security cameras in the parking lot were turned off," she laughed. When they kissed again, she tried to pull him back into bed.

"No, no."

"Only home for a little while and you're already denying me," she chided.

"You know better than I do that if I come back in there, I'll never get up."

"Sure you will," she laughed.

"You are sooo bad!"

"Hey, you left me alone here for two weeks. And while you were out doing who knows what, I was back here fantasizing about the pool guy."

"The pool guy? Claire, the pool guy is sixty years old."

"Desperate times call for desperate measures," she replied.

He laughed at her joke.

"Do me a favor, will ya?" she asked.

"If I can."

"Put off going on another of these little junkets for as long as you can?"

Ben thought about the request along with all that had transpired. The events of the last two–and–a–half weeks flooded his mind, especially the memories of Ericksen and Deitrich meeting their deaths. "No problem. No problem at all," he replied as he kissed his wife once more.

He gently pulled away and walked into the bathroom. Once there, he put on a T–shirt and shorts. He splashed some water on his face and set about the task of getting his life back in order. He heard Claire stirring in the next room.

As Ben had done on his previous trips to Japan and Korea, he'd bought a huge canvas bag on this trip to carry all of his presents. As well as making it easier in Customs, it also kept everything consolidated.

"Do you want me to empty out this bag?" she called.

"Yeah, thanks." While he was in the bathroom putting away his extra brush, razor and soap dish, Claire unpacked his present bag.

"Honey?" she called again.

"Yeah?"

"What's this?"

Ben pulled himself away from trying to figure out why all of his space in the medicine cabinet had disappeared. He came out of the bathroom to find her holding his newest acquisition. Like him, she now wore a T–shirt and running shorts.

"It's a Legion of Merit medal."

She squinted at the piece of metal and its attached purple ribbon, examining it closely. "It looks important."

"I guess you could say that," Ben replied. He tried to keep his tone casual. He turned to head back into the bathroom.

"What happened out there?" she asked.

"Out where?" Ben replied.

"Don't do this to me. I was back here worrying about you. Don't blow me off," she pleaded.

He sighed. "Honey, there were a bunch of people on an island in the middle of a tropical storm. I just helped get them off," he said as he put his hand on her face.

"Nothing to do with the Chinese?"

"The Chinese? What makes you ask something like that?"

She raised her eyebrow.

Ben raised his eyebrow, back.

"Not gonna tell me, are you?" she asked.

"Tell you what?" He headed back into the bathroom and the medicine cabinet.

"That you did something terribly heroic like you did on the *Devon*," she replied.

Her words stopped him dead. "Where did you hear about that?"

"Katelyn."

The doorbell rang.

"We'll talk about this later," she said. "Go get the door."

Ben nodded as he turned and walked out.

A few steps later, he looked through the peephole to see Adam, Vanessa and Katelyn. He smiled at the sight of the kids and opened the door.

"Daddy!" they both shouted.

Ben knelt to receive their hugs. They covered each other's faces with kisses. "God, I missed you guys!"

As the fervor of the children's affection cooled, Ben stood. Katelyn's eyes met his.

She took a step forward and embraced him warmly. "I'm glad you're home safe," she said.

"Thanks, Kate." Ben returned the gesture.

He felt Claire's presence behind him as Kate pulled away.

"Hey," Claire greeted in a very warm, friendly tone.

"Hi, Claire."

Ben mentally pinched himself as he refused to believe what his eyes told him. He glanced first at his wife, then Kate, and then back at Claire.

"Come on in," she invited.

"Are you sure? He just got home and I figured you two would need some time," Kate protested.

"No, no. We've got time for that. Besides, the kids

want to see their dad. I can make some margaritas," Claire offered. She extended her hand to Kate.

Kate slowly reached out and took it after a long while.

"Ben, honey. Close the door. You're air conditioning Plano," Claire said.

"Okay, hon," he replied. *What the hell went on here while I was gone?*

THE END

To order a copy of Ken Carodine's *All The Tea* in its
original trade paperback edition or convenient
audiobook format, or to order other Timberwolf Press
titles, please contact us in one of the following ways:

Phone: 1-888-808-0912
Or visit the Timberwolf Press website at:
http://www.TimberwolfPress.com

Timberwolf Press, Inc.
202 N. Allen Street, Suite A
Allen, TX 75013 USA